Murder
in the
Fens

BOOKS BY CLARE CHASE

The Tara Thorpe Mystery Series
Murder on the Marshes
Death on the River
Death Comes to Call

Murder
in the
Fens

CLARE CHASE

bookouture

Published by Bookouture in 2019

An imprint of StoryFire Ltd.

Carmelite House
50 Victoria Embankment
London EC4Y 0DZ

www.bookouture.com

ISBN: 978-1-83888-044-6
eBook ISBN: 978-1-78681-996-3

To Phil and Jenny, and David and Pat, with love.

CHAPTER ONE

Rachel watched her four-year-old son, Jamie, trot ahead of her, the warm late-September sun on his back. He knew where they were; a trip to the circular earthworks at Wandlebury was one of their staples. You could tell *he'd* had a decent night's sleep. She looked down at baby Fi, asleep on her front in her carrier. At three that morning Rachel had given up the fight against tears; she was desperate for a solid eight hours' rest.

The last day of the month. Rachel could feel the seasons changing, despite the balmy temperature. The leaves around her were just starting to lose their lush summer green, the first tinges of orange appearing here and there. But it was more than that: something in the air told her the year was dying, not waking up. As they entered the wooded area round the Iron Age ring, the warmth of the sun faded and the way ahead of her was marked with shadows. To her left and right, cross-orbweaver spiders staked their claim to the tangled branches she wove her way through. She put out a hand to protect baby Fi's head, but felt a cobweb brush her own face. It clung to her hair.

Jamie had dashed further ahead of her, down into the large ditch, dug more than two millennia ago. She followed him cautiously. Navigating the bank at speed might wake Fi. By the time she'd dipped right down into the bottom of the earthworks, Jamie was running up to the top again. He was way ahead now, and she enjoyed the peace as she followed him from a distance, keeping her eyes on his progress.

It was nice to find the track deserted. Most families were out in the open, picnicking in the grounds in the centre of the Ring. Sunday lunchtime had brought them out, with sandwiches and Thermoses full of tea. The weather was forecast to turn the following day. They were making the most of the Indian summer.

Walking the ancient ditch left her feeling removed from the exhaustion of everyday life. The Ring must have looked the same for centuries, and for a moment she could almost imagine that she was back in the old times.

The sound of a twig cracking somewhere behind her made her turn sharply. Fi gave a small whimper in her sleep.

There was no one there. It must have been an animal or something. But it had put her on high alert. And when she turned slowly forwards again, protecting Fi from more sudden movement, she couldn't see Jamie.

She upped her pace. Where was he? He'd have dashed to the top of the bank again, surely? But she couldn't spot him. She'd have to call. *Damn.*

'Jamie!'

By some miracle, Fi slept on.

There was no reply, so she began to climb the bank herself, for a better vantage point. Once she was at the top she'd be able to see him. There was no reason to panic…

She made it out of the ditch and stared through the undergrowth. It wasn't so far to the other side, and open ground.

'Jamie? Where are—'

But then she saw him, running towards her. *Thank God.* He'd only been gone for half a minute, but the feeling of relief was like a wave carrying her onto shore. She took a deep breath and swept forward, picking her way past twigs and low branches to meet him.

'There's a lady.' Jamie's brow was furrowed.

'A lady?'

Jamie nodded. 'I think she's asleep. But with her eyes open. Can that happen, Mummy?'

Rachel felt a chill crawl over her arms, and the hairs on her scalp rise. She took her son's hand and held it tight. 'Show me.'

Before they reached the spot where he'd been standing, through the tangle of undergrowth, Rachel glimpsed part of an arm, pale and motionless in the shadows under the trees.

CHAPTER TWO

Detective Constable Tara Thorpe felt her throat catch – a hard knot that made her swallow. Sorrow and anger set her eyes smarting. She clenched her latex-gloved hands and tensed her muscles to fight her reactions.

She'd been so young, this woman lying there before her in the early autumn warmth. Late teens? Early twenties at the most. She was pale and still, surrounded by the earthy browns and mossy greens of nature. A blackbird sang in a tree, and around her the CSIs caused twigs to crack and vegetation to rustle, but otherwise everything was quiet. The cordons were keeping families, out for a weekend walk, well away from the scene.

It wasn't obvious how the girl had died. It could have been natural causes, but it was clear that she'd been in torment at the end. There were scratch marks on her neck and blood under her fingernails, yet no sign that she'd been strangled. Her knuckles looked bruised, too. What had happened here? Her blue eyes were bloodshot, and she lay flat on her back, her black denim skirt rucked up. The black canvas lace-ups she wore reminded Tara of the shoes her school had made pupils wear for gym lessons. There was an even paler circle of skin on the third finger of the girl's right hand, Tara noticed. She'd worn a ring until recently. Signs of a boyfriend who was now an ex? But she might be jumping to conclusions.

The girl's blue T-shirt had a slogan on it. *Equal rights for others does not mean less for you. It's not pie.* She'd cared – had been fighting to make the world a better place, even if it was just through the clothes she'd worn. It crushed Tara inside that she'd been stopped in her tracks when she'd barely had a chance to get going.

She glanced sideways at her DS, Max Dimity. He was easy to get on with and until recently he'd been the same grade as her. His promotion hadn't put any distance between them; though another colleague – DS Megan Maloney – had kindly pointed out to Tara that it ought to. But they were all in it together, and Tara could tell that Max was battling the same emotions that she was. Looking any kind of death in the face was harder for him than for most. His wife had died in a car accident when she was just twenty-five. Five years had passed, but that must feel like no time when you were dealing with something so huge.

'Hell!'

The exclamation told her Garstin Blake, their DI, had arrived. As she turned, she saw he had the pathologist, Agneta Larsson, with him. Their protective suits only revealed their eyes. Agneta's were clear, blue and concerned. As for Blake, he looked as though he'd been up all night – the by-product of having a four-month-old baby. Though there might be other explanations for his lack of sleep too. There was a lot more to Blake's home life than met the eye. Why the heck had his wife kept her pregnancy from him for so long? And why had she told their daughter, Kitty, first? And lastly, why had Blake shared those facts with Tara? She was glad she knew, but it hadn't helped her put more distance between *them*… not that anything had ever happened.

Agneta ran her eyes over the dead woman's body, then crouched down and gingerly began a closer examination.

'Ah, dear God,' she said under her breath. 'She was hit with something. Here, under her hair on the left-hand side, near her temple.'

'Would that have killed her?' Blake was after instant answers, as ever.

Agneta gave him a look. 'I'll have to investigate more thoroughly when I'm back at Addenbrooke's, but first impressions – I would say not. It would have stunned her though. She might have been knocked unconscious.'

Agneta moved the woman's arm gently. 'Almost all of her muscles have contracted – I would estimate she died sometime between two and four this morning.'

'Late to be out here, whatever the reason,' Max said.

Blake looked at Agneta from under his dark brows. 'Any signs she's been moved? We're quite close to an access track. Someone could have brought her body here in a car.'

The pathologist shook her head. 'None that I can see, but I'll need to look more closely.'

'What about the marks on her neck?'

But Agneta wouldn't be drawn. 'I need to do the work, Blake. Guesses could lead you on a false trail.'

Larsson was right, but Tara empathised with Blake's urgency. Any trail felt better than none when you were faced with this sort of scene.

As she watched, Agneta bent to look more closely at the dead girl's skirt. She hadn't been wearing tights. Tara guessed they were all wondering the same thing. Had the attack had a sexual element? The way the skirt was rucked up like that, coupled with the bruises on her hands, made it look as though she'd fought someone off.

Agneta spoke, even as Blake opened his mouth. 'I'll be able to tell you later.' Pretty impressive mind reading, given she wasn't even looking in his direction. But Tara knew they'd been friends for years. 'There's something else though.' The pathologist glanced round at them and pointed at the patch pocket in the skirt. Tara could just see the edge of something pale and pink poking out of it, soft against the rough black material. The pocket was bulky – as though it had a tissue tucked into it – but the sliver of pink looked too delicate for that.

Blake frowned and caught the eye of one of the CSIs, who'd been on her way over to their group. The woman crouched next to Agneta, an evidence bag in one hand, and eased the pocket open. The sliver of pink was part of a flower. A Japanese anemone: beautiful, delicate, crushed.

'There are more,' the CSI said, looking down again. 'Her pocket's full of them.'

Max frowned. 'Could she have been collecting them? Or is this some kind of message?'

Tara felt goosebumps rise on her arms. She was guessing the latter. Who went to gather anemones in the dead of night? 'There's a language of flowers. I remember reading about it once. I'll look it up.'

'I was coming over to tell you we've found a black backpack,' the CSI said. 'It's just over there by that tree.' She pointed. 'Looks like it belongs to the deceased. There's photo ID – a student card. She's Julie Cooper – studying at the university, at St Oswald's College. It doesn't look as though anything's been taken. Her phone, purse, keys – all still there.'

Tara thought again of the pale band of skin on Julie Cooper's right-hand ring finger. Caused by an item the woman had discarded herself? Or had it been removed? She voiced the thought.

'If it was taken by her attacker it doesn't look as though money was the motive,' Blake said. 'Not if her other valuables have been left untouched.' He looked at the flowers in the CSI's evidence bag. 'Maybe her attacker took it as a souvenir.'

'Guv!' It was Barry – one of the uniformed officers who'd been first on the scene. He was over by the cordon. 'Call from the control room.'

Blake strode over to speak to whoever it was on the line, but two minutes later he was back. 'There's a Sandra Cooper at the front desk, back at Parkside. She was due to meet her daughter at her lodgings in time for lunch. When she couldn't find her, she got spooked.' His colour was as pale as the overalls he was wearing. 'Megan's with her now. I'm going to head over and join them. I've got the address where Julie was staying over the summer, too – her mother passed it on.' He turned to Max. 'I'd like you and Tara to get over there. There are CSIs on their way too. See what you can find out.'

As Max and Tara turned to make their way back to the cordon, she pictured Blake passing on the news. It was a terrible job to have, but nothing compared with what Mrs Cooper was about to go through.

She and Max took a few minutes to struggle out of their overalls. Tara had had to drag hers on over the deep-green jersey dress she'd been wearing; she hadn't stopped to change before responding to the call, which now seemed like a mistake. She pulled the white over-suit off carefully so that the hem of her dress fell back into place, without revealing her knickers to all and sundry.

Ten minutes later, she was sitting at the wheel of their car, waiting for a gap in the endless stream of traffic so that they could leave Wandlebury Ring. In a moment the queue would snarl up altogether, and she'd be able to edge out between the stationary vehicles. At last, she saw her chance and nudged her way forward, in front of a shiny VW which was indicating to turn in. As she made the manoeuvre she looked through the VW's windscreen and saw a face that she knew: her former colleague, Shona Kennedy from *Not Now* magazine. Trust her to get her grubby mitts on this story so quickly; feeding off the kill like a vulture.

Max's eyes were on the woman too, and her snide grin. 'She's not worth it,' he said.

Tara snapped her mind back to their mission and made it to the opposite lane. In a second she'd put her foot down and screeched out of Kennedy's line of sight.

CHAPTER THREE

Sandra Cooper had her head buried in her hands. Blake waited, next to DS Megan Maloney. He couldn't fault Megan – she'd said all the right things, followed every best-practice guideline to the letter. But her dedication meant she'd never come across as warm. She held all the bullet points she had to follow in her head, and her careful concentration prevented any ad-libbing. Following the rule book meant she'd probably avoid the sort of scrapes Tara got into, and spot things that got missed when you cut corners. But she'd never find the unexpected nuggets Tara unearthed by trusting the instincts she'd developed as a journalist.

Given all that, having each of them on the team ought to create the perfect balance. In practice, they didn't get on. Thank goodness for Max's calming influence and clear-headed insights. And now they'd got DC Jez Fallon on the team, their newest recruit. Great on paper, and DCI Fleming loved him…

Sandra Cooper's crying touched Blake to his core. He wished he could make up for Megan's lack of warmth; he'd have found it easier if they'd been alone.

The woman blew her nose on a tissue she'd pulled from the pocket of her jeans. 'I can't believe she was killed. Who on earth would do that?'

Blake leant forward a little. 'We don't know for sure that's what happened.'

'You said she was attacked.'

He nodded. 'That's right, but at the moment we don't think that's what caused her death. We should be able to give you some proper answers soon.' Nothing would ease her pain, but he was sure the not knowing must add to her living hell. Would the facts be any more bearable? He thought of the scratches on Julie Cooper's neck and her rucked-up skirt. 'Please, Mrs Cooper, could you tell me what time you were meant to meet your daughter at her accommodation?'

'Ms.' She looked at him through bloodshot, red-rimmed eyes. 'Julie's father's never been in the picture.'

He'd have to ask more about that when the time was right. Was Julie's mother certain she never saw her dad?

'I was meant to meet her at the house where she was lodging at eleven thirty,' Sandra Cooper continued. 'I rang her buzzer, and then' – she took a great gulp of air that turned into a sob – 'I rang her mobile. But there was no answer. I knew there must be something wrong. She was due to move back into her third-year accommodation today and I was going to help her shift her belongings in my car.' Her head was back in her hands again. 'I just can't take it in. I keep thinking there must be some mistake.'

He recognised the disbelief – he'd seen it before. That hope against hope that it was all some crazy misunderstanding. For a split second, he imagined himself in the same situation – being told that seven-year-old Kitty or baby Jessica were dead. He felt his core contract. 'Take your time.' But urgency was swelling in his chest. It was inhumane to question her in this state, but the clock was ticking. An attacker – probably a murderer – was benefiting from every moment they wasted.

'Are you all right to continue?' Megan asked. *Good, gentle tone. Tick.*

Sandra Cooper nodded.

'Can you tell us when you last heard from Julie?' Blake said.

'Earlier this week. It must have been Tuesday when I rang her and we arranged the visit.' A tear rolled down her cheek. 'A short while before the summer holidays she rang me to say she wanted to stay in Cambridge over the break. She'd got some part-time work on a project being run by one of the professors in her subject.' She blinked. 'I'd been looking forward to having her back home, but she was excited, and it sounded like a great opportunity, so I encouraged her. And I was pleased in some ways.'

Blake raised a questioning eyebrow.

'Her teachers at school persuaded her to apply to Cambridge, and when she got her offer, it was I who talked her into coming. She wasn't keen. She'd decided it was elitist and only for a certain sort of person. But I said if people like her turned down their places, then it always would be.' Her eyes looked hollow. 'It was my fault she came. If I hadn't put pressure on her, she'd have ended up somewhere else. She'd still be alive.'

'We don't understand the circumstances of her death yet,' Blake said, 'but whatever they were, you're not to blame. Awful things happen across the country. They're often entirely unpredictable.'

Sandra Cooper shook her head, fresh tears welling up and spilling down her cheeks.

'You mentioned she was staying behind to work with a professor,' Blake went on. 'Did she give you any more details? The academic's name, for instance, or the exact nature of the work?'

Julie's mother frowned. 'She said she was doing some research to help this person out. John, I think his name was.'

In a university the size of Cambridge, there would be a lot of Johns…

Blake took a deep breath. 'What was her subject?'

'Human, Social and Political Sciences.'

It sounded like the sort of degree where she'd have been taught across multiple departments. The words needle and haystack sprang to mind, but hopefully her friends or others at her college would know more.

'She didn't tell you anything else about the project?' Blake hated having to push, but it was essential.

Sandra Cooper's hands were clutched together on the table in front of her, her knuckles white. 'I didn't ask,' she said quietly. 'And now it's too late.'

'You would have asked her today,' he said. 'You couldn't know what would happen.'

The woman glanced up at him with watery eyes. 'Whatever it was, it had got her fired up. She sounded keen to stay and get on with the work. She was very engaged with the world around her. The environment, social injustice, politics – all of that.'

'And how did she like university in general?' Blake asked. 'Did she ever mention tensions with friends, or university staff? Anyone she was wary of?'

Sandra shook her head. 'Nothing like that.' She looked up at them with hollow eyes. 'Though I wonder if she'd have confided in me. There was one call we had a few months back when she seemed a bit quiet. I asked her what was up, but she just said I was being oversensitive, and not to worry. She was careful of my feelings – too careful.'

'She didn't tell you much about her friends, and other contacts here?' Megan asked.

Sandra Cooper frowned. 'I got the impression she kept herself a bit separate from her course- and room-mates. She was never in anyone's pocket. There was one particular friend I was aware of though – Bella. She was at the same college as Julie – St Oswald's.' She frowned. 'I didn't take to her, if I'm honest; she put me on edge, but I'm not sure why. As for the staff, I met her tutor at the start of Julie's second year. I was feeling a bit emotional – same as I always do when we're about to be parted.' She stopped short for a moment – no doubt feeling the permanent separation she was faced with now. 'I worried aloud to him about Julie,' she went on at last. 'He was kind – reassuring. It made me feel better.'

Blake nodded. 'Was Julie in a relationship with anyone, do you know?'

A sigh. 'There was a boy – Stuart. Stuart Gilmour. I met him earlier in the year when I visited. He was good-looking, but a bit aloof with me. They split up a while back now; March, it must have been.'

Not so long in Stuart's eyes, perhaps, Blake thought.

'He was a student too – at St Bede's College – but they met at some demo.'

'Did Julie say why they broke up?'

'Not exactly. He was politically engaged like she was, but she said in the end he wasn't as fond of fair play in real life as he was in principle.'

'Do you know what she meant by that?' Megan asked.

She shook her head. 'Either way, I don't think the break-up can have been that acrimonious. She was still wearing the ring he gave her when I saw her last.'

The ring that now seemed to be missing. Blake's glance slid sideways for a second and met Megan's. Stuart Gilmour was one to watch. And who was John, the academic behind Julie's decision to stay in Cambridge over the summer?

CHAPTER FOUR

Tara was with Max at Julie Cooper's summer lodgings. It was a rambling college-owned Victorian house out on Chesterton Road. A lot of the students had already vacated the place, ready to start the new term, and it felt half abandoned. Gloomy rooms stood empty, old-fashioned iron keys left in the doors for the cleaners. Everywhere they went floorboards creaked and their voices echoed in the sparsely furnished corridors. The CSI van was outside and, where students remained, Tara could hear their whispers as they talked about what had happened in hushed tones behind closed doors.

And then, from one of the rooms, Tara heard a gasp, followed by crying, as though the occupant had been trying to regain control, before giving in to grief again. They were hoping to speak to someone who'd known Julie well, and the raw emotion she'd heard made Tara pause at the door. She glanced over her shoulder at Max for a moment and he nodded, giving her the go-ahead. The crying had subsided to a series of sobs again, and she knocked gently.

'Who is it?'

Tara gave their names and titles. 'We're hoping to speak to someone who knew Julie well.'

After a moment, a young woman answered the door. 'I'm Bella Chadwick. I've known Julie since our first year.'

Tara took in Bella's appearance and felt her skin prickle. What she wore closely mirrored the outfit Julie Cooper had died in. A T-shirt and short denim skirt. They could almost be twins, even though they were non-identical. And yet there was a difference. The dead woman's clothes had all looked familiar to Tara – the kind she might have chosen herself as a student from somewhere affordable, like Camden Market. What was it about Bella's skirt that said designer? The subtle shaping? The stitch work? Tara wasn't sure but her actress mother, Lydia, had wafted around in front of her in enough haute couture gear for her to recognise it. Blake would understand – if he were there. One of the many unexpected things about him was that he had a fashion designer for a sister. It had finally explained the smart suits he wore, despite being an inveterate scruff.

Bella Chadwick's pale pink T-shirt left Tara wondering too. It had a slogan on it – championing feminism – but again, it shouted expensive. What kind of friendship had she and Julie had? And who had been imitating whom?

'Come in.' Bella stood back to allow them access to her high-ceilinged room. As soon as she'd closed the heavy panelled door behind them, her tone became agitated. 'What do you think happened to her? Who could have done such a thing?'

'We're still trying to piece together the details.' Max's eyes were friendly. At last, the student nodded.

'So, you've been here for the whole summer too?' Tara asked. She always preferred to begin with incidentals. When questioning seemed like a casual conversation, people tended to open up more.

Bella nodded. 'I've been doing shifts at the Eagle.'

One of the most famous pubs in town; it was where Watson and Crick had gone to celebrate when they'd worked out the structure of DNA. It irked Tara that people often talked about them without mentioning Rosalind Franklin, whose X-ray imaging had put them on to the truth.

Bella frowned. 'I could have gone home, worked there and saved on rent, but that would have meant three months with my parents, quizzing me about my academic achievements. They'd want to know why I wasn't studying the whole time.'

Tara could understand her being fed up with parental supervision and wanting independence. She guessed it was Bella's parents who funded her wardrobe, though.

She smiled, all the same. 'I know, right?' And she did. Put her under the same roof as Lydia and her stepfather Benedict for more than five minutes and the cracks started to show. *As for her father, Robin, who'd wanted Lydia to abort her...* 'Nice to be able to stay in college accommodation.' Tara knew the poshest lodgings on the central St Oswald's site would have been given over to summer conference delegates, paying handsomely for the privilege. Bella's room had seen better days. The paint was peeling in one corner and in the background, behind a whiff of cigarette and what must be Tiffany & Co (she could see the scent bottle on a shelf), there were undertones of must.

'It was good to find a room in the same house as Julie.' As she mentioned her friend's name, Tara watched Bella's eyes fill with tears again.

'You saw a lot of each other over the summer?' Tara asked.

The young woman hesitated. 'As much as possible. But we were both very busy, of course.' She spoke quickly. 'It was the same for Julie as for me. She was out earning money, working lots of hours. She had a job at Clifford's in town.'

A vegan restaurant.

'But I guess you caught up between shifts? We were wondering what Julie did in her free time.'

That pause again. What was on Bella's mind?

'She was doing other stuff too, so we ended up seeing less of each other than we would have liked.'

'Do you know what kind of "other stuff"?' Max asked. 'Was it more work?'

Bella frowned. 'I was busy as well,' she said after a moment, 'so I didn't manage to ask.'

Tara didn't believe that. Bella had the air of someone who'd have quizzed her friend. Had she been shut out for some reason?

But as if to prove the situation had been beyond their control, the student added: 'Julie was dashing around so much she even missed one of her shifts at Clifford's last month. Almost got the sack, so she said, but a colleague covered for her. Told the management she'd called in sick when she hadn't.'

That was interesting. Julie had clearly built up loyalty – even amongst temporary workmates. What had taken up her time? Tara reckoned she must have been reliable usually – if her colleague had been prepared to stick their neck out for her like that.

'Did you notice if Julie had any visitors here?' Max asked.

Bella looked down at her beautifully cut skirt. 'I think her ex, Stuart, came over once? But they finished with each other ages ago.'

'They were still on friendly terms, then?'

Bella gave Tara a quick look. 'Just in a casual way. She instigated the split, but he's well over it now. Julie wouldn't stop wearing his ring, which I thought was provocative. She said she liked it, and why should she chuck it away just because he'd behaved like an idiot. But it didn't seem to bother Stuart, so he must have put it all behind him.'

So, Bella might have wanted to be around Julie – and maybe it was she who'd emulated the other student's choice of clothes – but she hadn't approved of everything the dead girl had done. As for Stuart's reported recovery after the break-up – well, he wouldn't be the first man to hide his true feelings.

'Did you see Julie leave the house yesterday, Bella?' Max asked. 'Did she talk to you about her plans?'

'I…' She paused once more, and pulled a tissue out of a box on her desk. Her eyes were welling up again. 'I did happen to spot her go out. It was – I don't know – maybe eight forty-five p.m.?' She was being very specific, Tara noted. 'My shift at the pub yesterday was over lunch, so I was around. But I'd only just dashed in myself, so I didn't go out and speak to her. I don't know where she was going. We'd chatted briefly on the phone a short while earlier, and I knew she was busy.'

The room Julie had occupied was at the top of the house, as far away from Bella's as you could get. Yet Bella seemed up to date on the state of her friend's relationship with Stuart. Had Julie filled her in, or could Bella have come by the information some other way?

The CSIs were still busy, checking Julie's belongings. Boxes were dotted about the student's room, and a large rucksack was propped up in a corner, the contents half in, half out. Max and Tara put on overalls and gloves before they entered. Once again, Tara wished she'd taken the time to change – she'd been anticipating a quiet Sunday at home when she'd selected her outfit that morning. But when you were on call, you could never be sure of your time off.

'She'd already packed up,' the investigator nearest the door said. 'Everything was ready apart from her night things, make-up bag and wash kit.'

She must have done it all ahead of time, to be ready for her mum. Tara guessed they'd been close. She swallowed back emotion. As a child, she'd mostly been looked after by her mother's cousin, Bea – a stalwart and the best stand-in anyone could wish for. Tara couldn't help thinking of how each of them might feel if they lost the other to violence.

Now, thanks to the unpacking the team had done, small signs of the young woman Julie had been lay about the place. An incense burner – you could still smell it in the air too – a decorative tile with a design that looked North African, and a mug with the Campaign for Nuclear Disarmament logo on it.

Tara spotted an upturned object in an evidence bag on one of the tables in the room. She went to look and the CSI who'd spoken to them followed her.

'It's one of those Guy Fawkes masks, like they used in *V for Vendetta*,' she said.

Tara recognised it. She'd seen people wear them on various protests, including one in town recently which had focused on freedom of speech. People wearing them en masse looked eerie and threatening – you could feel the force of their feelings, without knowing their identity. The barrier meant you couldn't interact with them in the way you normally might. Tara knew it was illogical, but it felt as though they'd set you up as the enemy – even if you shared the same ideals.

Julie had customised her version of the mask. She – or someone – had added blood-red tears to its cheeks. They flowed freely near the blank, cut-out eyes, then extended down the mask's face, thinning out into drips as they reached its broad moustache. The additional decorations were effective. She must have used acrylic paint – or something with some texture to it. Tara shivered.

Julie had wanted to make the world a better place, using everything in her power to create a lasting impression. Had her strong feelings clashed with someone else's – equally strong, but without a shred of morality?

'Have you found anything that might give us a lead?' Max asked.

The investigator shook her head. 'Nothing personal that provides a clue as to who she met up with last night. It's a shame there's no revealing correspondence – all we found was a single postcard. But that's the way of it these days. Hopefully the contents of her phone will help, once you've accessed it. Most of what's here is just what you'd expect – except one oddity.'

She turned to pick an evidence bag out of a crate and lifted it so that Max and Tara could see. It contained scarlet paper, cut into bits.

'You can't tell, now that it's in there,' the CSI said, 'but we took a photograph before we bagged it. It formed a complete heart shape, until it was sliced to pieces.'

The news sent Tara's nerves jangling. Of course, Julie might have been given the heart by a boyfriend and cut it up herself, in a fit of anger. But it could have been the other way round. Had the heart been destroyed and then delivered to Julie as a message? Tara thought back to the packages she herself had been sent as a teenager – by a stalker who'd never been caught. The first envelope, which arrived on her sixteenth birthday, had been stuffed with handfuls of dead bees. At one point her tormentor had sent a pig's heart – and there'd been maggots too. Things had escalated, and when they felt they were being ignored they'd killed her cat.

After eighteen months the campaign had finally stopped, but by then she'd been a changed person – always on her guard, never trusting anyone, be they a friend or a stranger. She'd learnt self-defence from an ex-cop, Paul Kemp, and eventually regained some control. But then, earlier in the year, for the first time in more than a decade, she'd been sent a new delivery. Dead bees again. She'd been right back to her terrified sixteen-year-old self. The message with the bees had read:

Remember me? I'm still here. If you don't want me back, call off the dogs

She'd had no idea what had sparked it. There'd been nothing since, but she still approached her doormat each morning with a thumping heart.

A hot flush of anger rose up in her – not at her own tormentor, but at the thought of someone messing with Julie's head. As well as the lacerated heart, maybe it was they who'd stuffed her pocket with wilting flowers.

A final act, perhaps, after they'd killed her.

CHAPTER FIVE

Bella Chadwick stood just inside her closed bedroom door, listening. She still hadn't finished packing her things. With all that had happened, she couldn't focus. She'd have to do it later, then call a cab to transport her stuff to her new room.

She'd been by the window at first, watching to see when the two detectives left, but it had been ages now and they hadn't appeared. The CSI van was still outside. What the hell were they looking for? Julie hadn't had a lot of stuff. She'd always said people were more important than things. Bella had felt Julie's eyes on her smart clothes and her expensive belongings when she'd said that. She didn't seem to realise that it wasn't your fault if your parents gave you money to spend. Julie's mother wasn't wealthy, but long-term, Julie would have been a lot better off than Bella – if only she'd lived. She'd been clever, excelling at her studies. Bella was coming unstuck on that score.

She tensed; she could hear talking out in the corridor now. Thoughts of the future were banished instantly. A man's voice, and a woman's. Could it be the pair of detectives she'd spoken to earlier? The place was crawling with investigators, but the tone and pitch of their voices sounded right. She longed to open the door a crack but didn't dare. Instead, she went back to the window and stood to one side, her breath held.

After a moment, the pair appeared in front of the house. It *was* them. They were deep in discussion, as though they'd found something out.

Only when they got into their car did she pull her mobile from her skirt pocket. She didn't want to be interrupted – it was a conversation she needed to get right. And whilst the detectives had still been there, she'd been worried they might come back with extra questions.

Taking a deep breath, she dialled Stuart's number. As it rang, she practised her words. How should she put it? What precise tone should she use?

Stuart, you might not have heard. We've just had the police round here. You see, something awful has happened to Julie…

He was her best friend's ex, but nothing could hurt Julie now. Bella needed to be close to him and going in quickly, with sympathy, felt like the right way. But she didn't get the chance to recite her speech out loud. Stuart didn't pick up. Her heart was thumping as she hung up without leaving a message.

CHAPTER SIX

Blake had been reading the latest updates on his phone as he walked from his car to Addenbrooke's mortuary. The sliced heart might be significant. It seemed to fit with the flowers and the way Julie's clothes had been disturbed. If Julie's attacker had been sexually fixated with her, had they been an ex, or someone further removed? He wondered about Bella Chadwick's comments; that business about Julie still wearing Stuart Gilmour's ring. He'd left Tara to track him down and do all the usual background checks. She was working with Jez Fallon, who was speaking with other contacts of Julie's, including her colleagues at the restaurant where she'd worked over the summer… Blake frowned for a moment at the thought of the team's newest recruit. But it was early days; he needed to give the guy a chance. He couldn't currently sum up his objections to the bloke other than that he seemed too good to be true. Blake distrusted people who were aggressively shiny on the surface – in his experience, they were often hiding something underneath.

He knocked on Agneta Larsson's door and, hearing her mutter something that was probably welcoming in nature, walked in.

His old friend's eyes met his. They'd been out together once and it had ended well, with only fondness on either side. Now they were each married with kids, but the closeness hadn't faded.

'Not how you expected to spend your Sunday,' he said to her.

'Nor you yours.'

They both looked at the post-mortem table where Julie Cooper's body lay, covered by a green sheet.

Agneta sighed. 'Poor girl. She was so young.'

He nodded.

'Frans's parents are staying with us,' she said. 'They've taken Elise to feed the ducks. I saw the way they looked when I got the call to attend the scene at Wandlebury. It was like they'd each just drunk a glass of sour milk.'

Blake had got the measure of Agneta's in-laws from previous reports. 'Frans understands, though?'

A sad smile lit her face. 'Oh yes, he understands. And Elise will too, when she's older. Dear God – who could doubt the importance of something like this?' Then for a moment her eyes rested on his again. 'You look like you haven't slept. Those first four months are just the worst – if it's Jessica that's keeping you awake?'

She was the only person who knew the background to the drama in Blake's marriage. He and Babette had two children now. He was as sure as he could be that Jessica was his, but Kitty, their seven-year-old, was another man's. And he himself hadn't been aware until Babette told him when Kitty was eighteen months old – right before she'd scooped her up and left for Australia to be with her 'natural father'. The shock and sorrow had been overwhelming. There'd been no time for goodbyes. Babs had told Blake to let them go without a fight – it was better for Kitty.

Blake still didn't know what had made her come back a mere two weeks later. His wife had spent months persuading him to give their marriage another go. He'd done it for Kitty – he still loved her so much that it hurt. But he was increasingly sure he'd made the wrong decision. It was often the thought of Babette's lies – known and as yet unknown – that kept him awake at night. Jessica was a lot less stressful, though often noisy at 3 a.m.

'Let's just say it's a whole host of different things,' Blake said. 'But there's nothing fresh.' He nodded towards the body. 'This is what's going to keep me awake now.'

'I'm afraid you are right there, Blake.' Like most people she called him by his surname. He preferred it; 'Blake' managed to sound less formal than 'Garstin'.

Her intonation made him catch his breath. 'What have you found out?'

'Something like this is always horrendous, but what I am seeing here is the stuff of my worst nightmares.'

Blake thought of the flowers in Julie's pocket and the missing ring. Was there something ritualistic going on? 'Tell me.'

She nodded. 'So, we saw at the scene that Julie had been struck on the head, near her left temple. As I speculated at the time, that didn't cause her death. I would guess it knocked her out. She was hit with something smooth and not large – maybe seven centimetres across.'

Blake remembered the way the dead woman's skirt had been rucked up. 'Had intercourse taken place?'

Agneta shook her head. 'No, but her underwear was damaged – a few stitches torn. It looks as though someone had pulled her knickers down, and then they – or Julie herself – made some effort to yank them back up again. They were lopsided. The pictures are all in the CSIs' report – they followed-up here before I started work.'

Blake rubbed his forehead. What did that mean? Maybe whoever attacked her had had a very particular scenario in mind, and hadn't managed to enact it in a way that reflected their sick fantasies?

He shuddered and Agneta caught the movement.

'I'm afraid all that is just the beginning,' she said. 'You asked me if I thought the body had been moved.'

He nodded.

'My guess from the evidence I have now would be yes, and not long after her death. If she'd been left for some time, the way her blood had pooled due to gravity would make the position she died in obvious. But that effect can change up to six hours after death.

Nonetheless, there are signs that she died on her side. And there was bruising, Blake.'

'On her hands… I noticed it.'

'Not just there, as it turns out – those instances were just the most obvious. There'd been pressure on the outer surface of her legs too, around the knee and hip area, and on her elbows and forearms also.'

He swore. 'She was trapped? Kept in a very confined space?' Nausea crawled through his gut.

Agneta's eyes showed her emotion – and the fact the she wished she didn't have to pass on the news. 'She had fibres under her nails. Wool. Green wool.'

He frowned. *Why the hell would that be?*

'And then there are the blood results, and the scratch marks around her neck.'

He drew in a deep breath, preparing himself.

'There was a huge build-up of CO_2 in her body, Blake. She died of asphyxiation. Sometimes people in that situation claw at their throats instinctively.' She watched his face. 'They feel as though there must be something physical restricting their airway. I'm sorry.'

'So we're dealing with someone who knocked her out, either on purpose or in the heat of the moment, then trapped her somewhere airtight, or almost so, and left her to die. Again, we can't know for certain that they realised she'd suffocate, but they'd sure as hell have heard her trying to get free if they'd stuck around. And the signs point to someone who was sexually fixated on her.' He put his hands over his face. They needed to get this guy and get him quick. Both for Julie and to protect anyone else who might cross his path.

'Just one more thing, Blake,' Agneta said. 'Tara noticed Julie had been wearing a ring recently?'

He took his hands from his face and nodded.

'Well, I'd say that was removed during the course of what happened to Julie last night. There was a minute cut on her finger and bruising to the knuckle that suggests it was pulled off with some force.'

CHAPTER SEVEN

Tara looked up as Blake strode through the communal office door. He reached her desk in a fraction of a second and leant forward, his eyes haunted.

'Have you located Gilmour?'

What the heck had Agneta told him? It was bound to be awful, but she'd never seen him look so utterly desolate before.

'He was staying at this place over the summer.' She took the sticky note she'd used to record the details: a house on Atterton Road, just to the north of the city centre. 'His college gave me his mobile number too – eventually – but he's not answering. I understand he's due to move back into St Bede's accommodation shortly, but he hasn't picked up his keys yet. You think he's guilty?'

'I don't know, but he smells the worst so far.'

Her mind was full of questions he wouldn't want to answer until he had more time. She'd have to be patient. He took the note from her hand. 'Thanks.' The look in his brown eyes had hardened suddenly: anger and determination overlaid the torment.

He turned to Jez, who was at her side. 'Get over to St Bede's. See what they have to say about Gilmour and check he's not on site.' He glanced over his shoulder. 'Megan?' The DS looked up. 'We're going to Atterton Road.' Then his eyes were on Tara again. 'You and Max head over to St Oswald's. Find someone who can give you an overview of Julie's life there. Her mother mentioned a tutor. We'll meet back here at six thirty for a briefing – unless something significant kicks off. I'll want the background checks by then too.'

As Tara rose from her desk, she caught Megan watching her. The DS clearly didn't like her and Max being paired. Did she really still think there was something between them? She must be going around with her eyes shut. Anyone could see that Max returned Megan's romantic feelings.

Tara hadn't expected Julie's tutor to be at St Oswald's on a Sunday, but within five minutes of their arrival they were told the man in question – Lucien Balfour (*really?*) – would speak to them immediately.

The man who arrived was smart in a dark suit, with sandy hair and blue eyes. Tara caught the smile and appraising glance he cast her, just before the porter behind the desk introduced Max. She didn't miss his surprise as he realised she was also with the police. His initial look morphed into something more sombre as he held out his hand to her.

'Lucien, Julie's tutor. I heard what had happened to her as soon as I arrived, what with your people needing to access her room over on Chesterton Road. I can't tell you how shocked I am. Let me take you somewhere quiet where we can talk.'

'We weren't sure we'd find you here on a Sunday,' Max said, falling into step with Balfour as he led them along a stone walkway.

'I like to be around when the students arrive. It's a challenging time for a lot of them – especially the freshers, of course. Anything to make the transition to college life a little easier.'

Tara remembered the notes from Blake's interview with Julie Cooper's mother. The tutor had spoken to Sandra when she'd dropped Julie off at the start of her second year. She'd found his words reassuring. She mentioned it to the man now.

'Ah yes.' He turned to look at Tara over his shoulder. 'I well remember the occasion. There was a close mother–daughter bond,

I felt. I understand it was just the two of them at home, before Julie came away to study.' He put a hand to his forehead for a moment. 'This must be causing Ms Cooper unimaginable pain.' His words sounded genuine, but there was something theatrical about the gesture.

All around them the start of term was apparent. They were walking alongside a grassy court, surrounded by ancient stone buildings on all four sides, high and imposing. Tara could see students toing and froing, weighed down with boxes, carrier bags and rucksacks. One was dragging along a wooden trolley by an iron handle. It was loaded with bulging sacks and creaked as it went. Everywhere there was a sense of hubbub and she could almost taste the nerves in the air. Tara had had mixed feelings when she'd started university. Her stalker had stopped their anonymous mail campaign six months earlier, but she hadn't relaxed. She hadn't known why they'd gone quiet, or who they were. When she went off to study in a new city, she didn't know if they were still keeping tabs on her. She'd found it intimidating, moving into student rooms for the first time, in amongst all those strangers. In those days, everyone had seemed like a potential threat.

And here in Cambridge there must be extra pressures: to succeed academically in a highly challenging environment, and to fit in socially, too. It went way beyond simply standing on your own two feet, having left your family behind. You had the weight of their expectations on your shoulders. That was always the case, of course, but where expectations were high, you had further to fall. She thought of Julie's mother's desire to see her daughter blaze a trail for people of her background. The interview notes had made it sound that way. But equally, there'd been nothing wrong in encouraging her daughter. She'd wanted it for Julie's own sake, from what she'd said to Blake. For a second Tara wondered about her own half-brother, Harry. He was starting at Cambridge that weekend too – and had been pushed into it by his dad.

Lucien Balfour took them diagonally across the next court they came to, over the grass, whereas the students all walked round the edges, sticking to the stone pathways. Balfour turned and caught her gaze. He smiled. 'Fellows and their guests are allowed to walk on the lawns, as are the crows. Other than that, it's strictly forbidden. That said, we get some drunken excursions onto the grass every year. The last wise guy who tried it had to write a letter of apology to the Dean.'

At last they came to a door in the corner of the building that surrounded the court.

'This is my staircase. Second floor up.'

As they mounted the spiral stairs inside, shadowy in the minimal light let in by narrow windows, Tara looked at the nameplates next to the doors that they passed. It appeared that academics shared their staircases with the students – maybe so that they could keep an eye on things. The place felt timeless; nothing she could see placed the setting in the modern day. It was only when Balfour opened the oak door to his office, revealing a MacBook Pro on his desk, that the spell was broken.

The sun was getting low now and the heavy curtains blocked out much of the fading light. Their red velvet gave the place a theatrical air, and the whole room looked rich: full of oak furniture, darkened by age and buffed to a high shine. The place smelled of polish combined with a faint tinge of what Tara reckoned were spirits. She could see a half-full decanter on a side table, nestled amongst tumblers, turned upside down to escape the dust. Except there wasn't any. A cleaner must come in regularly – Tara couldn't imagine Balfour doing the job himself. He didn't look the sort to get his hands dirty – his suit was immaculate – and besides, she got the impression he enjoyed the college hierarchy. There'd been relish in his tone when he'd talked about the grass rules. He knew his place (relatively elevated) and probably thought everyone else should know theirs too.

'I presume I can't offer you a drink?' Balfour nodded at the decanter and reached to switch on a side lamp.

'No, thank you,' Max said.

Balfour nodded. 'I shan't want one myself until later. Much more to be done before the day is out.' He sat at his desk and motioned for Tara and Max to take seats opposite. 'How can I help?'

'It would be useful to know more about your role here, and how you knew Julie,' Max said.

'Ah, yes.' Balfour spoke slowly. 'The impenetrable Cambridge system. No reason you should know if you weren't educated here.'

Being patronised was one of Tara's least favourite pastimes. She took a deep breath and tried to relax her shoulder muscles.

'I have multiple roles in the college and the university,' Balfour went on, leaning back in his chair and running his hand through his thick hair. 'But in relation to Julie, I was her college tutor. To an outsider, the name might imply that I taught her her subjects, but that's not the case. College tutors exist to provide all-round pastoral support and guidance to students. We welcome them when they arrive, introduce them to college and university life, then offer advice on anything from health and finance to study worries or family problems. We tutors are a friendly face – a port in the storm, if you like. We're a dedicated bunch.'

He smiled and Tara inwardly gave up and acknowledged that she didn't like him; it wasn't something she could switch off. At least she realised she was prejudiced. She'd had her stepfather's views on the overriding superiority of the university rammed down her throat for years and that had been enough to make her kick back.

She always tried to look at the place in the round. She'd met the most wonderful people who were products of a Cambridge education, understood how its Nobel laureates had changed the lives of millions, and had encountered lively and enthusiastic academics who lit up the world.

But, Tara being Tara, she couldn't help noticing the *others*. The ones who seemed so conscious of their superiority. Those who were quite happy with the old-boy network. The ones who divided people up into the right and the wrong sort to attend a place like this.

She sprang to attention and switched it all off – at least, as best she could. 'That sounds like a very valuable resource for the students here.' She smiled at Balfour, thanking her mother inwardly for her inherited acting skills. 'And I can see that role would give you more insight into Julie's personality than other members of college staff.'

He smiled back. 'That's right – or at least, than any other *fellow*. When we say "staff" we tend to mean people who work to support us. I speak of administrators, housekeepers, cooks and the like.'

I stand corrected…

'So, Julie would have come to you with her worries?' Max said.

'I sincerely hope so. I like to think we had a good, solid student–tutor relationship.'

'I appreciate everything she told you would have been in confidence,' Max went on, 'but in situations like this it would help us a great deal to know if she had any particular worries.'

Balfour frowned for a moment, but then nodded. 'I understand.' He steepled his fingers, then shifted slightly in his chair.

Tara couldn't help thinking that he was filtering what he knew, mentally, before committing himself. She glanced at Max for a second, her eyebrows raised, and he nodded her on.

'Were you aware of Julie receiving any unwanted sexual attention – either from a student or a member of staff?' she said quickly, staring into his eyes. 'Or,' she paused a moment, 'from a fellow?'

She hoped Max had guessed she would go in hard. She wanted to pull Balfour out of his careful contemplations. By his expression, her tactic had worked.

'Good Lord!' The words came out with a splutter. 'Where on earth did you get that idea? I've never heard anything of the kind.'

A moment later, he caught up and closed his mouth. 'Oh.' A gulp. 'Oh, heavens. I see. Had she? I mean, when you found her? Had she been…?'

Max leant forward. 'You're reading more into my colleague's question than you should. But it's not uncommon for relationships to turn violent.' He paused. 'And that can be especially true if there's an imbalance of power in that relationship.'

Tara properly loved Max sometimes. He was able to cut to the heart of the matter in such a calming, deceptively innocent way.

Balfour leant back in his chair, heaved a sigh and straightened his shoulders. He'd recovered himself now. 'Of course, of course. Well, as I said, Julie never mentioned anything.'

'Would it always be up to her to come to you with a problem?' Julie had sounded like an independent type and Tara could relate to that. For her part, she wouldn't dream of going for a heart to heart with someone whose job it was to be her 'friend'.

'By no means.' Balfour looked affronted. 'I make sure I see my students at least twice a term, whether they request it or not. We have informal get-togethers over tea; I try to create an atmosphere that will put them at their ease.'

'And Julie attended those sessions?' Max asked.

Balfour nodded. 'Beyond those occasions, of course, I sometimes hear via other routes if there are problems that might affect my cohort.'

'Other routes?'

'For instance, if a student was struggling, academically, then I might get that information from one of their supervisors.'

So people told tales behind the students' backs? Tara could see it made sense – otherwise they might never have the courage to ask for help – but it made the trusting relationship between a student and their tutor feel less secure. What else might Balfour have been told about Julie? Had she been aware of all the knowledge her tutor had – perhaps relating to quite personal issues?

'Did Julie have academic worries?' Max asked.

Balfour laughed now. 'Oh heavens, no! She was one of the brightest in her year. And very sure of herself. You asked if she ever received unwanted attentions from any students or employees. Well, I can tell you now, she'd have given them short shrift if she had.'

She and Max exchanged a quick glance. They both knew that wouldn't be enough with a certain sort of person. Some men didn't understand that no meant no. Some might be determined to get their revenge…

'That was one comment on her personality that did come back to me,' Balfour said. 'She was headstrong. Wilful. Wouldn't take no for an answer. She did her work all right, but she was opinionated, and that wasn't always popular.'

'Headstrong' and 'wilful' sounded like outdated objections from supervisors who didn't like having their viewpoints challenged. Tara knew all about that. It made her think of her former boss, ex-DS Patrick Wilkins. 'Can you tell us who found her attitudes challenging?'

Balfour pulled back at her question. 'Oh, that was more of a general comment.' He stopped for a moment. 'I probably heard most of the people who taught her say it at one time or another. But she was young. Personally, I respected her for knowing her own mind.'

Was that really true? Perhaps they'd never know.

'Did she ever come to you proactively with any worries?' Max asked.

'None. I wish she had. If I'd had any inkling that she was in danger…'

'We still don't know exactly how she died,' Tara said.

'I'm afraid the rumours flying around and your presence don't leave much to the imagination.'

His words came quickly. It was a fair point, but she could tell he was rattled.

'And what about any other trouble you heard about, via the alternative sources you mentioned?' Max asked. 'We understand she was politically active – involved in demos, maybe, that kind of thing.'

He raised his eyebrows at that. 'That's not to be discouraged, I presume?'

Max didn't rise. 'Far from it. But things can get out of hand, occasionally.'

Balfour shook his head. 'I imagine she was too astute to get caught up in anything that might damage her future.'

'But you were aware she took part in that type of activity?' Max persisted.

'Vaguely. I knew she had passionately held beliefs. She had a boyfriend at one time, from another college. I think they egged each other on.'

'Stuart Gilmour?' Tara's eyes were on him.

Balfour frowned. 'Yes, that's right. Now *there's* someone who was on my radar for a while. I understand he found it hard to let go when they broke up. In the end, I discovered Julie had complained about him to his college. His name hasn't cropped up for a while, but he might be one to watch.'

That extra bit of information was interesting. Why had Julie let the guy into her room over the summer if she'd previously complained about him hounding her? And it proved Tara was right about Julie being the sort to tackle things independently. She'd dealt with the trouble direct rather than asking Balfour to hold her hand.

'What about any unhealthy friendships?' Tara was thinking of Bella. The student made her uneasy.

But Balfour opened his eyes wide. 'Oh no. I think Julie was too self-sufficient to get sucked into anything like that.'

'Do you know Bella Chadwick?'

'Ah.' A sour smile crossed Balfour's lips. 'Now I understand what triggered your question. I do know Bella. She was a great admirer and imitator of Julie's. I'm afraid I've found her to be something of a fantasist, but I believe Julie kept her at arm's length. A wise move.'

Tara wondered. Julie might well have done her utmost to keep some distance between them. But what did you do if you'd acquired someone like Bella – keeping an eye on your movements, copying the clothes you wore, moving into the same temporary accommodation you'd chosen over the summer?

Much of what Tara was considering was speculation – at the moment. There was more research to complete. But something about Bella Chadwick made her skin creep.

CHAPTER EIGHT

Veronica Lockwood put down the phone in the Master's Lodge at St Oswald's. Her husband – billionaire chairman and chief executive of Lockwood's Agrochemicals, and figurehead of the college – lowered his Sunday paper. He raised an eyebrow.

'Tony, calling from the porters' lodge. The CID pair have left, it seems.'

'Thank God for that. Last thing anyone needs, a load of police tramping about the place just as the parents and students are turning up.'

'They'll be plain-clothes detectives, Alistair. It won't be obvious.'

'But they're crawling all over the girl's room on Chesterton Road, I hear. The gossip will be rife.'

'And that is why I thought it would be best if you went over to the main college today. If you show your face, it will promote a feeling of calm control.'

He laughed. 'That's nonsense. As it is, people know a St Oswald's student died in suspicious circumstances *over the summer*. Who knows what she got up to during that period? It's nothing to do with us. If I dash out there and start issuing calming words to the parents, it's taking ownership of the thing. I intend to stand well back. And besides, most of the fellows know I went down to London yesterday to see old Westerly.' Lord Westerly. Alistair was trying to get funds out of him for a new library. 'They probably assume I'm still down there. They won't question my not being on the spot. The less I fuss, the quicker everything will die down.'

'What made you stay in London overnight in the end?'

He chuckled. 'You know how it is. You have to oil the wheels if you want to get money out of a chap. Westerly can put alcohol away like nobody's business without it mellowing him at all. I had trouble keeping up. Ended up toddling back to the flat. I couldn't possibly have used the car.'

It would have been useful if he'd let her know. Though she'd relaxed gradually, as she became increasingly certain he was telling the truth. He didn't know the tension he'd caused.

'So you really were there all night then, were you?' She watched his expression closely. She had his attention now.

'Yes, of course.' He gave an impatient sigh. 'Look, I know the gossip worried you, but I never saw the girl as a threat. If you're feeling tetchy, why don't you play something?'

Veronica glanced at her harp, sitting in the corner of the palatial, high-ceilinged room. 'I'm not in the mood.'

He was reading the paper again. 'Well, so long as you keep in good practice, ready for the students' welcome party.'

She didn't bother suppressing a groan. 'Alistair, I'm used to playing to audiences in international concert halls. I'm not going to get worked up about a gaggle of youths whose preferred listening is probably distinctly low-brow.' She walked over to the drinks table and poured herself a whisky instead.

'Get me one too, would you?'

She did so, and gave it to her husband. As he took his first sip, his eyes still on a news story about the economic forecast, she analysed his face. No trace of worry at all – he seemed entirely relaxed. She'd known him many a long year now, and that had to be a reassuring sign, surely?

CHAPTER NINE

Blake was perched on a beige sofa next to Megan in a bungalow on Atterton Road. Stuart Gilmour's landlady, Janice Lopez, sat opposite them, her hands clasped together. Stuart himself was nowhere to be seen.

'I've been away for the weekend – my sister's hen party, down in Brighton – so I don't know where he's got to,' she said.

She looked very post-hen party: eyes bloodshot, skin pale. She'd probably been hoping for a quiet evening…

'But it's odd, because he was meant to be moving out today – back into college accommodation.' She pulled a face. 'I still don't have anyone to replace him. This place might not look like much but the mortgage is almost killing me. Having a lodger just about keeps the bailiffs from the door.'

'What's Stuart been like as a tenant?' Blake asked.

The woman shrugged. 'Fine. Keeps himself to himself. Turns his music down if I yell at him.'

'Did he ever bring this girl back here?' He showed her a photo of Julie.

The woman looked at the image through half-closed eyes, frowned and then winced as though the action had hurt her. 'No, I don't think so. She's a girlfriend?'

Blake didn't answer. The report of a suspicious death was already on all the regional news sites he'd checked, stating that the victim was being 'named locally' as student Julie Cooper. Photos of the dead woman were being posted. But he guessed

Stuart's landlady had been too busy nursing her hangover to read the latest headlines.

Janice Lopez sighed. 'Well, I'm guessing by your faces that Stuart's in trouble. Shall I tell him to call you when he reappears?'

He and Megan exchanged a glance. 'I'll get one of our people to come and wait outside,' he said. 'We'll keep trying his mobile too.'

'Oh, Lord.' Lopez put her head in her hands, her long, dark wavy hair falling forward. 'A friend of mine did ask if I knew what I was doing when I agreed to have him here.'

Blake leant towards her. 'Why was that?'

She looked up at him slowly. 'He needed a place after he was suspended from college for the rest of the academic year. You didn't know?'

Blake took a deep breath. 'No. I didn't know.' From what his own academic mother said it took quite a lot for someone to get suspended – or 'rusticated', as she called it. Antonia Blake had had to deal with discipline once upon a time, when she'd acted as a college tutor. Nowadays she'd escaped that sort of irksome role and concentrated on her research and teaching as a professor of art history.

Megan sat forward, notebook in hand, eyes alert. 'Did he tell you why?'

'Oh yes, he was quite open about it. He's very active, politically, and he got caught after a protest that went too far. It wasn't a first. I think he said he'd been fined for criminal damage once, and there was something else. I can't remember what.'

Would that be enough to get you suspended? Blake wasn't sure. Maybe the repeat offences had finally pushed the college authorities over the edge. The background checks Blake had asked for would include everything they needed to know. Shame he hadn't got the information already.

'The college obviously took the matter seriously.' Blake frowned. 'But you weren't too worried about having him here?'

'St Bede's housekeeping department and his tutor gave me a reference to say that he'd never been known to cause trouble in his college accommodation. He's clearly very idealistic, but I didn't have any reason to think he'd cause me problems.'

She leant to one side, grabbed a handbag from a coffee table and set it on her lap. A moment later she'd retrieved a bottle of water and a packet of painkillers that had been inside. 'Why did you want to talk to him again?'

As they pulled out of the bungalow's drive, Blake turned to Megan. 'If Gilmour had brought Julie back here last night he could have attacked her without anyone hearing. No landlady at home, and there's enough space between this and the next house for a scuffle or her cries to go unnoticed.'

'And if it's not him, then why has he gone AWOL when he's meant to be moving back into his college?' Megan said.

'Good question. We need an update from Jez.'

Megan called the DC, putting him on speaker, and Blake asked him for the latest.

'I'm about to come back for the briefing. No sign of Gilmour at St Bede's, yet. One other interesting thing.' He paused.

'Go ahead.' *It's not the movies. I just need the information…*

'Someone else has been asking for him too. A student from Julie's college. She was a bit het up, apparently, and left a note for the porters to deliver. They weren't keen to let me see it, but I managed to persuade them.' Blake wondered what methods he'd used. *'Turned out the message was from a girl called Bella Chadwick. She wanted Stuart to get in touch.'*

'Useful to know. We're aware of her.' A second later he rang the station. He needed Tara to contact Chadwick again – find out why she was so desperate to reach the dead student's ex.

CHAPTER TEN

Ex-detective sergeant Patrick Wilkins was sitting in the Grain and Hop Store pub, next to Parker's Piece – the square expanse of grass that separated Regent Terrace from Parkside police station. He glanced at Shona, her red lipstick gleaming, long red nails in pristine condition. How did she chase around all day, yet still look so immaculate? He half admired and half mistrusted her for it. Shona was the kind of person who got other people to do her work for her. For a long time, he'd provided her with leads for the scoops she wrote up for *Not Now* magazine. He'd always wondered if their affair was based on anything more than her career ambitions and the bitterness he felt towards his colleagues. And yet here they still were. As for the leaks, Patrick felt he'd been entirely justified. His old boss – DI Blake – had always been down on him. And then, when Tara Thorpe had joined the team as a detective constable – supposedly working under Patrick, but with no sense of respect whatsoever – he'd been all the keener to feed Shona information that would make both his colleagues' lives difficult.

He and Shona had come up with a wonderful article the previous year. It highlighted a crazy theory Tara had been following and threw the nauseating 'special relationship' she and Blake clearly had into sharp focus. As Tara's former colleague, Shona had revelled in the results as much as he had.

But that high point had come just before the fall. An old friend of Tara's – with some inexplicable sense of loyalty to her – had caught him out. Seen him drinking with – and recorded him talking to – Shona's editor, Giles Troy. Thorpe's spy – Paul Kemp, an ex-cop no less, who'd left the force under a cloud – had handed the evidence over to Blake. And that had been that. Umpteen disciplinary meetings later, Patrick's patience with the force had run out. It had felt good to resign – a form of revenge. They deserved to be without him.

He'd planned to make Tara pay personally, too. He'd had an angle to pursue, and the promise of hard cash from Giles Troy if he came up with the goods. But it hadn't been as straightforward as he'd hoped…

A moment earlier, Patrick and Shona had seen various cars turn up at the station. The idea that Thorpe might be in one of them twisted a knife in what was still an open wound.

Shona had had her eyes on the activity across Parker's Piece too, but now she turned towards him. 'They'll be in there for ages. The murder of a young student will keep them up into the night.'

'You're sure it's murder?'

She smiled her cat-like smile. 'The official statement said the death was being treated as suspicious. How often does that sort of announcement get downgraded? Besides,' she ran her tongue over her bottom lip, making the gloss there glisten, 'I managed to grab a quick word with a young PC earlier, who's clearly in the know.'

'And who clearly doesn't know you!'

She stroked his cheek with a long-nailed finger. 'It's not my fault if he was… too revealing when we spoke. People often are. I don't know what comes over them.'

He wasn't going to flatter her ego by showing his jealousy. He knew her tactics of old. He peered again at the station. For a moment he had the urge to walk over there. He'd like them to see him as they entered the building, to make them feel uncomfortable. But would his appearance have that effect? Or was he insignificant to them now? The thought made his heart rate ramp up.

If only he hadn't failed in his plans to get back at Tara. Giles Troy had been excited at the prospect at first, and invited him in to *Not Now*'s offices for some 'cosy chats'. Patrick suppressed a shudder. There was nothing cosy about Giles. He was the sort of man who was your best friend until he wasn't – and at that point you'd better watch your back. Patrick had been busy setting up his new business, but he'd spent all his free time on the Tara project – slowly, bit by bit, he'd been sure he could get what he needed. But the results hadn't come, and Troy had started to treat him with contempt.

How dare he? He must know what a difficult task their project was.

'Darling,' Shona sipped her gin and tonic, 'the look in your eye. Thinking about Tara and Blake?'

Back in the spring, he'd hinted to Shona that he and Giles had plans to get even with them, but he'd never shared the details. He'd wanted to keep something for himself. The moment you told Shona about anything it felt as though she owned it. And if it was sensitive information then it felt as though she owned you, too.

Giles had approved of him keeping the crux of the matter secret. He'd told Patrick he was monitoring Shona's performance. He was curious to see how she'd do, now she no longer had a contact inside the police. Privately, Patrick thought most of Shona's success in the last couple of years had been down to him. He wouldn't be surprised if Giles came to see that too, and eased her out of her comfy job before long.

What a back-stabbing lot they were!

And now, he was very glad he'd played his cards close to his chest. At least Shona wasn't aware of how he'd failed.

'Tara and Blake don't bother me,' he said at last, tearing his eyes away from the station.

'But you had something up your sleeve, didn't you?' Under the table, Shona had slipped off one stiletto shoe and was now rubbing her stockinged foot against his inner leg. 'You hinted you'd cooked up some way of getting your own back. But you've been mighty quiet about it ever since.'

He jacked up a smile, and hoped it looked convincing. 'That's all in hand. It'll take time – it's quite… complex.' Hopefully she'd forget about it if he kept fobbing her off.

'Ooh – you're full of mystery! Go on, let me in on the secret!'

She could beg all she liked; he was keeping the washed-up project to himself. 'My lips are sealed.'

Shona's eyebrows arched and she pouted. 'You used to be willing to tell. What have I done wrong?'

It was good to have the upper hand for once – even if there was no real secret that was worthy of her interest. 'When I've got what I need to move forward you'll know all about it, believe me.'

He had a nasty feeling that she saw right through him. But what was the worst she could do?

CHAPTER ELEVEN

Tara called Bella Chadwick as soon as she got Blake's message. The news that she'd gone to Stuart Gilmour's college to try to track him down made her pulse quicken. Was there something going on between Bella and Julie's ex? Either a relationship, or some other connection she'd kept quiet? It wasn't her only omission; she'd said nothing about Stuart being suspended. But that might not be relevant, of course, and there was no particular reason she should have. She managed to get the girl straight away. Five minutes later, with Bella's latest words fresh in her head, she was ready to join the briefing.

Blake was at the front of the room. His eyes looked hollow, his five o'clock shadow dark against unusually pale skin. Tara took a seat next to Jez. He didn't look like the new boy. He had an air of confidence – relaxed in his surroundings. His sidelong glance met hers for a second before Blake started to speak.

As he relayed Agneta's findings the room went absolutely still. She heard a sharp intake of breath and realised that it had come from DCI Fleming. Tara knew the woman cared, but she normally maintained a poker face. It went with her persistence and discipline, which Tara reckoned was driven in equal measure by the desire to help people and an absolute need to make it to the top of the tree.

'I've been thinking about the type of container the killer might have used to imprison Julie,' Blake said quietly. 'The green wool under her fingernails might indicate a trunk, or hard suitcase of some kind, that had at least one bit of clothing in it.'

Tara raised her hand. 'The students. They've all been packing up to come back over this weekend. It might be someone who arrived yesterday and was in the process of unpacking. Or someone who's been staying locally and getting packed up, ready to move over to their new college accommodation.'

Blake nodded. 'We haven't got enough to arrest Stuart Gilmour but I've requested a warrant to search his room. Barry's stationed outside his lodgings on Atterton Road in case he shows up there, and Sue's briefing everyone at St Bede's in case he goes to the college direct.'

'Has Kirsty got anything extra from Sandra Cooper?' DCI Fleming's tone was urgent.

DC Kirsty Crowther was acting as family liaison officer and was with Ms Cooper now. Julie's mother was staying locally until she felt strong enough to travel home. Tara couldn't begin to imagine her pain.

'She managed to ask about Julie's dad' – it was Max who spoke – 'just to rule him out. Julie did meet her father once, but the guy made it plain he didn't want anything further to do with either of them. He ended up marrying a US citizen and he's been living in Arizona for the last seven years. We're checking that's where he is now, for the record.'

Fleming nodded. 'What more do we have on the boyfriend?'

It was Blake who spoke first, to relay the information he'd got from Stuart Gilmour's landlady.

Jez raised a hand. 'That also ties in with the background checks that Tara and I did.' He glanced down at his notebook. 'Several charges relating to direct action protests in the recent past: aggravated trespass, breach of the peace. And one for harassment.'

Fleming raised an eyebrow.

'Repeatedly doorstepping a local councillor who supported the development of a new animal testing facility on the outskirts of the city. He was in the habit of speaking to the woman's children too – asking them if they realised how evil their mother was.'

'I wonder whether he took to doorstepping Julie as well – once they'd broken up,' Tara said. 'We've got evidence that she felt threatened – or at least bothered by him. According to her tutor she complained about him to his college. But Julie's "friend" Bella Chadwick also told us that Julie allowed him to visit her over the summer.'

'What's the story with Bella?' Fleming must have picked up on her tone.

Tara gave her the background, before adding in the latest details. 'Jez found she'd been asking after Gilmour at his college this afternoon. Apparently she was agitated. I called her to ask why.' Tara had gone in hard, knowing that Bella would be unprepared. 'She stumbled over her words and it took her a moment to come up with a coherent story. Eventually she told me she'd been trying to contact him in case he hadn't heard about Julie. Although they'd broken up, he'd known her well – and who would bother if she didn't? She said it would be cruel to leave him to find out by accident. I pointed out that we've been trying to break the news to him all day.'

Fleming nodded. Her slick black fringe didn't move. She must use gel or something on it. Its fixed position increased Tara's feeling that the woman was Teflon-coated. 'And what's your impression of Bella so far?'

'I'd say something wasn't quite right about her relationship with Julie. Her tutor implied as much when we spoke to him. And he called her a fantasist.' Tara paused for a moment. 'She dresses like her, and I wouldn't be surprised if she deliberately arranged to stay at the same digs in Cambridge over the summer in order to be with her.'

Megan looked up. 'Isn't that a bit speculative?'

Surely that's what Fleming had just invited her to be? But sharp retorts were out. On this case, Tara was going to keep the moral high ground by behaving like an adult. Something she hadn't quite managed on their last major enquiry...

'You're right – I need to do more digging. I'm going to check who booked the accommodation first and I'd like to know more about how they interacted too.'

For a split second, Tara saw the ghost of a smile cross Blake's face. He'd probably guessed the feelings she'd damped down.

'Good. Speculate some more then,' Fleming said, which was greeted with a frown from Megan. 'If you're right, what do you think we have? Did she idolise Julie?'

Tara frowned, reanalysing everything they'd learnt that day. 'I think so. I get the impression Bella's quite conventional. Maybe she was fascinated by Julie's edginess, and her dedication to her causes. It was odd that she "just happened" to be watching at the time Julie went out last night too. My guess is she wanted to spend more time with her and her plans to keep her close over the summer hadn't worked out as she'd hoped. I'm starting to wonder if she envied her too. And maybe the adoration she got from Stuart Gilmour – even if it was oppressive. Bella might feel he's mad, bad and dangerous to know.'

The question was, how dangerous? And if Bella had wanted to be exactly like Julie, might she also have wanted to replace her?

'Did Julie have a record?' Fleming asked.

Jez shook his head. 'Nothing shows up.'

'But it sounds as though she was involved in similar protests to Gilmour,' Max said. 'On top of what her mother told us, there's the mask the CSIs found in her room. And her tutor seemed vaguely aware of her being politically active, too.' He filled the team in on the details.

Jez looked up. 'I managed to speak to some of the people she roomed with at college last year, and some contacts from the societies she joined too. Sounds as though she was quite reserved, socially – kept herself to herself. But they noticed that Bella tended to hang around her. I got the impression Julie was ambitious. She wrote for the St Oswald's newspaper. The guy who edits it reckons she wanted to go into journalism. I've recorded the various pressure groups she belonged to on file.'

'If she had an eye to the future, she'd probably avoid getting caught up in anything too damaging,' Fleming said, echoing Lucien Balfour's thoughts.

That fitted the DCI's own sense of priorities, but maybe it was simply that Julie's idea of how to promote change hadn't matched her ex-boyfriend's. After all, would doorstepping a councillor and harassing their children change anyone's mind over how things should be run? Tara could imagine the action might put other people off standing for public office, but other than that, it didn't sound likely.

'Anything on the flowers that were found in Julie's pocket? Or the cut-up heart in her bedroom?' Blake asked.

'The heart was coloured in by hand in red felt-tip on standard eighty gsm paper.' Megan had the CSI's report in front of her. 'I wondered if it was something Julie had made – which had been destroyed and returned to her by a disgruntled ex.'

'I checked,' Max said, 'but there were no felt-tips at all amongst Julie's belongings. Kirsty asked Julie's mother and apparently she wasn't into drawing or crafts.'

'The cuts were done quite neatly,' Tara said. 'You'd think someone acting in anger might have made a rougher job of it – torn the thing up or made the bits tiny, so that it could never be mended.'

Megan frowned. 'I suppose we can't expect people to act like stereotypes all the time.'

How long was it going to take for the woman to stop resenting her? Tara had ignored protocol on a previous case. It had certainly put Tara in danger, and Megan still thought she'd played fast and loose with her own safety, too. Tara had already apologised. And the third time, she'd actually meant it… more or less. 'If someone sent her the heart, maybe Julie had never seen it before,' she said. 'Perhaps they cut it up neatly because they wanted her to piece it back together and get their message.'

Megan was silent.

'I looked the flowers up,' Tara went on. 'Anemones have several different meanings according to the site I found, so that muddies the waters. They can symbolise positive things like anticipation for the future, or be a talisman of protection against evil.' She paused, tucking her red-gold hair behind her ear as she read her notes. It needed a cut. 'But they can also signify forsaken love or the death of a loved one.

'Or the loss of them to someone else.' Once again, she felt the hairs rise on the back of her neck.

'Do we know of any other relationships Julie had, as well as the one with Stuart?' Fleming had been walking up and down the room, but now she paused and perched on the edge of a desk, her patent leather shoes gleaming in the overhead light.

'I wondered if Balfour knows of or suspects a relationship with one of the college employees.' Max glanced at Tara, his eyebrows raised.

She nodded. 'I got that impression too.'

'There's no hard evidence,' Max went on, 'but he was desperate to assure us nothing of the sort would *ever* happen. And sadly, we all know that's not true. It wasn't a crazy question to ask. As for Balfour, he ended up gushing.'

'Any ideas who might be involved, if your hunch is right?' Fleming asked.

'We still haven't found "John".' Blake was leaning against the wall at the front of the office. He looked a bit dishevelled in his beautifully cut suit, but his eyes were sharp enough.

'John?' Fleming's questioning glance met his before he'd had the chance to carry on. She was as impatient as the DI.

He nodded. 'If he exists. Julie told her mother she was staying in Cambridge for the summer to help a professor called John with some research.' He glanced at Tara and Max. 'We now know Julie was working at a local restaurant whilst she stayed in Cambridge, so it's not clear how official this other "research work" was. It's possible she made it up. Maybe she fancied staying in town over the summer and didn't want to hurt her mum's feelings. She might have felt a worthy research project was a better excuse than waitressing.'

'But?' Fleming said.

'From Bella's statement,' Blake turned to Tara and Max again, 'it sounds as though Julie did have *something* extra on the go over the vacation. Something she kept to herself, and that made her miss a shift at work once – assuming that information is accurate.'

Jez looked up. 'One of her workmates at the restaurant gave me the same story – and the manager mentioned she seemed preoccupied. But they didn't know what else she had planned for the summer, any more than her college contacts did.'

'I'd say there's more to find out on that score,' Blake said. 'And that "John" is probably out there, whether or not that's his real name.'

CHAPTER TWELVE

Max was with Jez and Megan at the Tram Depot pub. It was mid-evening, and they'd all have to be in work again early, but he hadn't been able to face the thought of sitting alone at home with the image of Julie Cooper's body in his mind's eye. The student had been five years younger than Max's wife when she'd died, but seeing the body still brought back memories. A beer and company was good – especially when the company included Megan. If Jez hadn't been there, he could have relaxed properly, but he wasn't being fair. He knew he needed to make an effort.

'Does Tara ever come along to the pub?' Jez lounged against the bar next to Megan. His thick blond fringe had fallen forward and he looked at Max's fellow DS from under it, a light in his blue eyes. A confident swagger; that was what the guy had.

Nothing wrong with that, of course.

Megan raised an eyebrow. 'Sometimes.'

Jez gave a slow smile. 'She said she had a "prior engagement" this evening. I wasn't sure if she was teasing me. She had a look in her eye.'

Megan's expression was wry now. 'Ah yes, I think I know the one.'

'It *is* Sunday though,' Max said, taking the beer the bartender had poured him. 'Not unnatural for people to have other plans.' He paused. He knew what Tara was up to, but if he said, would he be sharing her private life with Jez in a way she wouldn't want? It sounded as though she'd been holding back. Whether she'd been playing hard to get, or had reservations about the new

DC, he wasn't sure. 'I think she might have been seeing family,' he said at last.

Megan glanced at him as he spoke and he took in her beautiful dark eyes. She'd asked him out, earlier in the year, but instead of saying yes, he'd panicked. He'd been kicking himself ever since, but her move had taken him by surprise. He hadn't been in a relationship since Susie had died. For a second his gaze slid to Jez. He bet the guy hadn't known a moment's anxiety in his life. And he was smiling at Megan right now.

'What about the DI? He doesn't hobnob with the likes of us?'

'There's no arrogance to Blake,' Max said. He had Megan's attention again now, but for the wrong reasons. She felt he defended their boss too quickly, even though the DI treated them both with respect. It was one of the few things they disagreed about. 'He'll have dashed back home to help his wife with their children. Kitty's only seven and they've got a four-month-old baby too.'

Jez took a sip of his beer. 'That explains it. I didn't know he'd got kids. The day after I arrived, I almost wondered if there was something between him and Tara.'

Megan opened her mouth to speak and Max decided to leap in.

'They got to know each other before Tara joined the force.' He set down his beer for a moment. 'She was a journalist back then, and they investigated the same murder. Tara was one of the killer's targets, so it was pretty intense. Her old boss here, Patrick Wilkins, had it in for her and spread rumours about the pair of them, but it was all rubbish.'

The smile spread across Jez's face once more. 'Good to know. Thanks.'

Megan had closed her mouth again. Max knew she found it hard to dismiss the accusations Wilkins had bandied about, and he couldn't entirely blame her. There *was* a spark between Tara and Blake, that was the trouble. He'd seen it at work: watched as his DI had held the DC in his arms after she'd escaped from a burning building. But that didn't mean they were having an affair. Blake was one of the good guys, and Tara wouldn't break up a family. Her own background – which he'd gradually picked up on – meant she knew childhood could be a tricky time. Her actor mother – the now-famous Lydia Thorpe – had had her as a teenager. Her father, Robin, hadn't wanted to know. He was now a well-established architect in the city, happily married with three children he and his wife Melissa much preferred to Tara. Lydia's career took off when Tara was small, and so she'd mainly been looked after by a cousin of her mum's – Bea. Max had met Bea once. The bond between her and Tara was as strong as any he'd seen, but he reckoned the distance her mother had kept still rankled. Knowing your father had tried to persuade your mother to abort you couldn't be easy, either…

Max picked up his drink again. 'I can't imagine what it must be like for the DI, to go from discussing the results of a post-mortem, to playing with his kids.'

Jez raised an eyebrow. 'Sounds like a challenge. Mind you, the thought of having kids at all would have me running for the hills.' He made it sound like something to be proud of.

Megan had stuck with a lemonade and she sipped it now. 'Ah, you'll change your mind. Find the right woman, and before you know it…'

It sounded as though Megan must want kids, then. Max was disconcerted to find himself interested in the fact.

Jez's slow smile was back in place. 'Not me. I like my independence. Besides, I've already been married once. Big mistake. Once bitten, twice shy.'

Megan looked discomfited for a moment. She wasn't sure if she'd put her foot in it, Max guessed.

But Jez seemed entirely relaxed. 'Sure you don't want a shot of something in that drink?' He was leaning forward, coaxing her. Max felt all his muscles tense.

She grinned, and shook her head, making her glossy chestnut curls dance. 'Quite sure, thanks. I'm running on empty as it is.'

An hour later, they were all still there. Eventually, they'd managed to secure some bar stools, but Max was knackered now. All the same, he didn't want to leave first… which was ridiculous. He wasn't even managing to contribute to the conversation – unlike Jez, who was coming up with witty comment after witty comment. At last, Max got up.

'Right. I'd better be off.'

He didn't like to acknowledge the relief he felt when Megan glanced at her watch, raised her eyebrows and slipped off her stool as well.

'Heck, me too. I might be on sugary drinks, but they won't replace sleep.'

Jez gave her what Max felt was a knowing look. Did he think something might happen if the two of them were left alone together?

'My car's still at the station,' Jez said, 'so I'm going to cut back through Adam and Eve Street. Would either of you guys like a lift?'

It was Megan who shook her head first. 'I think a walk might help me sleep.'

He nodded, a smile still playing round his lips. 'I'll see you tomorrow then.'

Max hesitated. 'You haven't had too many to drive home?' He couldn't leave it unsaid.

Jez laughed. 'Good God, no. I'm a big guy, don't forget. Besides, I've not got far to go.'

Max knew he'd moved to Cambridge from Newmarket when he'd joined them, but he was also well aware that accidents could happen within minutes of home. He thought again of Susie. As he and Megan started walking, he wished he'd kept track of what the DC had drunk.

Max lived on the north side of town, further out than Megan. It had been pure luck that he'd already been in town earlier when the call about the body at Wandlebury came through. He might nip on a bus once they reached her place.

'What do you think of him?' he said, nodding over his shoulder in the direction Jez had taken.

Megan glanced sideways at Max, a twinkle in her eye. 'A charmer.'

That much, I'd noticed. But he hadn't warmed to the guy himself. He wondered about the story behind Jez's marriage break-up. Normally, the mention of it wouldn't have made him pause, but he couldn't imagine the DC being faithful for five minutes. He gave Megan a look. 'I think Blake's got reservations. Not that he's said anything.'

Megan raised an eyebrow. 'Well, I think Jez has got designs on Tara. That might be what's putting the DI on his guard.' He opened his mouth but she held up a hand and smiled. 'Even if it's only a subconscious reaction.'

'Back there in the pub I thought it might be you he had designs on.'

Her smile broadened now and she cast him a sidelong glance. 'I think it's just his way. Why? Would you mind?'

He cocked his head to one side. They were walking along East Road now, one of the least romantic locations in Cambridge. A drunk guy was lolling against a wall outside a kebab shop, making guttural sounds in his throat. They made Max want to pass him at speed. If he and Megan got spewed on it would definitely ruin the moment.

He moved a couple of inches closer to her. 'What do you think? I only stuck it out in the pub for so long because I thought he'd leap on you the moment I left.'

Her eyes met his. 'So, if I suggested the cinema again…?'

The last time she'd asked he wasn't convinced he could manage an evening out without getting emotional. Plus, he hadn't been sure if she'd meant as a date. He got it now.

'I'd say it was an excellent suggestion.'

She moved closer to him as a fire engine sped past, its sirens blaring, and the guy behind them finally threw up.

'Plenty more suggestions where that came from.'

CHAPTER THIRTEEN

John slumped towards his landline's base station and tried to put the handset back into the charger. The phone slipped and fell to the tiled floor below, cracking across its cheap plastic backing.

He didn't glance at it; didn't even see it, consciously. Julie's face was clear in his mind's eye: her pale complexion, her raven-black hair and those eyes. They were like deep pools of the purest water. He'd looked into them and seen her conviction; seen the fire under the surface. He'd been too tired to share that feeling. He'd spent so many years living a half-life, caught in a place removed from reality, because reality was too painful.

He'd damped down his guilt for a long time. He was ashamed that he'd managed to lock it away for such an extended period. After a rocky patch as a child – when he'd almost gone under – a teacher at school had made him believe for a while that he might have a normal life. He'd studied, and somehow managed to drink his way through university and still get a first. More of the same followed as he'd completed his PhD. He'd been able to work and to party and to blank it all out. But then – when life slowed down and he got a steady job – the cracks had started to show again.

He imagined them – small and hairline at first. But he couldn't quell the taint that was inside him. It pushed its way into the fissures and made them wider. And they spread, until they covered every part of him.

It was true. The police would come. Maybe not tomorrow. It might take them a few days. But they would find out about him, and they would come. The advice that he should be ready was intended to protect the reputations of others, not his own. He knew that.

His recent actions would have a knock-on effect.

He should never have— He tried to block out the memory of that day in his office. His lips on Julie's. Her kissing him back. And then his hands…

She'd offered him the chance to try to suppress the past again – to block out the evil that was inside him. But you couldn't stopper something like that.

Dimly, he remembered her telling him it wasn't too late. Whatever it was, it couldn't be that bad. People would understand. He wasn't a bad person.

That was what she'd thought. But she'd been wrong.

His house was about to be repossessed, but as he picked up his bottle of whisky, homelessness wasn't on his mind, any more than his broken phone was. He swigged from the bottle, the liquid filling his throat with fire.

As he closed his eyes the visions in his brain flickered between Julie and a dark and lonely road, high up in the mountains.

CHAPTER FOURTEEN

Tara's mum, Lydia, had texted her to let her know she, Bea and Kemp had let themselves into her house. Bea had a spare key.

Tara's cottage stood in a bit of no-man's land, close to the River Cam. As she walked across the dark, deserted meadows to reach it she could see Lydia's elegant figure, framed in a brightly lit window. She'd got a glass in her hand. They'd clearly opened a bottle then… and that would be Tara's mum's doing. Bea would have waited and Kemp liked his beer. Tara had put four in the fridge earlier that day, before she was called over to Wandlebury.

The collision of home and work life was always hard to handle. She couldn't imagine hooking up with a partner permanently; someone who lived a normal life and would expect her to bounce home – bright and cheerful – at the end of a long day. Amongst her visitors, at least Kemp was an ex-cop, so he'd understand. And Bea would get it too, just because she was like that. But her mother – well, her actress mother was more familiar with on-screen detectives.

Tara put her shoulders back and unlocked the front door. She found Bea in the kitchen.

'I brought something to heat up,' she said. 'It's in the fridge. Nothing special – just leftovers from the hungry hordes.'

Bea ran a traditional boarding house, just across the river in Chesterton. She was the best cook Tara had ever been fed by, and she'd been training Kemp up quite successfully too – somewhat against the odds. He lacked the air of a domestic god.

'You're a saint. Thank you.'

Tara still wasn't exactly sure where Kemp fitted into Bea's domestic set-up. He'd started by staying at the boarding house because he needed to be in Cambridge. Bea was a big fan of Kemp's and had insisted that he pay friends' rates. Her hero-worship stemmed from the support Kemp had given Tara when she'd been stalked. His calm practicality, and the self-defence tricks he'd passed on, had combined to put Tara back on the rails again. Over the last few months he'd found time to help Bea renovate some of her guest rooms – to help pay his way, so he said. And earlier that year, Tara had got the impression that things had moved on between the pair of them. He was at the boarding house more often than not now, helping with the clientele. It had been just over a year since Bea's husband, Greg, had died. Tara guessed she and Kemp were taking things slowly. The set-up made her happy and nostalgic at the same time. At one point she'd been in a relationship of sorts with Kemp, but that was a long while ago now. And he and Bea were much closer in age.

'I've been keeping up with the news.' Bea gave Tara's shoulder a squeeze. She knew of old that Tara wouldn't want to talk about the murder, but her eyes said it all.

Tara put her hand on Bea's for a moment and squeezed back. She hesitated. 'Was there any post for me when you came in?'

Bea frowned. 'I'm not sure. Kemp was first through the door. Probably not – not on a Sunday – but were you expecting anything?'

Since the packet of dead bees that had arrived six months earlier, Tara hadn't been able to switch off the adrenaline that hit her when she came home at night, even on days when there was no official delivery. She'd had parcels and messages sent by hand in the past. 'No, nothing special. I just wondered.' She went to the fridge to get the food Bea had brought with her. 'Has everyone got drinks?' She called the question through to the sitting room where her mother and Kemp must be lurking, even though she already knew the answer. *Pointed, but fair.*

'Doing well thanks, mate.' From the fridge contents she could see Kemp was on his third beer.

'*Excellent.*'

'And I am too, thank you, darling.' Lydia appeared now and leant in to give Tara a kiss on the cheek, holding her glass to one side. 'We went straight ahead. I was feeling the need.'

She was staying over at Bea's that night. Tara still had no spare bed and at times like this, that was an advantage. Lydia probably felt the same – she wouldn't want to rough it at Tara's isolated, draughty cottage. The cows on the common could make a racket in the early mornings too. The lack of a bed provided them both with a polite excuse.

Tara's mind was still on the drinks. 'Wonderful. Do keep on going. I might even have one myself.'

'Oh, good idea.' Lydia gave her a smile, clearly oblivious to any undercurrents. She leant against the kitchen wall, a move Tara reckoned was designed to show the level of her exhaustion.

'Here, let me get you one.' Bea moved towards the bottle Tara had, sitting on the worktop.

But that wasn't fair. Bea would have been coping with all her regular paying guests and now she'd got Lydia to look after as well.

'You sit down,' she said to Bea. 'Honestly. I'll stick your food in the oven.' She peered at it. Chicken in a sauce that smelled of cider. 'It looks amazing.' She turned to her mother's cousin. 'You're a lifesaver.' Tara meant it. She was just that – and had been for Tara's entire upbringing. 'So how did it go with Harry's drop-off?' She turned to her mother as she unscrewed the lid on a bottle of gin.

'Fine, fine. Everyone at Bosworth College was charming.'

That tended to be the case when you were a star of stage and screen. But Tara had really wanted to know how it had been for Harry. He was her half-brother – wanted from birth in a way that she hadn't been. They'd only started to get to know each other better just recently, and she was now prepared to overlook the fact that he was treasured.

'What did Harry think?'

'Well, his room's quite poky,' Lydia said. Tara's mother lived in a mansion, out in the Fens. 'But a nice second year student told me the accommodation gets better, later in your degree. And the other freshers seem friendly. I'm sure he won't regret coming here.'

He'd had a good, hard think about it, though. His father – Tara's stepfather, Benedict (currently in Munich on business) – had encouraged him *very* heavily to take up his offer. Bosworth was Benedict's old college. Lydia and Benedict had tried to enlist Tara as their PR woman, wanting her to convince Harry how nice it was, living in Cambridge proper. She'd thought he ought to make up his own mind. She made a mental note ask him out for a coffee soon.

Lydia returned to the sitting room (to take the weight off her feet) and Tara made Bea go and join her, but Kemp came to help lay the table. A nice gesture, but she knew there was more to it than met the eye.

'So how was it today then?' he asked, glancing at her with a ready grin. He looked like what he was: a rough diamond.

She gave him a repressive glance back. 'Just as you'd imagine.'

He heaved a sigh. 'Yeah, I got that. Bloody awful. But how's the investigation going?'

'You resigned from the police, Kemp – it's not my job to share titbits with you because you secretly miss it.'

He opened his eyes wide. 'I can't believe that's why you think I'm asking. Nah. Don't miss it at all. After all, I'm still a detective, and now I get to run my own show.'

Kemp had turned to private investigative work when he'd left the force. And he'd excelled himself when he'd secretly decided to look into the affairs of her old boss, Patrick Wilkins. He'd known the DS was a thorn in her side, intent on causing her trouble. You'd never guess that someone as big and ungainly as Kemp would be so cunning and adept at trailing their prey. He'd been looking out for her interests, but she couldn't help feeling he'd also embarked on that little project to relieve the tedium. Since Wilkins had left the force, he'd committed the cardinal sin of setting up as a PI himself. Kemp spat blood every time he was reminded of the fact.

'Don't you miss the variety of police work though?'

He gave a low chuckle. 'Maybe. Just occasionally. But the lack of a boss breathing down my neck more than makes up for it. Sure you can't tell me anything about the case?'

'Quite sure. I can only discuss what's already in the public domain – you know that.' She loved baiting Kemp. But after a moment the levity brought on by banter and a single swig of gin and tonic was gone. Her mind was back on the scene at Wandlebury. 'And to be honest, I'd rather block it out over supper.'

His shoulders went down. 'Fair enough. Can't blame you there.'

Tara was fighting the urge to ask her next question, but in the end her nerves won. 'There wasn't anything waiting for me on the doormat when you came in, was there?'

Of course, he'd have said if there had been. Probably. Unless he'd put it down in a corner somewhere, got stuck into the beer and forgotten all about it.

Kemp put his head on one side. 'Is this still about the package you got sent in the spring? You're still on edge about it, even on a Sunday?'

It must be high in his mind too, then – even six months on.

'I can't quite switch off until I know there's been nothing.' There weren't many people she'd have admitted that to.

For a second the thunder clouds rolled over Kemp's readable face. 'I could still try and find the bastard for you. I wish you'd let me.'

He'd had a go, way back when she'd first met him, just as he'd started working as a PI. His former CID colleagues had got wind of his activities and warned him off. It hadn't stopped him at first, but when they'd threatened him with court action things had got tricky. Then, back in the spring, when she'd had her latest delivery, it had been Blake and her colleagues that she'd turned to. She'd asked them to abandon the case when the attempts to trace the buyer of the dead bees had gone nowhere. It felt as though she was wasting police time on a deeply personal matter.

'I hate the effect the bastard's had on you,' Kempt went on. 'It's like that one package has wiped out the intervening years. Go on. Let me have another go at catching him.'

At last she nodded. 'Maybe. I just need time to take stock. Once this murder case is over, we can think it through.'

He sighed. 'All right.'

'But it's way different this time,' she added, 'thanks to you. I've got the means to take control now.'

Yet still she hadn't – not quite.

It was just as her visitors were about to leave, shortly before midnight, that Tara heard a text come in on her phone. She reached it out of her bag and Kemp caught her smiling.

'Who's sending you messages in the dead of night?' he asked, shamelessly leaning towards the screen.

She snatched it away. 'Do you mind?'

'Spoilsport. You wouldn't tell me about the case earlier and now…' He looked mournful.

'Oh, for heaven's sake. It's just from Jez, that's all.'

'The new DC, eh?'

Kemp hadn't met him, but she'd passed on the latest office gossip.

'There's no need to say it like that.'

'Like what?'

'In that leery tone. As though there's dirt to be dished.'

'Isn't there?'

'He's just being friendly. He went to the Tram Depot after work with Max and Megan and he was messaging to say they'd missed seeing me there.'

'*They* did? Or *he* did?'

She smiled again as she stuffed the phone back in her bag.

'Stop looking for gossip when there isn't any. It's time to wrap the evening up, anyway. I'm knackered.'

Bea looked done in too. She'd been making noises about going for a good hour and a half as her mother had sat back in her chair, her laugh ringing out at the stories Kemp regaled them with. The time for polite hinting was over.

At last, Tara was alone in the cottage, watching her extended family tramp through the darkness, over the tussock-humped grass towards the Green Dragon foot and cycle bridge that led to Chesterton. As they reached the path by the river Cam she could see them better, lit by the lamps that were placed at intervals next to the water. Bea and Kemp walked close together and her mother still had a spring in her step, despite the hour. She'd had practice, Tara supposed, after years of late-night parties and receptions.

Tara drew the threadbare curtains of the sitting room, noting a new tear near one of the hems. The wind had got up. It rattled the sash and stirred the thin material she'd just adjusted. She wasn't going through another winter with the house in this state. She'd had someone in to quote for new windows two weeks earlier. The price had made her toes curl and they couldn't fit her in until February. She should have asked way back in the spring, so they'd told her. She'd have to rig up something temporary, even if it looked hideous.

She dragged herself to bed and lay there, the only sound that of the wind. The cottage might be crazily impractical, but she loved the feeling of distance it gave her from the mayhem of the world. It was one of the few things that made her feel peaceful.

But tonight, the isolation wasn't enough to make her feel separate from the chaos out there: the violent disturbance to the natural balance of life that had led someone to kill. She couldn't banish the thought of Julie Cooper from her mind. As she stared up at the ceiling she was back at the crime scene at Wandlebury Ring.

So, Julie's body had been moved: she'd been left to die in an enclosed space, not out in the open. Which begged the question: why choose to dump her body at Wandlebury? The spot where she'd been found was close to an access track, so it wouldn't have been that hard to carry her from a vehicle. She'd been slight in stature, too. But there'd been more risk taking her body there than to open countryside, for instance. There were a handful of houses inside Wandlebury Ring. They were nowhere near the crime scene, but someone returning home late at night *might* have driven past. It was unlikely, but not impossible.

What had made the killer take that risk?

CHAPTER FIFTEEN

On the upside, baby Jessica was asleep. On the downside, her chosen resting place was Blake's shoulder. For some reason she seemed impervious to background noise, but not to her position. If he tried to lay her down, her eyes flew open. Under other circumstances, he might have sat by her cot and waited for her to settle, but she had a cold so she was more fretful than usual. He didn't want her to wake Babette, who'd gone to bed hours earlier.

He wished that concern was as selfless as it sounded. Sure, he wanted to take his turn with Jessica. He'd been out all day – Babette would have been hard at it, coping with all the feeding and nappy changing, as well as keeping Kitty happy. But also, he was enjoying being on his own, with only a sleeping baby for company.

He'd just decided to end their marriage when Babs broke the news of her pregnancy – a good couple of months after she'd become aware of it herself. Suddenly he was trapped with a woman who'd betrayed him and who – he was convinced – was still lying to him.

He thought of the man who was Kitty's father but he had no mental image. He'd never set eyes on the guy – as far as he knew. Earlier in the year, Babs had finally given him a name: Matt Smith. *Really?* He still wasn't sure he believed that detail. What had happened out in Australia? It had been such a drastic move on Babs's part to head out there. Okay, so she'd done it to be with Kitty's biological father, but he'd only been a brief fling, according to his wife. And then – after all that – she'd rushed home to England again after just two weeks. She claimed this Smith guy hadn't been paying eighteen-month-old Kitty enough attention. It would certainly have riled Blake – to see his beloved daughter being ignored by her biological father. But why hadn't Babs taken a bit longer to try to fix things? Surely you didn't make such a wrenching life change only to give up after fourteen days?

Now, when he and Babette were together, he found it increasingly hard to ignore his nagging doubts. And there was her continued lack of honesty, too. They hadn't been trying for a baby – she'd told him she'd forgotten to take her pill. But it was always half-truths with Babette.

Through the resentment he felt, he became aware again of the warm bundle on his shoulder and a stab of guilt shot through his chest. *I don't regret you, little one.* He stroked Jessica's back through her brushed cotton babygro and nestled his head for a second against hers. *How could I?*

He walked the sleeping baby through to the kitchen. He ought to try to put her down again soon – get some rest himself – but maybe he'd leave it five more minutes in the hope that she'd be more deeply asleep.

He sat down with her at the round oak table, next to where he'd left his laptop, and flipped it open. In a moment, the room around him faded and his mind was one hundred per cent back on the case. The techs had reported on the contents of Julie Cooper's phone.

The pictures from her camera roll came first. A lot of them were what you'd expect – shots of the woman he recognised as Sandra Cooper, outside a terraced house, and several he assumed were of friends in various locations. Then, about eighteen months earlier, ones of a self-confident-looking young guy started to appear. He seemed about Julie's age. Stuart Gilmour? And then there were various shots of demonstrations. One in particular struck him. It was after dark, and the scene was lit by the torches and ignited cigarette lighters that the protesters held. They were all wearing Guy Fawkes masks like the one that had been found in Julie's room. Then Blake realised that one of the glints of silver in the photo wasn't coming from a flame or a bulb. It was reflected light, off a sharp piece of metal. One of the protesters had been carrying a knife.

Absently, his hand went to Jessica's back again, stroking it. He thought ahead to when she'd be old enough make her own decisions.

The person with the knife – man or woman, there was no way of knowing – might have had it for any number of reasons. They could have been a troublemaker, intent on using the occasion to cause mayhem. You got that sort – ones that the genuine protesters bitterly resented but found it hard to weed out. Or it could be someone who'd wanted to create real fear in the heart of the opposition. He noted the date of the photograph. Had trouble broken out that night? Who or what had the protesters been targeting?

The camera roll also contained selfies of Julie with a girl superficially from the same mould – similar hair and make-up. This was Bella, Blake guessed. He'd confirm it with Tara and Max the next day. It was clear that it had been Bella who'd picked up the phone and taken most of the shots.

The weirdest photos went back twelve months and were in amongst pictures of a college bedroom. Had this been the start of Julie's second year? Maybe she'd taken the shots of her room to show a friend or relative. But the odd images next to them in the roll made no sense at all.

They were of a cat. Not a real one – a statue. Could it really be made from gold? That was what it looked like. Would it be solid? Blake had no idea about that sort of thing. Babs watched *Antiques Roadshow* sometimes but it wasn't his scene. It was an evil-looking creature. A wildcat with its mouth drawn back in a snarl. The maker had managed to make its green eyes – formed with jewels that might actually be emeralds – look fierce. Angry even. In that first photo the creature was sitting on a shelf. In a second, Julie had clearly picked it up with one hand whilst photographing it with the other. It showed the underside of the statue, on which there was a porcelain plaque bearing a coat of arms and some writing.

Familia supra omnia.

Blake hadn't done Latin at school, but he'd picked up enough over the years to guess the translation. *Family above all else.*

The notes on Julie's phone didn't tell him much. Some were clearly shopping lists, from which he gathered that she'd been a healthy eater. Some seemed to be reminders about things she needed to do. 'Pass research over to Graham.' 'Sort out banner.' 'Ring Ava.' And one just said 'Scotland?' Thoughts about a holiday, perhaps?

After that, he ran his eyes down the list of people who she'd been in contact with by text recently. The exchanges with her mum were the most heartbreaking. Fond messages a week or two back – and then increasingly concerned texts going only one way, as Sandra Cooper had tried all the methods she knew to reach her daughter earlier that morning.

Next on the list was Bella Chadwick. The girl might have been living in the same house as Julie over the summer but she'd clearly made contact electronically too. Maybe because Julie had kept her distance in person? He scanned the messages.

Fancy meeting up later?

Lots of that sort. Julie had often made excuses, but occasionally she'd said yes. They'd spent some time together over the summer. And she'd sent one text the previous afternoon, before Julie had left her lodgings for the final time.

What's up? Fancy a chat? I've got news.

But the reply from Julie had been discouraging.

Sorry. I'm a bit busy. Hey – text me your news though.

She'd been trying to let the girl down gently, Blake guessed. Bella hadn't texted again but there was a call from her later that day. It was very short.

After Bella's messages, Stuart Gilmour came next on the list, despite their break-up. Blake scrolled back in time, rewinding Julie's life until he reached the spring, when her mother thought she and Stuart had parted company. It took a while. They'd remained in frequent contact.

There were texts back in February which were mainly practical: details of where and when to meet, for instance. He found the occasional one that seemed to refer to a recent sexual encounter… *You were amazing tonight – can't wait to be with you again.* She'd replied *Thank you for having me*, with a winky face.

And then he paused for a moment over an exchange that focused on Bella.

The first text was from Julie to Stuart and just read *Bella!* It was accompanied by an alarmed face emoji.

IKR? he'd replied. Blake had to look that one up – I know, right? *Was she following us, do you think?*

Either that or it's one hell of a coincidence, had been Julie's response.

It's like I said, Stuart had come back. *You're her idol.*

She'd put in a laughing face. *Hardly. Reckon she fancies you. That's why she copies the way I dress and keeps an eye on us.*

He'd signed off with a scared face emoji. Blake wondered what he'd really thought. If there was anything in Julie's assertion, he might have been flattered. Though maybe Bella's behaviour was a bit over the top.

It was only a week or so later that the tide had turned.

It's not what you think, Stuart had written.

I bet it's exactly what I think, Julie had shot back.

Was it Bella who had come between them? Or had this been about something else? The sniping went back and forth but, of course, they both knew the problem, so there hadn't been any need to spell it out. He rubbed his stubbly chin. Where the hell was Stuart Gilmour now? He might not tell the truth about the break-up, but at least Blake could look him in the eye as he pressed him with searching questions.

Jessica let out a soft sigh in her sleep as he read on, down the list of texts. He was almost drifting himself – thanks to the repetitive sniping in the messages – when he came across one that caught his eye. It was from Stuart to Julie.

Read this! I know about John. And I've got evidence. Now tell me you don't want to talk.

John again. The name of the academic Julie's mother had mentioned. The one her daughter was supposed to be working for over the summer.

I've got evidence...

If Stuart had information Julie wanted to hide, why was she dead and not her blackmailer – if that's what Stuart had been?

At that moment he was aware of a soft footstep behind him, from over by the kitchen door. He turned to see Kitty, looking at him through half-closed eyes, her hair tousled. 'I'm not sleepy either, Daddy.' She spoke quietly, through a yawn.

'Either?' He closed the laptop lid and went over to her, Jess still on his shoulder. 'But I *am* sleepy, Kitty.' He smoothed a hand over her hair. 'And Jessica already *is* asleep, so she must be as well, mustn't she?'

Kitty nodded slowly. 'Maybe.'

'Perhaps that means you might be too, really.' He crouched down to give her a kiss. 'Shall we *all* go on up?'

'It really *is* about time.' She turned on her heel and led the way. Her words echoed a favourite phrase of Babette's. Spoken by Kitty, the mimicked adult sentiment made him smile, but it came with a sting in its tail.

CHAPTER SIXTEEN

The weather had changed overnight, and the sharp drop in temperature had brought a fine mist with it. It gave Bridge Street an otherworldly feel. As the imposing chapel of St John's College became visible in the moist air, Tara tightened the belt on her coat to stop the chill damp working its way in. She wished she'd checked the weather forecast before she'd set out, and worn trousers instead of a dress and jacket.

DC Jez Fallon was striding next to her, just inches away. 'You were right: "family above all else". I'm impressed.' He switched his phone screen back off and stuck the instrument into his trouser pocket.

Tara glanced sideways at him. She knew that look: appraising eyes, a cheeky, confident smile. It was appealing, but for a moment her thoughts still strayed to Blake – married with a child and a baby, Blake. Whatever had gone on between them in the past – even if it had only been in their heads – it was well and truly time to put a lid on it.

She grinned back at her new colleague. 'All those pub quizzes haven't been entirely wasted.'

'Pub quizzes? I assumed for Latin you'd have to watch *University Challenge*.'

She raised an eyebrow. 'Well, you know, we *are* talking about Cambridge hostelries.'

He rolled his eyes. 'Oh yeah, of course.'

They were on their way to Beaumont's, an auctioneers based in the ground floor of a seventeenth-century timber-framed merchant's house. A Mr Phelps had agreed to help after Blake had sent them to investigate the cat pictured on Julie Cooper's phone. Tara couldn't imagine what the meeting would tell them. She was curious, but it seemed like a side angle.

The real action was going on elsewhere. Blake and Megan had gone to find Stuart Gilmour, who'd finally turned up at St Bede's. Meanwhile, Max was continuing to track down the myriad of student and academic contacts Julie had had.

Mr Phelps had asked them to use the back door. It involved going down a narrow, dark passageway to one side of the building, under a bit of the premises that jutted out above.

'Wow. This place is like something out of Dickens,' Jez said as they passed into the shadows.

Tara nodded and pulled on an old-fashioned bell to announce their presence. A moment later the door opened, and a man of around her height with salt-and-pepper hair, wearing a dark suit, stood back to let them in.

They showed their badges as they moved past him.

'Thanks for seeing us, Mr Phelps.' Jez got in first.

'You're welcome.'

The auctioneers was attached to an antiques business, with items on sale to passers-by. As they followed their host, Tara noticed several curiosities towards the front of the building – an ancient-looking teddy bear, a beautiful mirror and a walking stick with a marble handle. So many objects associated with so much history, and yet the place felt oddly static and quiet. A sales assistant sat on a high stool behind a counter to her left, so still that he looked like a waxwork.

The office Mr Phelps took them to housed a large oak table, inlaid with dark-green leather.

'Please,' the man said, 'let's look at the photograph you've brought.'

The tech team had blown up the image of the cat and that of the coat of arms and motto, too. Tara had stowed the printouts in a board-backed envelope. Now, she pulled it out of her bag and set each picture down on the surface in front of them. Mr Phelps' eyebrows went up.

'Good heavens. That's quite an ornament.' He switched on a strong lamp, its beam focused on the picture. 'May I?'

'Please.' Tara watched as he picked up the second shot.

'The coat of arms might help us.' He turned to one side. There was a laptop sitting on a wooden cabinet. It looked out of place in the traditional setting, but Mr Phelps flipped open the lid, called up a website and entered some login details. 'There are very specific terms we use to describe the different elements of the design. If you understand the description, you can create a coat of arms accurately from scratch, and equally' – he paused a moment as he typed – 'if you know the correct terminology to describe an unidentified coat of arms, you can find a record of the family that the design belongs to.' He glanced at them over his shoulder for a moment. 'The order is important. In the description, every element mentioned before a particular colour is of that colour.'

Tara peered at the screen. 'Gules?' Her pub-quiz knowledge didn't stretch that far.

'That's red.' The man turned back to his work.

A moment later, a result came up. She and Jez were either side of him now – looking at the screen.

'It belongs to the Lockwoods, and that's their motto. *Family above all else.*' Mr Phelps frowned. 'When I say the Lockwoods, it doesn't just go with the name. It's a specific lineage I'm talking about. The right to this coat of arms was granted to a Hubert Lockwood for services to the crown in 1940, and anyone descended in the legitimate male line has the right to use it. Still recent enough for the family to find it a novelty, I'd imagine.' He smiled. 'Your own research will tell you more, but I can help assess the statue itself.'

They all turned back to the photos on the table.

'It's certainly a striking piece.' Tara couldn't argue with that. It was one fierce-looking cat. 'And by the look of it, of some considerable value. Given everything else we can observe, I would guess that the eyes might be made from emeralds. The hallmark on the statue is a little blurred, but I think it gives us what we need. The object is gold and there's a maker's mark. I think' – he turned to his computer and checked a new website – 'yes, I'm right. It was designed by Francesco Gallo.' He whistled.

'Does that affect its value?' Tara asked.

Phelps nodded. 'I'd judge it would fetch around twenty thousand pounds today. The hallmark shows us it was made soon after Hubert Lockwood was granted the right to the arms. I might be able to find out more.'

He set to work on his laptop again and logged into yet another site. 'If it's in one of the online catalogues… aha!' He was beaming when he faced them again – a man who loved his work, clearly. 'He made three of the things, apparently.'

'Three?' Hubert Lockwood must have been loaded if he'd commissioned them all.

Mr Phelps nodded. 'Perhaps one for each of his children? It's the kind of thing people do. If they're wealthy enough, of course.'

As soon as they were back at the station, Tara googled Hubert Lockwood. 'I want to know how Julie would have come across that type of object.'

Jez appeared at her side and crouched so that he was nearer her screen. And her. 'Me too. It seems so unlikely. The cat looks like something from a museum or a stately home and the background in the photo doesn't give anything away.'

Tara nodded. 'I'm hoping the Lockwood connection will tell us. Wikipedia's got the original owner of the coat of arms, who Mr Phelps mentioned.' *Hubert Edward Lockwood*. She clicked the link to 'personal life', skimming the details of his parents, who he'd married and then of his offspring.

Eldest son, Alistair Lockwood, billionaire owner of Lockwood's Agrochemicals and master of St Oswald's College, Cambridge. Knighted for services to industry and charity work.

She felt her skin prickle.

'He's master of the college Julie attended?' Jez was staring at her screen. 'Why do you reckon she was so interested in the statue? From what we know of her so far, she doesn't sound the sort who'd be an antiques freak. Unless...'

Tara glanced sideways at him. 'Unless what?'

'Well, I suppose she might have wondered how much it was worth. It could be quite a tempting object if it was just sitting on a shelf, somewhere at St Oswald's College.'

It was quite possible that it was at St Oswald's – though Tara guessed it would be in Lockwood's private residence at the college. Most masters were in post for several years and a master's lodge usually went with the role. They tended to be grand places where the post holder would live for the duration of their tenure. She guessed Sir Alistair would probably have moved his belongings into the lodge – especially anything valuable. All the same, she didn't like the train of thought Jez seemed to be following.

'You mean she might have been thinking of stealing it? She doesn't sound the sort, from what her mum and tutor have said about her.' She thought again of how the student had packed up all her things, ready for her mother's arrival. She came across as a considerate person, with values.

'But it's worth a heck of a lot of money, as we now know. And the fact that she took a photo of the base and the hallmark makes it look as though she wanted to find out more about it – not just that she admired it as a piece of art.'

He did have a point. But Tara felt it was an affront to the dead woman to suggest it. Then again, Julie had been politically active. One of the pressure groups she'd been part of was focused on the growing gap between rich and poor. What if she'd been horrified at the amount of money Hubert Lockwood had spent on flaunting his wealth and his new coat of arms? What then?

'If she'd been planning to steal it, maybe she'd have used the money to support the causes she was fighting for.' Jez's words echoed her thoughts. 'And anyway, maybe she thought it belonged to the college, rather than to the master specifically. In that case she might have seen it as a victimless crime.'

But Tara shook her head. 'That won't wash. The coat of arms on the statue is quite different from the one belonging to St Oswald's, and Julie would have spotted that. The colleges put theirs all over everything. My stepfather's still got a plate he pinched from his college buttery when he was a student, with Bosworth's coat of arms on it. And the motto on the statue makes it sound like a family possession, anyway.'

As she spoke, Blake walked into the room and glanced from one of them to the other.

Jez took a deep breath and stood up as Tara raised her eyes. She spent a moment updating their boss on the cat and its connection with the master of St Oswald's College, before switching topic. 'How's it going with Stuart Gilmour?'

Blake's look was sour. 'He already knew Julie Cooper was dead when we finally caught up with him. He refused to talk to us at first – unless we arrested him – but at the last minute he consented to a voluntary interview – solicitor, recording and all. His college made it clear his return to his studies might be short-lived if he didn't cooperate. Consequently, he's not in the best of moods – and neither am I. I'm heading to the interview room now.'

But he detoured via the coffee machine. *Another rough night*, Tara guessed.

CHAPTER SEVENTEEN

The coffee hadn't soothed Blake's ire. Stuart Gilmour had spent some time with his solicitor – a woman he probably knew quite well now, thanks to his previous run-ins with the law. Had they stretched the meeting out longer than they needed to, just to wind him up?

Gilmour's expression was confident – cocky and self-assured in fact – but his face was pale, which made Blake feel slightly better.

Megan was at Blake's side, looking organised. As soon as the formalities were done, he got stuck in.

'Where have you been for the last twenty-four hours? Your landlady and your college were both expecting you to shift your stuff from Atterton Road to St Bede's, and Bella Chadwick's been calling you almost as often as we have.'

Gilmour's cool gaze met his. 'None of you is my keeper.'

'You weren't worried about returning to your university accommodation on time? You must be on thin ice after being suspended last year.'

His features twitched sharply. 'I was *that* close to telling them to shove the rest of their course.' He held his forefinger a millimetre away from his thumb.

It figured. He didn't look the sort to toe the line. 'What changed your mind?'

Gilmour shrugged and there was a moment's pause. 'I'm a thorn in their side. They'd have loved it if I walked and I'm not here to give them an easy time.'

Blake pitied the guy's lecturers. 'So where were you yesterday? Why didn't you return to your college room or your digs last night?'

Gilmour put his head on one side. 'I didn't feel like it.'

He heard a faint sigh from the man's lawyer and guessed he wasn't following her advice. It probably meant she felt there was no reason that Gilmour shouldn't commit himself, and that he was just being obstructive for the sake of it. Blake felt his blood pressure rise. He'd get it out of him in time, but Gilmour wasting it made him want to thump something.

Blake forced himself to sit back in his chair. 'Mr Gilmour, your ex-girlfriend was attacked and murdered. We know that she made an official complaint to St Bede's about you harassing her after you broke up. We also know that you managed to persuade her to see you at her lodgings over the summer. And we know that quite recently you were still sending her messages that implied you weren't over the split.'

He left it there, and Megan stayed silent too.

Gilmour opened his mouth but so did the lawyer, at precisely the same time.

'That isn't a question, Detective Inspector,' she said. 'Please ask my client something directly if you would like him to comment.'

Blake tried to ungrit his teeth. 'Tell us about the latest texts you sent to Julie Cooper, Mr Gilmour.' It would be interesting to see what he said. Unlike Blake, he hadn't got the precise wording in front of him as a prompt.

For the first time, Gilmour looked uncomfortable, though he reinstated the swagger in half a second. 'I can't think what you're referring to.'

Like hell you can't. 'The ones about John.'

The lawyer was frowning. They hadn't covered this in their pre-interview discussion, Blake guessed.

Gilmour took a moment, acting out his response, his eyes widening as though he'd only just remembered. 'Oh, those.' He pulled a face. 'I was being a prat.'

'Oh well, that's just fine then.' Blake took a deep breath. 'The message sounded threatening to me.'

He glanced at Megan, who started to read Gilmour's words aloud.

'"Read this! I know about John. And I've got evidence. Now tell me you don't want to talk."'

Blake let his eyes bore into Gilmour's. 'If someone sent me that message I'd feel coerced into seeing them. You had a hold over her. How did you hope to benefit from your secret knowledge?'

Gilmour rolled his eyes. 'I just wanted to see her, that's all. I thought if we talked it would give us the opportunity to clear the air. She'd either decide to give me a second chance or tell me to go to hell. But at least we'd have it out properly.'

'Why didn't you do that when you first split up?' Megan asked.

'She didn't give me the chance.'

Blake thought back to the text messages that looked as though they'd been sent in the immediate aftermath of the split.

It's not what you think, Stuart had written.

I bet it's exactly what I think, Julie had replied.

'Why didn't she give you the chance?' Blake said.

'She was too angry. She thought…' He paused a moment, his eyes on the middle distance, somewhere over Blake's shoulder. 'Well, it was the usual. She thought I'd started seeing someone else, behind her back.'

'Someone?'

'Her friend. Bella Chadwick.'

'And you hadn't?'

'No.' Gilmour's expression was bland.

The lawyer shot him a sidelong glance.

'So you used the secret knowledge you'd acquired to force her hand. Who's "John"?'

He smiled now. 'Just another student. But he had a girlfriend who wouldn't have been best pleased to see him mucking around with Julie. Plus, Julie was normally so upstanding and principled – the fling would have made her look like a right hypocrite, and she would have hated that.'

'It was pretty mean of you to threaten to expose her.' Megan's expression was icy. Gilmour had got under her skin and she'd become more natural.

The student looked unmoved. 'All's fair in love and war.' He folded his arms and leant forward on the table.

'I'd like John's full name, please,' Blake said. 'And his girlfriend's.'

The student rolled his eyes. 'Jeez. I don't even know his surname, and as for the girlfriend, I've got no idea. It was only luck that I happened to see Julie necking with him in the shadows on Jesus Lane. I followed him after that and saw him meet up with the woman I took to be his regular date.'

Blake put his head on one side. 'A moment ago you spoke as though you were aware of John's girlfriend's character. You said she wouldn't be best pleased about what had been going on.'

Gilmour raised his eyes to heaven. 'Oh, come on! Who would be?'

But Blake was sure he was lying – inventing a story at speed that didn't quite hang together.

'So you took a photo.' Megan's eyes were on the printout of his text again. 'That was your evidence?'

Gilmour nodded. *Easy enough for him to agree.* 'I'd had a few drinks, or I might not have done something so crass.' He shrugged.

He didn't look weighed down by guilt as far as Blake could see. 'In the end, Julie and I met up. We had it out. I apologised and deleted the photo.'

'Where did you meet?' Blake asked.

'Round at her summer lodgings on Chesterton Road.'

'Did you visit her often after that?'

The guy shook his head. 'That was it. I managed to convince her she'd been wrong about me and Bella, but we both decided it was best to move on.'

Seriously? The transition from obsessive ex to mature former lover was hard to believe.

'She still wore your ring.' Once again, not a question, but it was worth it to check the look in Gilmour's eye. And that – in fact – was interesting. No reaction at all.

'I gave it to her. She was welcome to carry on wearing it.'

'How did you and Julie first meet, Mr Gilmour?' This from Megan.

'I don't see how that's relevant.'

'We want to check every detail we can. The more background we have, the more likely we are to pick up on something that gives us a lead.'

He rolled his eyes. 'All right then. We met at an animal rights demo in spring last year and we both wrote stories for student newspapers too. After that we kept bumping into each other at similar events and eventually we ended up going for a drink.'

'You've crossed our radar before.' Blake glanced at the list Jez had pulled from the files. The action brought up the new DC's image momentarily, crouching by Tara, his head close to hers. 'Was Julie with you on any of the demonstrations where you were arrested?'

'Sure she was. We supported the same causes.'

'Yet we never brought her in. Was she against the more extreme direct action that you took?' He was wondering what the dynamics had been like between them.

'Not at all. She got stuck in. She was at the demo that got me suspended, for instance – doing much the same as I was. Even though I avoided arrest that time, the college authorities were on to me. Some arse took photos after I'd taken my mask off and circulated them on social media.'

'You wore a Guy Fawkes mask for the protest itself?' Blake remembered the photos on the dead student's camera roll.

'That's right, just the same as Julie. And she was caught in the same photograph as me, so her college got wind of her starring role as well. Which just shows you how unfair discipline is here. Her treatment was totally different to mine. No suspension for her.'

There was bitterness in his voice.

'Why was that particular march so contentious?'

'She and I – and a few others – had taken baby dolls with us and we held up knives to their throats. It was to symbolise the cut-throat attitude of the company. They don't care who they hurt and it's often the innocents who suffer.'

Blake thought of the glint of the knife blade he'd seen in the photograph. The dolls hadn't been caught in the image. 'I'm surprised that was one of the occasions you escaped arrest.'

'They were only folding knives. And we were using them for "theatrical purposes". That's allowed, isn't it?'

He'd been reading up on the law. His smug expression had Blake fighting to keep his temper.

'It's a bit more complicated than that,' Megan said. She sounded calm. 'Especially if there are several of you in a crowded area. It's illegal to use a knife in a threatening way.'

'Even if it's against a doll?' Gilmour laughed. 'You've got to do these things, otherwise no one takes any notice. The company needs to be put in the spotlight.'

'What company is this?' Blake's eyes met Gilmour's.

'Lockwood's. And because their chairman, Sir Alistair Lockwood, is master of St Oswald's, the university authorities were paying especially close attention.'

Blake was sure his reaction had been slight – outwardly at least. He'd thought instantly of the cat with its Lockwood coat of arms. But Gilmour had caught it – he could see it in his eyes. The student's expression was hard to read.

'We'll need to know your whereabouts from Saturday evening until you reappeared this morning at your college,' Blake said.

'I don't see why.'

Blake tried to keep his tone controlled. 'You had a painful break-up with a woman who has now been found murdered. You badgered her so hard that she made an official complaint about your behaviour. You blackmailed her into seeing you. Your ring was torn from her finger on the night she died. Would you like me to go on?'

Gilmour gave a deliberate sigh. 'I was at my lodgings on Saturday evening and overnight.'

When his landlady was off getting hammered at her hen party. *Great.* 'Anyone vouch for you?'

'I shouldn't imagine so.' That smile again. 'Then, yesterday just after lunch, I went out to meet a mate about a protest we're organising.'

'Details?'

Gilmour rattled off a name and a number as though it was a huge inconvenience.

'On my way home, I saw the news about Julie.' He paused. 'We might have called it a day, but you can imagine it hit me in the gut. I went and bought a bottle of vodka and walked. I'd been on Hills Road, and I don't even remember my route after I left the supermarket, but I ended up hiding out on Coe Fen. I wanted to block it all out.'

'Do you have the receipt for the booze?' It would at least give some credence to his story.

Gilmour stretched in his chair and dug in his jeans pocket. 'There.' He put a crumpled bit of till paper on the table and smoothed it out for them to see.

'I saw Bella's number come up on my phone but I didn't answer. I knew why she'd be calling and I didn't want to talk.'

'And where did you go after that? Did you eat supper? Where did you sleep?'

That sigh again. Heaved out for effect. 'Bella didn't stop at one call. She kept on going. I switched my phone off for a while but when I put it back on she'd left messages and then she rang again. I picked up that final time. In the end I went to see her.' He gave them a look. 'I mean, she was upset too, clearly. And she knew I must be. We ate pizza in her room, finished off the vodka between us and crashed out. It was only when I woke up this morning – with a cracking hangover – that I started to connect with reality again.'

He'd stayed with Bella? Bella who Julie had thought he was seeing behind her back? Bella who they'd asked to inform them immediately if she managed to track Gilmour down... *Right.*

'Nothing happened.' Stuart's look was withering. 'I know the old cliché – in the heat of the moment, and all that. But I was plastered. Even if I'd wanted to have sex with Bella it most certainly wouldn't have worked. And besides, whatever Julie thought, I still think Bella was obsessed with her, not me. She was beside herself last night. Couldn't stop crying.'

'Do you have access to a vehicle, Mr Gilmour?'

The young man lounged back in his chair now, his eyebrows raised. 'Yes. Okay – I do currently have access to a vehicle. What's all this about?' He looked from one of them to another. 'Wait. You mean Julie wasn't killed where she was found?'

Again, there was something exaggerated about his reactions. Was he trying to hide the fact that this wasn't really news to him? Or was he just someone who loved to be the centre of attention?

'I can tell you I'd have struggled to get a body into the back of my brother's Ford Fiesta, but if I put the rear seats down, I guess I could have managed it. And before you ask, I borrowed his car so I could shift my stuff back to my college rooms.

'Julie and I might have broken up, but I was fond of her.' His voice was quieter now, but Blake didn't buy his sudden attempt at emotion. He'd seen the look his lawyer had given him. 'I'm gutted that she's dead.'

Blake nodded at Megan. He'd heard enough. As she wound up the interview and ended the recording a fresh wave of anger at Bella Chadwick washed over him. Keeping quiet about tracking Gilmour down made it clear they couldn't trust her. Might they both have been involved in Julie's death? He sure as hell hadn't warmed to Stuart.

The lawyer was shifting in her chair. She'd probably got better places to be, and Blake felt just as impatient. There were a million and one facts to check, but as he stood up, his mind was focused on one small detail of Gilmour's statement. St Oswald's College had known about Julie's involvement in the march against Lockwood's – the company managed by the master of their institution. That almost certainly meant her tutor, Lucien Balfour, had all the details, and yet he'd sat on them for some reason, when he spoke to Max and Tara. Blake wanted to know why.

CHAPTER EIGHTEEN

It wasn't like Shona to suggest a meet-up with Patrick during the day. She was normally hell-bent on her work – saving their diverting liaisons for late at night, when she'd filed all her copy. He wondered what was up.

She was late, of course. He hoped to God she didn't just leave him sitting there, having forgotten all about their appointment. He couldn't get up and walk out without looking like a loser. Another person entered the café, failing to close the door properly behind them. The weather had turned colder and misty overnight, and each time someone came in or went out, cool air pooled near his table, the draught working its way up his trouser legs. The door, which was now ajar, was only a couple of feet from him, but he presumed no one was expecting him to sort it out. You didn't pay to sit in someone else's establishment only to have to leap up every two minutes to keep the place habitable.

He'd been glancing at the news on his phone as he waited, sipping his latte. Not much more about the death out at Wandlebury. His ex-colleagues at Parkside probably had no clue as to who'd done for the girl. He imagined Fleming in the team briefings, rapping out her predictable orders, putting all her faith in Blake to find the truth. Eventually. When he could take his eyes off Tara Thorpe for long enough to get on with the job. What with that and distractions for the DI at home, his old boss would be even more useless than usual. Thanks to a chance encounter with Blake's wife, Babette the Babe, Wilkins knew there was something odd about that marriage.

Why didn't Fleming see him for what he was? And how was it that other members of the team stayed loyal? He knew Megan Moany Maloney had her doubts about Tara, partly thanks to some well-chosen words from him. And yet they all muddled along.

He was glad *he* hadn't settled for the status quo. Some of the PI work he'd taken on since resigning had been a bit dull. Not like being involved in something really important. He'd done a couple of investigations into errant partners. For a second, he wondered about either Blake or Babette as future clients. That would be a good joke. Blake would never hire him of course – but the idea of investigating the skeletons in his cupboard was very appealing.

At that moment, the flapping door opened wider, and Shona dashed in, a bag from a designer boutique on her arm. It hadn't been work that had held her up, then. As she moved gracefully towards him, the breeze carried a waft of her scent. Behind her, a tall guy was on his feet, closing the door properly, with an admiring glance in Shona's direction.

Typical.

She dropped into her seat, kissing her fingers, then brushing Patrick's cheek. He could tell the tall, door-closing guy was dumbfounded to see that he was her date.

'What can I get you?' Patrick caught the eye of a waiter. He'd take command of the situation and show the onlookers the reasons for Shona's preferences.

'A cappuccino, please.'

The waiter overshot their table and took an order from a middle-aged woman, sitting by the window. Patrick took a deep breath. In the end, he had to wait a full minute before he could request Shona's drink – and it was a look from her that brought the waiter over.

He switched off his irritation and turned to his girlfriend. 'So, it's good to see you. But unusual, at this hour. Is everything all right?'

She smiled. 'Absolutely. I've got something for you.'

For a moment he glanced at the bag she was carrying. This wasn't like her.

Her smile broadened. 'Not material goods. This is information. You've passed plenty in my direction in the past – I thought it might be time to return the favour.'

What on earth had she got up her sleeve? She met his puzzled look.

'Aw.' Her hand was on his cheek again. 'You looked so down, yesterday at the pub. I got the impression your plans for getting even with DI Blake's golden girl might have hit the buffers.' Her eyes were on his. They saw far too much.

'Not at all. It's just slow, intensive work.' He knew he couldn't lie as well as she could.

She raised an eyebrow. 'There's no need to explain. But – just in case it's useful – I wanted to let you know that I had another chat with my pet police constable this morning. Purely to get more information on the Julie Cooper case, of course.'

'Anything new?'

She took a deep breath, and he could tell she'd come away with less than she'd wanted. 'They're being cagey. My man claimed he'd heard very little.'

'So what is it that you have to pass on, then?'

She leant back in her seat as the waiter delivered her coffee. 'Information on Tara specifically. I don't know what it means, but I found it quite… diverting.'

She was really drawing this out. He hoped it was good. He swigged his latte and waited for her to get on with it.

'I mentioned to the pet PC that Tara and I used to work together, and so we got chatting.' She glanced down for a moment, with mock modesty. 'I think he's taken to me, if I'm honest. Anyway, I managed to get him to open up about Tara's life at the station – and Tara in general, in fact.' She cocked her head. 'I gather there was some kerfuffle about that case she worked on in the spring. Talk around the station about her having behaved recklessly. But overall – don't get upset – my PC says she's quite well respected. It might not be long before she goes for promotion.'

'Is this supposed to be helping?' At least if she went for DS, she'd probably have to move away. There was no opening at Parkside, as far as he knew.

'I haven't finished yet. He also said that, back in the spring, her personal and professional lives collided. He mentioned about how she was stalked, and sent weird packages, way back when she was a teenager – which of course we know. But apparently, she got a delivery recently. In March. From the same stalker, as far as anyone's aware. She called the police in, and they started an investigation, but it didn't go anywhere. Apparently, Tara told them to leave it after a couple of weeks. She didn't want to waste their time, and there's been no delivery since. They assume it was a one-off.'

Patrick's heart was beating faster. 'And she was sent this latest package in March, you say?'

Shona leant forward, her eyes sharp. 'Apparently so. Why? Is the timing significant?'

He was thinking hard. 'Did your contact mention a message with the delivery?'

A satisfied smile crossed his lover's face. 'He did. He couldn't remember exactly what it was, but he said it was a threat. Something like: "Remember me? If you don't want me back, call off the dogs." Nice and dramatic. It made me wonder if she's been doing some digging – making a fresh attempt to identify her tormentor.' Her eyes were knowing. 'Unless someone else was doing that, of course.'

She waited.

My God, she sees it all. She'd guessed what he'd been up to and his reactions would have confirmed it.

Patrick watched the reflection of the café's overhead lights in Shona's eyes. 'To think, you might have found all this out months ago.' The fact that the information about the March poison pen letter had been sitting there on the police files all that time rankled. Shona was apt to ask her contacts on the force about Tara. Their status as sworn enemies meant she was always keen to get the latest dirt on her. It was a shame she hadn't put the effort in sooner; it would have saved Patrick an awful lot of time and disappointment.

Shona raised an eyebrow. 'That sounds a little ungrateful. I've no doubt I would have unearthed it earlier, only there's been no big police case to take me onto their territory until now. But this is a breakthrough. At least you know that… if someone *was* looking into the matter of Tara's stalker' – she gave him another meaningful glance – 'they got a definite reaction. They must have been on exactly the right track.'

The facts were even more telling than she knew. Patrick thought back to the spring. He'd only just resigned from the force. He'd barely started his attempts to track down Tara's tormentor – in fact, he'd only been to talk to one person.

He felt a wave of heat rush over him. From being certain he'd never identify her stalker, the field was suddenly narrowed down to a single suspect. All he needed to do now was to find proper evidence – something he could hand over to both Giles at *Not Now* and to the police. Okay, so it still wouldn't be easy, but it was entirely possible. And if he succeeded, he'd be the hero of the hour. Solving a case that the force had bungled would be a shot in the arm to his new PI business, to say nothing of the other emotional satisfaction involved. He'd be able to put Tara in an unwanted spotlight after all – rake up her painful past and every ounce of dirt he'd ever managed to get on her.

He grinned to himself as he imagined the carefully crafted headlines in the magazine that used to employ her. It was helpful that she'd made so many enemies there.

He'd resume work on her case the very next day – reinterview the suspect, and go in hard, armed with this extra knowledge. And, when he'd got what he wanted, he'd invite Giles out for a drink. The editor had written him off, convinced he'd been all talk. Patrick was about to regain the man's respect.

Shona looked at him, a smile playing round her lips, one eyebrow raised. 'Darling! You do look cheerful. Now, one good turn deserves another. I've told you what my pet policeman said. How about you tell me exactly what you're planning?'

She leant forward. Information was like a drug to her.

Wilkins sat back in his chair and returned her look. 'All in good time, Shona. All in good time.'

CHAPTER NINETEEN

'Everything about Gilmour makes my skin crawl.' Tara watched Blake, who was perched on a desk at the front of the incident room, bringing them up to date. 'But there's something odd going on. On paper he sounds like the classic obsessive ex who wouldn't let go. In that role, I'd imagined him pestering Julie yet again, striking her when she rejected him, then locking her up in a confined space and waiting for her to run out of air.'

The idea of him listening to Julie, fighting for her life, left Tara with a mental film clip she'd never be able to erase.

'You say those scenarios fit with Gilmour's profile *on paper*?' Fleming sipped a coffee from a tiny white cup. Tara wondered how she could stomach anything – even coffee – whilst they were discussing something so horrific. But as Fleming herself would say, you had to compartmentalise to be effective. Tara hadn't quite mastered the art yet. She wondered what Blake felt.

The DI nodded. He was standing now. 'The reality doesn't match up. Gilmour was detached in the interview. I'd expect a lot more emotion from someone who's lost the object of their obsession – whether he killed her or not.' As Tara watched he went absolutely still, his jaw taut. 'He's still a potential killer in my eyes, but he comes across as a psychopath.'

Tara felt a chill creep over her skin. Of course, you could have those sort of tendencies without ever resorting to murder. She'd read an article not long ago that suggested psychopaths did especially well in certain careers. It hadn't pleased her to find that two of the ones she'd worked in so far were mentioned: the police and journalism. For law enforcers it was the psychopath's ability to do an intense and dangerous job whilst staying calm that benefitted them. She immediately thought of Fleming again. *Let it go…* And for journalists it was the way psychopaths could turn on the charm, coupled with a ruthless and focused streak, that made the difference.

'The story about this other student, John, whom Gilmour supposedly saw Julie kissing, sounds thin too. Didn't know his surname, didn't know the name of the girlfriend who would supposedly be so upset with Julie if the truth came out.'

'Julie doesn't come across as the sort to be swayed by that kind of threat anyway,' Tara said. She'd been made of sterner stuff, by the sound of things.

'I agree. It'll be hard to disprove Gilmour's story – given the lack of details to check – but I want people on it. And I need Bella's statement.' Blake had been pacing the room, but now he stopped. 'I'd like to know why the hell she didn't report Gilmour's reappearance as we asked her to – if they were really together last night. And I want to meet her anyway; her relationship with Julie warrants further inspection.'

'It's possible she and Gilmour worked together to kill Julie.' Fleming put her cup down on the table next to her.

'Yes, ma'am.' Blake's expression was weary. Tara guessed he'd worked that one out for himself.

'So, Megan, you're with me for the interview with Bella Chadwick. Jez?'

Tara watched her fellow DC raise his blue eyes to Blake's. 'Boss?'

'I want you to get over to Atterton Road. See if you can find any neighbours who saw or heard Gilmour on Saturday evening or overnight. It's a relatively quiet street. If any of them noticed he had a visitor – or that he went off for a drive in the small hours – we'd have grounds to arrest him and search his brother's vehicle.'

Tara saw him glance at Fleming for a moment and she nodded her approval. It made sense. Gilmour had said he'd been alone and that he'd stayed in. Catching him out in a lie would certainly leave him with some explaining to do.

Blake strode over to stand between her and Max's desks now. 'I want you two to visit Sir Alistair Lockwood at the Master's Lodge at St Oswald's. The picture of the cat seemed like a side issue until we interviewed Gilmour. Even now, it might not be relevant, but the fact that Julie was on the march against Lockwood's Agrochemicals is another link between her and the master. I want to know how Julie got the photo of the statue and how well the master knows his students. Dig and see if anything smells off.' His eyes flicked to Tara's as he finished his last sentence. She hadn't left her journalist's reputation behind. Max was the polite face of policing, getting answers by lulling their interviewees into a false sense of security. He was so nice they got caught out when he tied them in knots. And she – she laid traps and snares. She knew her gender still meant she got away with asking questions that sounded like nosiness too. She hated the fact that certain male interviewees seemed to find her deep interest in the minutiae of their lives entirely understandable. But the fact that they seldom questioned her – or took her all that seriously – had its benefits. She suspected Alistair Lockwood wouldn't be so easily fooled though. You didn't make billions without having your head screwed on and your eyes wide open. CEO had been high on the list of jobs for psychopaths too. They ought to be evenly matched…

As she nodded she noticed Jez behind the DI, getting ready to leave the room. His eyes were on them both. When he realised she'd caught him staring he gave her a grin. She grinned back, causing Blake to turn and glance behind him. 'Glad you two are getting on so well,' he said.

There was just a hint of resentment in his tone, and that made Tara smile again.

CHAPTER TWENTY

The Master's Lodge at St Oswald's, huge, imposing and shrouded in mist, looked like the perfect setting for a ghost story. Tara and Max had parked on the gravel drive, next to a Mercedes E-Class and an Aston Martin. The Gothic-looking building was set in spacious grounds, away from the noise and hubbub of the main college. It was topped off with tall chimneys and crenellations and its mullioned windows were set well back in their surrounds. For a second, as they approached the house, Tara thought she caught movement in one of them. She stared at the dark glass, but everything was still now. The place was distancing. No one could doubt the occupant's position of power. Whoever had designed the place had clearly wanted to ensure that each successive master was revered – and maybe feared, too. She wondered if new post holders were ever dismayed at having to move into such a forbidding-looking place. But perhaps that hadn't been the case with Sir Alistair. His family's unusual heirloom seemed to fit the style of the residence. Both the lodge and the cat said 'keep back – we'll defend our territory.'

They rapped a lion's head knocker on the dark, heavily varnished oak front door. As they waited, Tara noticed a stone grotesque over the lintel: a snarling beast that she couldn't identify. Half a minute passed before a woman answered. If she'd been at the other end of the house it would have taken her that long to reach them. She had silver hair, streaked with strands of iron-grey, swept up into a French pleat. Tara tried to judge her age. Somewhere in her fifties? She was dressed in an impeccable 1930s-style suit – up-to-the-minute retro, rather than old-fashioned. She looked like someone who'd throw on a fox fur at a moment's notice. Tara wondered how much the suit had cost.

They introduced themselves and showed their badges.

The woman didn't smile or hold out a hand. 'I'm Lady Lockwood – Sir Alistair's wife. He's just finished a conference call for Lockwood's, so I can take you to him.'

Tara had googled the family on their journey over. Lady Veronica Lockwood was a virtuoso harpist, no less well-known than her husband. Tara wondered if he would be more friendly than she was.

The hallway they crossed was cavernous and panelled in dark wood. They followed the woman up a wide flight of stairs and along a shadowy corridor. Through a doorway Tara could see an upstairs sitting room, occupied by a woman who might be around her age. The stranger glanced at them for a moment before looking quickly away. Was it her movement Tara had detected as they walked up the drive? The windows in the room faced the right way.

'Give me a moment, please.' Lady Lockwood went ahead of them through an open door and shut it behind her.

A minute later, she reopened it and ushered them into a large study. As they followed her inside, Tara saw a man she recognised as Sir Alistair, thanks to the internet research she'd done. There was a younger man next to him.

Tara was slightly ahead of Max and the master put his hand out to her first, turning to the DS a moment later. 'Welcome. My wife has explained who you are.' His handshake was warm and firm. She could feel the strength of character behind it, but also his physical strength. 'I'm devastated to hear about our student, Julie Cooper. I assume she's the reason you're here.' He shook his large head. 'To be robbed of her future so young. It's unthinkable.'

His tone was sincere, but Tara was sure he'd be able to perform in any situation life threw at him. You couldn't be the figurehead of a company like his – or of an institution like St Oswald's – without unshakable PR skills. Calling Julie 'our student' made it clear he was speaking for the college, rather than himself. Did he know Julie had protested against his firm? Underneath his smooth façade his feelings towards her might have been far from friendly.

Sir Alistair turned towards the man who was by his side, standing rigid next to a mahogany work table. 'This is my son, Douglas – second in command at Lockwood's.'

He looked around Tara's age – early to mid-thirties maybe? – with smooth chestnut hair, dark-rimmed glasses and a tidy suit.

He nodded. 'I was here for the conference call.'

'It must be hard to fit everything in,' Tara said. She wondered how much of Sir Alistair's time St Oswald's took up.

The master nodded. 'It can be. I'm meant to devote half a working week to the college. But of course, with my background I'm used to working round the clock as required. It's part of the job when you're head of a company, and part of the thrill. I wouldn't have it any other way.'

He motioned for each of them – including his family members – to take seats round the large table. Party time.

'Is it common for St Oswald's to choose industrialists for the role of master?' Max asked.

Tara had wondered about that too. The protest in town couldn't have made life any easier for the college's PR people.

'It's a tradition of this particular college. Every other master is someone with an academic background who has excelled in business. We alternate with figureheads who've stayed in academia.' He smiled for a moment. 'St Oswald's has a good reputation for science. It's beneficial for the students to see someone who has used their knowledge in business. But also, of course, people coming in from industry tend to be quite adept at bringing new money into the college. We have good contacts and a few words in the right ears can reap dividends. It encourages legacy giving, too. If you've been a master of a place, you feel a certain obligation to recognise the fact in your last will and testament.' His smile was broader now. 'I'm not blind to the fact, and I heartily approve of the fellows' use of psychology.'

'I expect the sergeant's wondering about your appointment because it's been controversial, darling.' Veronica Lockwood's tone was dry. She looked in Tara and Max's direction. 'I've had people accost me in the street to take me to task about my husband's business.'

Some people would have found that intimidating, but Tara reckoned Veronica was too tough for that.

'Do you have any involvement in the firm at all?' she asked.

'None whatsoever. I come from a long line of writers, artists and musicians. I have my own career. Though I'm proud of our partnership.' She looked at her husband. 'I like the mingling of arts and science – a meeting of minds. And Alistair's heritage is just as impressive as mine. He comes from generations of innovators. As for the company, the protesters fail to look at the big picture. Lockwood's products ensure that crops flourish and millions are fed.'

'Thank you, my dear.' Sir Alistair smiled again. 'I'm sure the police don't wish to be treated to a Lockwood-sponsored broadcast.'

Douglas leant forward, his elbows on the table. 'Mother's right though.'

'I know.' Sir Alistair patted his son's arm. 'The protesters are young and passionate. Nine out of ten of them will realise the truth of what Veronica is saying by the time they reach thirty.'

'Were you aware that Julie was amongst those who protested?' Max's tone was gentle.

'I was.' Sir Alistair looked at them from over the top of his steepled fingers. 'Julie's tutor, Lucien Balfour, brought the matter to my attention, because of the connection with my firm. She wasn't the only St Oswald's student involved. A girl called Bella

Chadwick went along too. I don't know any of the students well, but Lucien explained the background. It was clear that Julie's beliefs were passionately held. There's no point in trying to crush views like that. You have to provide information to change minds. And as for Bella, Lucien gave me the impression she only went along because Julie did. She wanted to be part of the gang. It's not unusual, that fervent desire to belong. I can't blame for her for being a typical youngster.'

'So you advised Lucien Balfour to be lenient?' Tara asked.

Lockwood shook his head. 'I just said the link with my company shouldn't affect his actions. He should treat the matter just as he would any other.'

Was it standard, then, to take no action at all? That seemed to be what Lucien had done. It had been a peaceful protest as far as Tara knew, but you'd think the carrying of knives might have provoked a response.

'Did you ever chat to Julie one to one?' Max's tone was casual, but the master's eyes widened all the same.

'If you mean about the protest—'

'I didn't specifically. I wondered if you'd spoken to her enough to get an idea of her character?'

Tara noticed a slight relaxation of his facial muscles.

'I'm afraid not. I wondered if you'd ask and I looked at her photograph before you came, to make sure I was remembering the right person. I do make a point of passing the time of day with the students I bump into – in the dining hall perhaps, or out in the grounds. But I'm not good at putting faces to names and I don't get to know any of them well.'

Presumably he hadn't looked her up after Balfour had told him she'd been on the protest, then. Assuming he was telling the truth. They needed to ask about the cat Julie had photographed next. She glanced at Max and he nodded for her to go ahead.

'Sir Alistair, do you own a gold statue of a cat?' She glanced round at each of them as she asked. The surprise was there, in all their eyes.

It was the first time she'd seen the master frown. 'Yes.' He paused again. She guessed he liked to anticipate the way a conversation was going, and they'd robbed him of the chance. 'Yes, I do. It was given to me by my father. A symbol of family unity, and his love for me and my brothers. We had one each. Why do you ask?'

'Julie Cooper took some photographs of it. They were found on her phone.'

The man sat back in his seat, the frown deepening. 'How extraordinary.' And then his focus was back on Tara. 'How did you know it belonged to me?'

'One of the shots showed the Lockwood coat of arms.'

'But that's on its base.' Douglas sounded just as confused as his father.

'We wondered how she got access to it. Do you have it with you here at the lodge?' Max asked.

'Oh yes. When I agreed to accept the role of master, I signed up to the standard tenure of eight years. We moved all of our personal belongings here. Our permanent home is occupied by tenants at the moment, though we have a pied-à-terre in London.' Sir Alistair got up from his seat. 'I'll show you the room where the cat is kept.'

Tara and Max followed him out onto the landing. Once again Tara saw the woman in the upstairs sitting room, watching them. They turned right and then through the last door on the left, into a relatively small room, lined with books. It had a display cabinet next to the window and in it sat the cat. It was quite small – only about the size of Sir Alistair's hand.

'There.' He was still frowning. 'When was the photograph taken?'

Tara glanced at her notes. 'Almost exactly a year ago.' She gave the date.

He nodded, though the frown was still present. 'The Michaelmas term party. Each year we get the students in and ply them with cake. It's a way of making ourselves available to them – after all, they're the reason we're here. I would probably have chatted to Julie on that occasion, but she would have been one of many.'

'I'm surprised the students were allowed in this room.' Tara smiled.

The master returned her grin. 'I certainly didn't intend for them to poke about upstairs, but with large numbers coming in, it's hard to keep track of them all. Our main public reception rooms are downstairs, and the students always mill about in the kitchen too.'

She nodded. 'Can you think of why she might have wanted to photograph the cat?'

The frown was back again. It was more intense this time, and it was a moment before he answered. 'As we both know, Julie wasn't a fan of my firm. Perhaps she resented the cat as a sign of my family's wealth. I can't deny that it's rather ostentatious.'

Tara could see that was possible, but Julie couldn't have happened upon it by accident. What had she been doing, sneaking into this room? And if she'd simply been struck by the showiness of the statue, why examine it so closely? It was odd that she'd photographed the base. It would fit with her wanting to find out its value, as Jez had suggested. But not – Tara reckoned – in order to see if it was worth stealing. She'd had a prime opportunity to take it then and there if that had been her aim. The cat was small enough to fit into a handbag, or the backpack she'd had with her when she was killed.

'Do you often hold student parties?' Max asked.

The smile was back now. 'Once a year is as much as we can manage – logistically and in terms of the wear and tear on our nerves and the carpets. Shall we go back to my workroom now?'

Back at his table, Sir Alistair picked up an invitation card and handed it to Max. 'If it would help, you are welcome to drop in to this year's Michaelmas student party. It's tomorrow at five. Just turn up.'

It might be interesting to see what the students got up to – though whether they could afford the time on a case like this was another matter.

'Thank you.' Max didn't commit them, one way or the other. 'Just for the record, sir, could I ask you each to confirm your whereabouts on Saturday evening and overnight?'

Tara saw a look of anger cross Veronica Lockwood's face.

'It's just procedure,' Tara said. 'If we're thorough now there's less chance of us having to bother you again.'

Sir Alistair held up a hand. 'Of course. I drove down to London on Saturday afternoon on college business. I had a dinner date with Lord Westerly. I'm hoping to get a significant donation out of him to build a new library here at St Oswald's. We ended up making a night of it, so I stayed at the pied-à-terre I mentioned, in Notting Hill.'

'Can anyone vouch for you?'

The master's smile didn't dim, though Veronica's face was like granite.

'I'm afraid not. I walked back to the flat – I don't remember much about the journey, to be frank – and slept it off. I drove home at lunchtime on Sunday and the first person I saw was Veronica.'

Max turned to the man's wife.

'I stayed behind. Drinking into the night isn't my forte. I'm leaving for a concert tour in a couple of days, so I spent my time practising. I doubt anyone heard me. The grounds here are so spacious. I find it hard to sleep before I go away, so I went to bed early and took a pill. I went to buy a newspaper on Trumpington Street on Sunday morning and came home to wait for Alistair to return.'

Max turned to Douglas. 'Sir?'

Douglas almost jumped. 'You want mine too?'

Tara could see what was behind Max's question. Julie had tried to cause trouble for the firm. And why had she been digging around in the Lockwoods' private quarters?

'Just for the record.' Max echoed his earlier words.

'I was at our house on Brookside.' He gave them the address. 'My wife, Selina, was with me. She's here in the house now, so she can confirm.'

The woman in the upstairs sitting room?

He called out her name. A moment later, the eyes Tara had twice met, peering through the sitting room door, locked onto hers once again.

'We're just confirming where we were on Saturday night,' Douglas said. '"For the record".' His distaste was plain.

Selina looked nervous. 'Douglas was at home with me,' she said. 'We live just over the road. You've said?' She looked at her husband.

Douglas nodded. 'I've said.'

They prepared to leave. As they reached the doorway of the study, Tara looked over her shoulder to find Selina's eyes were still on her. And she still looked scared.

What was it they weren't being told?

CHAPTER TWENTY-ONE

Bella knew the police would come to see her. They were bound to – she hadn't followed their instructions and reported Stuart when he'd knocked on her door the night before. But she hadn't been able to bring herself to. He wasn't quite as upset as she'd anticipated – shaken, yes, but not wracked with tears like she was. She'd been holding it together, but on seeing his face she'd crumpled. It had taken her all day to get him there. How could she report him to the police when he finally arrived? She'd been so desperate for company. To have him there, to speak to him about Julie, simply to block out endless hours on her own – was just too desirable to give up. What difference did it make that his talk with the detectives had been postponed?

But now that the officers were here, she could see they thought differently. As she sat on the edge of her bed, glancing up at the fierce-looking guy with the unruly dark hair and angry eyes, she realised her hands were shaking. The woman who'd come with the man was sitting in Bella's desk chair, whereas the male detective was pacing up and down in front of her. It felt as though the woman was only there to make sure the guy didn't thump her.

They'd told her their names, but she'd gone blank. The woman might be Megan something? She must have been trying to seem approachable by mentioning her first name, but it hadn't worked. Bella blinked away her tears now. They'd never understand. She'd spent so much of her time with Julie, doing everything she'd done, pretty much ignoring the other people in their year. And now there was just a blank. A feeling of emptiness.

'I'm going to ask you again, Bella,' the guy said. 'Why didn't you call us when Stuart arrived?'

'He's lost his ex-girlfriend! When he showed up at my door it just seemed… inhumane. I knew he'd talk to you this morning.'

'Did you ask him to do that?'

'I told him you needed to speak to him urgently.'

'Yet he decided it could wait.'

'He was cut up.' Both the guy and the woman frowned at that, but Stuart must have been – underneath it all. She wondered how he'd seemed when they'd interviewed him. Had they also been surprised at his lack of emotion? 'It didn't seem right to push him.'

The man sighed impatiently. 'So, what did the two of you find to do all night?'

The female detective's mouth twitched slightly. *Bastards, the pair of them.*

'We talked, of course!' Bella's voice was embarrassingly uncontrolled and high-pitched. She paused a moment before continuing. 'We'd both had a terrible few hours.'

'You have my utmost sympathy.' The man's frown was deepening further now. 'But time makes all the difference in a murder enquiry. If either of you want us to find out who killed your friend, then you might want to help instead of concentrating on your own needs.'

He wasn't shouting. Not quite. Bella clutched her stomach. She felt sick. She and Stuart had both drunk a lot of vodka the night before. She'd thrown up three times that morning. It would be a long while before she could face any food. How could something so gut-wrenchingly appalling have happened?

'You have to consider your own safety too, Bella.' The woman looked at her from under glossy brown curls. 'Julie's attacker is out there and more often than not, victims know their killer. You spent a lot of time together. You might know them too.'

Bella swallowed. The nausea was getting worse. Did they reckon Stuart had done this? She thought back to the way he and Julie had interacted. They'd seemed devoted at first, but they each had their own, very firm, agendas. They were driven in a way she'd never been. Bella tried to look at the situation through the eyes of the police and shivered. Perhaps that *was* what they thought. Stuart could be an unnerving person. He'd got violent at times, when he'd been protesting, and he'd made her uneasy on occasion. She wouldn't want to get on the wrong side of him, but, given all his principles, he'd never stoop to murder. Besides, he was too canny to let things get out of hand.

'I understand,' she said at last, to the female detective. 'I hadn't thought it through.'

The woman nodded and turned to the man, whose shoulders went down a little. He paused with his pacing.

'So, you and Stuart talked. What else?'

'Got drunk and passed out.'

'That's all?' His brown eyes looked deep into hers. It was a disconcerting feeling.

'That's all. Knowing Julie was dead didn't leave either of us feeling sexy.' She regretted the words as soon as they were out. She sounded bitter. He'd think he'd got to her now – and probably that she fancied Stuart.

'We understand Julie and Stuart broke up because Julie thought you and he were seeing each other behind her back.' The woman spoke gently.

She had to take a moment before answering. Guilt gnawed at her insides. She felt the truth was lit up above her head in neon, and that they would read her mind. 'She was wrong. We weren't.'

'Bella, we also have evidence that you followed Stuart and Julie on at least one occasion, when they were still together.' Even the guy sounded more sympathetic now. He was weirdly good-looking when his face relaxed – rough around the edges though, despite his smart suit. For a second, she imagined pouring her heart out to him.

She took a deep breath. How to explain it? 'I— Well, I felt a bit left out, to be honest. I knew Julie before she got together with Stuart and we used to chat a lot. And then suddenly they were living in each other's pockets. Spending all their time planning protests or… well, you know.' She wasn't going to mention sex again. 'I sometimes went off into town when I knew they had. Not because I wanted to see them or make them feel guilty. It was just because I'd got nothing to do. Cambridge is a small place and I realised they'd seen me once.' She looked down at her lap. 'I was embarrassed.'

'Were you jealous of Julie?' the woman asked.

'No. I didn't – don't – fancy Stuart.'

'Did you fancy Julie?' The man's voice was even gentler now.

'No. Honestly. I found her fascinating – inspiring. That's all.' The tears came again but surely they'd expect that. She'd be crying over Julie's death for a long time yet, and what she'd told the officers was true – all true. Except the bit about not fancying Stuart.

'Bella – for the record, we need to ask you where you were on Saturday evening, and overnight.'

She'd already told the other detectives that she'd seen Julie leave the house on Chesterton Road from her bedroom window. Presumably that wasn't enough. 'I was in my room at the house where I lodged over the summer.'

'Can anyone vouch for you?'

She shook her head. 'Most of us who stayed there didn't know each other well. I bumped into another of the students, Martina, early on Sunday morning when I went to make a coffee in the kitchen, but not before then.'

The woman wrote it all down in her notebook. 'Do you drive, Bella?' she asked after a moment.

'No. I took a couple of lessons in the summer vacation after my first year but then I broke my wrist. I haven't gone back to it yet.'

The woman nodded.

'And as DS Maloney said,' the man went on, 'there's a chance you might know Julie's killer. Is there anyone you can think of who might have wanted to harm her?'

She paused a while before she answered, reviewing the names she might mention but then mentally crossing them off, one by one. 'No.'

The man had picked up on her expression. 'If you're worried about getting someone into trouble, Bella, please don't be. If you confide in us, we can investigate discreetly. And you'll be helping your friend.'

She remembered him looming over her when he'd first come in, looking as though he wanted to punch something. 'No, honestly. There's no one.'

There was a long pause but at last the guy sighed again. 'Last question then. Can you tell us about John?'

She felt a small shiver run through her and clasped her hands together. 'John who?' She tried to meet his eye, but as before, his look made her uncomfortable.

'John who Julie was… involved with – a little while back.' It sounded as though the detective was feeling his way.

'I'm sorry,' Bella said, 'but I can't help you.'

CHAPTER TWENTY-TWO

Blake had called the team together. Tara, Jez, Max and Megan were already gathered round a table in the incident room, huddled over steaming mugs of coffee. The heating at the station hadn't caught up with the sudden drop in temperature outside.

As he walked over to join the others he glanced out of the window. The trees lining the expansive green of Parker's Piece were just starting to turn, the edges of their leaves tinged with gold – the summer's growth breaking down and dying. That day, the Piece was occupied by student clubs and societies, showing off what they had to offer to the incoming cohort. In the area just opposite the station a group were doing folk dancing, watched by a gaggle of faintly embarrassed-looking youths he took to be freshers. In one corner of the green there was even a glider. He wondered how much it cost to join that club. The mist was lifting, displaced by the rising wind which made the trees twist and turn. Blake didn't like autumn. It was the season where he felt change most keenly, and after several years of the sand shifting uneasily beneath his feet, he didn't like the sense of uncertainty it brought.

'All right,' he said, calling them to attention. 'We'll talk about Bella Chadwick first.' He took a deep breath, trying to batten down his feelings of frustration, then gave them a summary of that morning's interview. He turned to Megan. 'Is there anything you'd like to add? What were your impressions?'

The DS glanced at her notebook, even though they'd only recently left the student. He'd rather hear what was uppermost in her mind, off the cuff. But Megan would want to be precise – it was in her blood. 'Her comments about Stuart Gilmour jarred with the impression I got of him. She said it would have been "inhumane" to call us when he turned up, because he was so upset. But at our interview he was fully in control of his emotions.'

Blake nodded. 'I agree.' He rubbed his chin. 'And assuming he wasn't bottling up his feelings when he spoke to us, then I'd guess she's lying about his state when he arrived. Which means that's not the real reason she failed to call us.'

'Do you think she could be frightened of Gilmour?' Max said.

'It's possible. She said something about it not feeling right to "push" him. Maybe it wasn't out of concern, but because she was scared of his response. Then again, she didn't try to deny that they were together in her room all night. She could have clammed up because they were both involved in Julie's death.'

'Is that what you think?' It was Tara who'd spoken. He met her green-eyed gaze. 'Gut instinct, I mean?' she added.

He caught Megan's look of disapproval out of the corner of his eye and wished for a moment that he could chew the case over with Tara alone, over a whisky in a pub somewhere. As for Megan and her dislike of hunches, it wasn't as though anyone was suggesting they head out, all guns blazing, to act on his thoughts.

He shook his head. 'I don't know, but I'm certain there's something that Bella's not telling us. And I don't like Gilmour.'

Megan wouldn't like that subjective judgement either – though he was sure she felt the same. 'Did you notice Bella's reaction when I asked about "John"?' he said, turning to her.

'She hesitated.'

'Yes, and the way she asked for clarification made me think she was playing for time. When she finally said she couldn't help she didn't meet my eye. If she was in the habit of trailing after Julie, my bet is she knows all about him. I want to know why she's not telling us.'

He turned to Max. 'What have you and Tara got?'

Max filled them all in on the visit to the Lockwoods' college residence. A lot of interesting information there – from the fact that Julie seemed to have nosed her way into rooms that were off limits, to the scared look in Douglas Lockwood's wife's eye, when she'd confirmed his alibi.

'And I've just had the results from the tech team who've been looking at Julie's laptop,' Tara said. She glanced down at her computer. 'Along with the kind of stuff you'd expect – essays related to her course and so on – there are various documents she was putting together for that student newspaper she worked for – *Uncovered*.'

Blake looked up quickly. 'Anything on Lockwood's?'

Tara nodded. 'She'd been preparing an article when she died, by the look of it – last saved just the day before. But the file had been created a whole year earlier. So, it looks as though it was a long-term project.' She frowned. 'Maybe she was waiting for – or even expecting – something big to add to it.'

'Could be. What about the content so far?'

'The article's written in a provocative way, and some of the information is quite shocking, but I've checked, and it's all in the public domain already. And the scandals that she wrote about have been explained away by Lockwood's PR people – sometimes with independent scientific backing. And sometimes not so much.'

Jez's blue eyes were thoughtful. 'She was probably waiting for new information that would put her on the map. Assuming she was planning to pursue journalism as more than just a hobby.'

'I don't think "putting herself on the map" would have been her goal.' Blake's words sounded harsher than he'd meant them to. 'She strikes me as someone who worked on principle. Either way, I imagine her aim was to find something that would really hit Lockwood's where it hurt.' He turned to Tara. 'What does her search history tell us?'

'That Lockwood's wasn't the only big corporate she had in her sights – but all the same, there's a disproportionate number of searches for the master's firm. Of course, she wouldn't have found anything new or secret on the net, but it looks as though she was diligent. She wanted every scrap of background information – so that she could be sure of her ground, I guess.'

'Any oddities?'

'Only one that I've found so far. Several of the searches were for Lockwood's and a specific location. For instance, Lockwood's and São Paulo or Lockwood's and Mumbai. And when I cross checked, I could see there'd been some kind of legal challenge for the company – or accusations of malpractice – in each of those places. I'd guess Julie had heard about them on the grapevine and was doing some digging. But one of the searches was for Lockwood's and Scotland – only the company doesn't have a base there.'

'Scotland?' He frowned.

Tara looked up. 'Yes, why?'

'It might be coincidence, but Scotland was mentioned in the notes on her mobile. Just that one word, with a question mark.'

It was a small thing, but an odd one – and Blake had learnt not to ignore those.

CHAPTER TWENTY-THREE

Tara had gone back to checking through Julie Cooper's laptop contents when her desk phone rang. It was Gail on reception.

'There's a woman here to see you.'

Tara usually preferred a bit more information than that. 'No name?'

'She said she'd rather not give me one, but she asked for "the female detective who visited the Master's Lodge at St Oswald's College this morning".'

'I see. Thanks, Gail.' She ended the call and got up, wondering who it could be. A student, who'd seen her enter the building and had something to say?

She paused a moment when she reached the doorway to the reception area. There were several people sitting on the padded upright chairs there, and one that she recognised. Tara took a moment to watch the woman before she went to announce herself. Douglas Lockwood's wife, Selina, looked just as twitchy as she had earlier. She was glancing repeatedly at the front desk, and then towards the exit, as though she was tempted to leave again without waiting.

Tara wasn't about to let that happen. She was almost at the woman's side when Selina turned and realised she'd been spotted. 'It's good to see you again.' Tara put out a hand. 'Shall we find somewhere private to talk?'

The woman nodded without speaking – her eyes still flicking towards the exit – and Tara led her to an interview room.

'Can I speak to you off the record?' Selina's words came out in a rush the moment the door was closed. She had to be pretty damned nervous to be that breathless.

'We don't have to record anything. But because of what we're investigating, I'm afraid I can't absolutely guarantee to keep everything you tell me quiet. What I can do is treat what you have to say with discretion and do my utmost not to involve you, if that's what you'd prefer.'

Selina stood by the table for a moment, one hand on its surface, half down into the chair next to it. But her eyes were still on the door.

'I could tell there was something wrong when we visited earlier,' Tara said, slipping into the chair opposite as though their discussion was a fait accompli. She hoped Selina would feel less able to walk out that way. 'Perhaps you'll feel better if you get it off your chest.' The woman must be tempted, otherwise she wouldn't be there.

After a moment longer, Selina faced Tara properly and dropped into the seat nearest to her. 'I suspected you'd seen something in my expression. I didn't know your name – and if I'd asked the others it would have looked odd – but the fact that I'd already given myself away made me want to come.'

Tara nodded. 'I'm Tara. DC Tara Thorpe. Whatever's on your mind, I'd be hugely grateful if you'd share it with me.'

Selina sighed. 'All right then. Well, I know the dead girl used to go on protest marches against my husband and father-in-law's firm, Lockwood's.'

That was interesting in itself – not news to the police of course, but why should Selina be aware of it? 'Who told you that?'

'My husband mentioned it in passing. I think he and Alistair must have discussed it. Douglas was complaining about the sort of students the university gets these days, and how misinformed young people are. All the sorts of things you'd expect really.' Selina still sounded breathless. 'He didn't seem cross with Julie personally, of course. I'm sure he never met her, so his ire would have been at the protesters as a whole.'

Tara nodded. She'd expect Selina to put that spin on it, whether it was true or not.

'But judging by your visit earlier, you associate Julie Cooper with Alistair directly, because she disapproved of his business. I'm not saying you think he was involved in her death, of course – that would be unthinkable. And he wasn't even in Cambridge when she was killed. But if you're looking for a connection between Lockwood's and Julie Cooper then you need to know about Alistair's son.'

Tara paused a moment, confused. 'What, your husband?'

She shook her head. 'No – Alistair's younger son, John.'

CHAPTER TWENTY-FOUR

'*John* Lockwood? How the hell did we not pick up on that?'

Tara was sitting opposite Blake in his office. Deep inside, she knew she should have found the information, somewhere. 'I guess researching Sir Alistair's offspring wasn't top of our agenda. Douglas and John weren't mentioned on Hubert Lockwood's Wikipedia page, and then our' – she paused and took a deep breath – 'my focus was on Alistair as part of Lockwood's, rather than him as a family man. I'd been looking at his biography on the firm's website – it mentioned Douglas, but I don't recall any details of a younger child. And then I reviewed his wife's biog on her own website, because I knew we'd meet, but the kids aren't mentioned at all there. And the rest of the family didn't let on about the extra son, or that he and Julie were connected.'

Blake's thoughts on that were abundantly clear from his expression. 'There's no doubt that they were aware?'

'None at all. Selina says Douglas had been worrying about it. John lectured Julie for one of her courses and took her for supervisions – again, just in one subject. He's based at another college and not at Julie's main department. But someone had warned Sir Alistair that their relationship might have gone further than was proper.'

'Hmm. So, when Julie told her mother she was helping this academic, "John", with his research, that was entirely made up. But he was probably the reason she wanted to stay in Cambridge over the summer.'

'It looks that way. Selina didn't know of any project where John might have recruited student helpers.'

'If this is all true, it's surprising that Julie fell for him – given her views on Lockwood's.'

Tara had been thinking the same.

'And who would have warned Sir Alistair about the possible affair, I wonder? Let me guess, Lucien Balfour, who was so keen to assure you and Max that there was no hint of any improper relationship between Julie and a member of university staff?'

'Seems more than likely. We thought he was lying at the time.'

'I remember.' Blake put his head back for a moment and looked at the ceiling. 'I bloody well hate it when it's like this. People closing ranks and staying silent. So, do we take it that Sir Alistair thinks his son might have killed Julie, and that's why he's kept shtum? Or simply that he doesn't want a family scandal threatening his position at St Oswald's?'

Tara thought back to what Selina had told her. 'Hard to say, but if Julie and John were sleeping together, he has to be a suspect for her murder. Maybe Julie tried to break it off with him. Or perhaps their relationship hadn't got that far but John wanted more. He could have lashed out at her, then panicked, locked her up and…' The image of Julie was so clear in her mind.

Blake's brown eyes met hers. 'I know,' he said. 'It's horrific.'

There was a moment's pause before Tara spoke again.

'Realistically, I guess we can't possibly judge whether John's a likely candidate until we've talked to him. Or you and Megan have, rather.' She cursed inwardly. Somehow it had come out as accusatory – as though she felt left out. In truth, she was jealous of Megan – but only of her seniority. She wanted the next step up. She'd taken the right exams now – but there was no opening for her. In her heart of hearts, she reckoned she'd do a better job than Megan, too. She'd tried to bury that thought deep; she knew it was wrong. She and Megan both had their skills and their Achilles' heels. But wasn't worming information out of people more important than writing up your notes correctly? *Blimey.* She was at it again – behaving like a five-year-old. And it was she and Jez who'd failed to pick up on John Lockwood's existence. Megan would have found him.

'You're right,' Blake said. He sounded normal. Hopefully her inner thoughts had passed under his radar. 'We need to talk to him urgently. Do you know where to find him?'

She nodded. 'I called his department, but he's not in today. After they'd verified my identity by calling me back, they gave me his home address.' She handed over the sticky note she'd written the details on, glad that she'd come prepared for that question, at least.

CHAPTER TWENTY-FIVE

Blake was dragging his coat on as he stood amongst his team. They were all talking about Selina Lockwood's revelation.

'Megan, you're with me. We'll go to John Lockwood's address – he's over on Cardew Street, off Chesterton Road.' He'd lived just round the corner from Julie's summer lodgings. Convenient. 'Tara.' He paused a moment, thinking on his feet. 'I want you to catch up with Bella Chadwick. Make it informal, work your way under her skin and find out why she didn't tell us what she knew about John.' He remembered the scared look in the girl's eyes again, as he'd mentioned the man's name. 'I'm sure as hell she did know.'

He turned to Max. 'Given Tara's occupied, I want you and Jez to interview Gilmour again. He lied to us about John – all that rubbish about him being a student. If he had evidence that Julie was sleeping with a university academic that puts a very different light on things.' John Lockwood had a lot more to lose than some two-timing undergraduate. And if Julie minded about him, Gilmour's knowledge would have been important to her too. But he still couldn't see how all that might relate to her murder. They needed to keep digging – at breakneck speed. Something had to slot into place.

Megan was on her feet, grabbing her bag, and Tara was up too, a look of zeal in her eyes. She was probably glad to be leading on something. He was still slightly worried about the dynamic between her and Max; they weren't quite the right balance for each other – Tara always ready to take over, Max a little too accommodating. Then again, the alternative of Tara and Megan would test everyone's resolve.

Max and Jez were talking tactics – Max's voice quiet, Jez's louder. He didn't wait to hear what their approach would be. Fleming was always telling him he should stop being a control freak.

Cardew Street was narrow, and lined with two-up two-down terraced houses. It was off the same road as his mother's place. Despite being significantly further out of town, the homes there would still fetch three or four hundred thousand, Blake guessed. Crazy.

John Lockwood was at number twenty. The paintwork on the door was cracked, and there was a hairline break in the sash window at the front, too. The short path to the front door was paved, but there was grass coming up between the stones, and the tiny area of garden next to it was unkempt. He and Megan exchanged a glance. Were these the signs of an absent-minded academic with his mind on higher things? Or was something else at work? He'd certainly never have guessed the house belonged to the son of a billionaire.

Blake rapped at the scuffed brass knocker. There was no bell. The action was met with absolute silence. He tried again, but his hopes weren't high. The place looked empty somehow. The windows were dark, and everything was still. He glanced at the sticky note Tara had given him. There was a mobile number on it, and he dialled. Would the man pick up? Could he be on the run, having killed Julie?

After a few rings, he got shunted through to voicemail. There was no personal message, just his network's pre-recorded one. He left his details for what it was worth and moved closer to the window to peer inside. The interior was crowded with books, papers and an assortment of oddly matched furniture. Every surface was covered, and Blake could see unopened post on a table. It looked as though John Lockwood had let his life get out of control.

'He was there last night.'

The voice made him jump. A man had approached Megan. He had one hand on her sleeve, now, his eyes bright.

'You spoke to him?' Megan asked, showing her warrant card.

But the man shook his head. 'Heard him. I live next door. I think he must have dropped something. There was an almighty crash. I listened out, in case he'd hurt himself, but I heard him moving about after a moment. I haven't seen him today.'

Blake moved forward. 'Is that unusual?'

The man gave him a sharp look. 'I don't spend my time spying on my neighbours. But I eat breakfast in my front room, and if people come and go I usually spot them. The soundproofing is the main thing in these places.' He nodded at number eighteen. 'The walls might as well be made of tissue paper. I know someone rang John late last night, for instance. I didn't hear what was said, but I expect if I'd put my ear to the wall I would have.'

The man made Blake feel uneasy. Suddenly he saw Tara's point, when she said living in an isolated cottage had its advantages. 'And what about this morning?'

'It's been quiet as the grave.'

The expression didn't make Blake any happier.

'He drinks,' the man said, nodding. 'It's not a happy situation. He might be sleeping it off.'

'You haven't got a spare key, I suppose?'

The man shook his head. 'Keeps himself to himself, that one. There's a footpath down the end of the gardens – for access, so we can take our bins round. You might be able to get a look round the back.'

And Blake guessed John Lockwood's neighbour would watch their every move. All the same, he didn't fancy breaking off to request a warrant at a time like this. It might come to that, but maybe they could find out more first. Or raise John Lockwood from his stupor by shouting up at his rear windows.

He thanked the man without sharing his plans and walked off up the street with Megan. 'Let's do as he suggests, but access the path further along the road. If we're lucky, he might have gone to make a cup of tea by the time we approach Lockwood's garden.'

They walked almost the entire length of Cardew Street. Every so often there was a passageway between the houses. When they'd rounded a bend in the road, Blake nodded. 'Let's go up this one and see if it leads to the path the neighbour was talking about.'

He strode ahead. They were travelling between two long, well-tended gardens. The one to his right contained a couple of rowan trees, their blood-red berries striking against the overcast sky. The mist had finally lifted, but the day was still dank and darker than usual. At the end of the passageway they found the path the man had told them about. It ran behind the gardens on that side of Cardew Street, and regular gates gave house-owners access to their own plots. Blake turned left and began to count, knowing they'd started at the rear of number fifty-four.

But when they came to the access to number twenty, he realised he could have guessed the right house without keeping track anyway. Number eighteen – the one that belonged to the neighbour they'd spoken to – was a bit untidy at the end. But John Lockwood's looked like an abandoned wasteland. The nettles were waist high. The fence was thick with ivy, interwoven with brambles. What kind of life was John Lockwood living? Blake's mother was an academic. She didn't set much store by household tasks, or gardening either, but she did the minimum – before things got out of hand. And even if Lockwood hated odd jobs, he could surely get someone in to help. This – this was the sign of someone who couldn't handle life. It was the only conclusion Blake could draw.

He turned to Megan. 'Shall we?'

The garden gate opened inwards, towards the house, but it fouled against the build-up of grasses and tangled vegetation. It took him a moment to force it back, but at last they were through. He and Megan held their hands high, away from the stinging nettles. Out of the corner of his eye he caught movement in the window of the neighbour's house. *Ah well.*

The back of John Lockwood's place was L-shaped. Blake was familiar with the standard Cambridge terrace layout. There was normally a kitchen, and sometimes a downstairs bathroom, right at the rear of the house, where once the outside loo would have been. Then, if you walked past that, down an area behind the main house and next to the kitchen, there was a rear reception room that most people used for dining.

He rapped at the back door which led into the kitchen and peered inside as he waited. It didn't tell them anything new. The sink was full of dirty crockery.

Beyond, Blake saw a depleted loaf of bread on a board. Had he been down to eat that morning? Or was it there from longer ago?

Once again, he listened, but there was nothing. The door was locked when he tried it, after pulling on a pair of latex gloves. He called Lockwood's mobile again. No answer.

They'd have to get a warrant. He cursed and walked towards the window of the rear reception room for a quick peek before they left.

It was dark inside, and at first, all Blake could see was a table, and an empty whisky bottle. But as his eyes adjusted, he realised there was something else. A man's leg... He moved quickly, as far left as he could get, hard up against the boundary fence. From that angle he could see more. The man's whole body. There was a pool of something that looked like vomit on the wooden floor next to him. Blake's immediate instinct was to break the window, climb through and check for a pulse, but in his gut, he knew there was no point.

If this was John Lockwood, he was dead.

CHAPTER TWENTY-SIX

It was mid-afternoon as Tara walked across Coe Fen with Bella Chadwick. The place was a traditional site for grazing cattle – Coe came from cow, she'd heard. Charles Darwin had reputedly done beetle surveys there too. The ground was close to the river and at the mercy of seasonal floods. For Tara's purposes, it was perfect: just behind St Oswald's, and currently almost deserted, thanks to the damp, shivery day. She could see why people had retreated indoors. As she watched, the wild wind forced the ancient willows to bend and twist.

'I thought it might be easier to talk outside college.' Tara tucked her red-gold hair behind her ears and glanced sideways at Bella. She wanted her off her own territory – but the location was also informal and as good as private. 'I was having a chat with DI Blake, who heads up my team, about the talk you had earlier today.'

Julie's friend – if that was what she'd been – looked back at her. She was still wary, and her eyes were puffy. She hadn't been holding up well, by the look of things.

'Was that the man or the woman who came?' she said at last.

'The man.' Bella shut down slightly in response. Tara guessed Blake had got under her skin, even if he hadn't managed to make her tell all she knew.

'Bella, I know this is hard for you. I can't imagine any worse circumstance. But we do need to ask you to help us as much as you can, for Julie's sake. And what's more, I got the impression you were in trouble too.'

Bella's eyes, which had been on hers, moved quickly down to the path under their feet. 'What do you mean?' she said after a moment.

'DI Blake saw your reaction when he asked you about John Lockwood. He could see that you knew about him and Julie.' Tara saw her flinch at the mention of the academic's name. 'You might feel better if you tell me all about it. And whatever happened, telling the truth is one last thing you can do for Julie.'

The young woman was still silent, her eyes on the thrashing trees ahead of them.

'Given what we already know, letting us have your take on it can't hurt, can it? You've got a lot of weight on your shoulders. This is one thing you can offload.'

She heard Bella take a gulp. She was fighting emotion again. 'I knew that Julie had classes with John. And that they were spending time together. I think she liked him.'

'She didn't mind that he was one of the Lockwood family?' She knew Bella had joined Julie and Stuart on the anti-Lockwood's march, so she must be aware of Julie's views on the firm.

Bella shook her head. 'John doesn't do any work for the company.'

Tara was still surprised. 'So, you don't think Julie got involved with John *because* of his family connections? He would have been a contact on the inside.'

Bella shook her head. 'I think she just hit it off with him when they talked about the course she was doing.'

But Tara didn't feel the student was telling the full story. She needed to be patient. 'How did you find out that they'd got friendly?' It wasn't as though Bella was doing the same courses as Julie had been. There'd be no reason for her and John Lockwood's paths to cross. Perhaps she'd only known about the two of them because she'd followed Julie. Maybe that was why she hadn't confessed to knowing who John was – it would highlight the strangeness of her own relationship with the dead girl. The way she'd behaved had been tantamount to stalking.

'She told me.' Bella's words were almost lost on the wind. 'That's how I found out.'

'Julie confided in you?' Tara tried not to let her tone give away her scepticism.

Bella nodded.

Tara didn't believe it. She'd looked at the records the tech team had got from Julie's phone – seen the way the dead student had tried to distance herself from Bella, noticed how often she'd made excuses to avoid meeting up. Would she really have invited Bella in for a glass of wine and regaled her with stories of her relationship with John – whatever stage it had got to?

'Did she tell you how far things had gone? I'm sorry to ask personal questions, but it's important. Do you know if they had a physical relationship?'

Maybe John had wanted one, but Julie hadn't.

'She didn't say. I don't think it was a big deal. That was why I didn't mention it. Julie wouldn't have wanted to get John into trouble.'

But her excuse didn't fit. Tara had seen fear in her eyes when she'd mentioned the man's name, just as Blake had earlier. What if Bella *had* followed Julie? And what if John Lockwood knew she'd seen the pair of them together? What if he'd threatened her to keep her quiet? What then?

She thought back to the flowers in Julie's pocket, the mutilated heart in her room and the tears in her underwear. They made this look like a crime of passion.

And one way or another, John Lockwood had plenty at stake.

CHAPTER TWENTY-SEVEN

'I'm very sorry for your loss.'

Blake was sitting next to Megan in the Master's Lodge at St Oswald's. Sir Alistair and Lady Lockwood were opposite them, he on an upright chair and she on a chesterfield sofa. The master's face was devoid of all colour.

Lady Lockwood looked blank for a moment, but at last she straightened her back and took a deep breath. 'It's not unexpected.'

Blake had guessed that might be the case. It was clear from their son's home that he'd been on a downward spiral for some time.

'Do you know the precise circumstances of his death?' Her voice was still steady and her eyes dry, but he'd seen that before – learnt it could come from an almost trance-like state of shock on hearing the worst news.

'We're waiting for medical reports, but it looks as though your son became ill after drinking heavily.' He'd be interested to hear what the man's doctor had to say, and if there was any role for the coroner and Agneta in all of this.

Lady Lockwood sighed. 'I've been afraid of this for a long time. He was making himself unwell.'

'Through alcohol consumption?'

She nodded.

'I understand you both knew that your son had become close to Julie Cooper.' He watched them intently.

'I'd been told that was the case.' Sir Alistair rose from his chair and walked towards one of the tall mullioned windows that ran along the south side of the room. 'But people here do like to bring me unsubstantiated gossip. I looked into it and came to the conclusion that's just what it was. It's not unnatural for a student to admire a fellow. They're inevitably interested in the same academic fields, and the supervisor is everything the student hopes to be – intellectually, I mean. A sort of hero worship – if you like – develops. That doesn't mean there's something untoward going on behind closed doors.'

'Was it Julie's tutor who raised concerns about the situation?'

Sir Alistair turned to face him. 'It was. But Lucien wasn't expressing his own personal fears. I gather it was someone in John's department who'd seen him having coffee with Julie, or something similar. It was hardly incriminating.'

'But I assume it was your uncertainty about the truth that made you hide John and Julie's connection from us.'

'You have it the wrong way round, Inspector. I was sufficiently relaxed about the suggestions to be sure my son's fleeting connection with Julie was irrelevant.'

'You still made the conscious decision to withhold information, sir. You must have known we'd be interested.'

The large man looked him straight in the eye. 'I did. But John was troubled, Inspector, and I didn't want to make his life more difficult.'

'Sir Alistair, we both know Julie Cooper was a passionate campaigner. As well as taking part in a demonstration against your firm, we now find she was associating with your son. And her laptop search history shows she read every scrap of online information relating to Lockwood's.'

Blake hadn't managed to ruffle the man. In fact, he smiled. 'I'd expect nothing less, Inspector. We develop bright and enquiring minds at St Oswald's. All our students need to have that sort of dedication to their pursuits.'

He was either genuine or well-polished. Blake tried not to feel cynical as he concluded the latter. 'It occurred to me, sir, that if she was spending time with your son, over and above what was required for her studies, she might have been driven by the desire to get inside information. Something she couldn't access on the internet.'

He shook his head at that. 'That simply won't wash. John had nothing whatever to do with Lockwood's. He's never worked for the firm – not even in the summer holidays whilst he was a student. It was only ever Douglas who wanted to get involved. And no member of the leadership team at Lockwood's would discuss business with an outsider, family or not – it's a cardinal rule.'

It made sense. Blake couldn't imagine Sir Alistair's approach being influenced by sentimentality.

As for the master's declared reasons for keeping John's connection with Julie quiet – well, they might be genuine. But if there was any truth in the rumours it would make John a murder suspect, and threaten Sir Alistair's reputation by extension. And it was quite a coincidence that John had been found dead the day after Julie. They hadn't ruled out suicide. He could have taken his own life out of sorrow. But, of course, it could also have been from guilt.

CHAPTER TWENTY-EIGHT

'What is it?' Selina had walked in on Douglas whilst he was still on the phone. She'd seen his jaw go slack and his face turn pale, but nothing he'd said had told her what the caller wanted. He'd just kept nodding and muttering: 'I see.' Now, at last, the call was at an end.

Her husband let out a long breath. 'It's John. He's dead.'

Selina felt gooseflesh rise up on her arms. She'd only told the police about Douglas's brother and Julie a few hours earlier. Was this somehow because of her? Because she'd put him under suspicion? Would Douglas find out what she'd done? And if he did, would he be furious, or glad? It all depended on the truth…

'How? How did it happen?'

'They're not sure yet.' His eyes met hers. 'The police saw him through a window, collapsed on the floor of his study. It looks as though he'd got ill after a drinking session.' He paused. 'So those detectives must have made the connection between him and Julie – that was why they visited. When they got no answer, they went round the back.'

'Do they think— do they think it might be suicide?'

'I just said, didn't I?' Douglas's outburst made her jump. 'It's too soon to tell.'

'I'm sorry.'

He was pacing up and down the room. She'd read that the death of an estranged family member could have far-reaching consequences. Her husband was meant to feel guilt – and sadness that the last chance of reconciliation had gone.

She wondered whether to put an arm round Douglas, or offer to get him a drink or something. But seeing his hunched shoulders and rigid jaw told her all she needed to know. She left the room quietly. It was often best to let the dust settle.

Half an hour later, she arranged to walk past the sitting room. Her husband was still in there, but sitting now, rather than pacing, relaxed back in his chair, the tautness gone from his muscles.

She ventured in, still standing near the door. 'Are you all right?'

He glanced up at her. 'Yes. Look, I can imagine what you were thinking before. But Lockwood's has bloody good lawyers and the best public relations people. Whatever John did or didn't do – it will all be forgotten in a year or so.'

Though not by the student's family and friends. Part of her felt it was horrific that that didn't cross his mind – but it wasn't his fault. He'd had that mindset ingrained from birth – it was spelled out in the Lockwood motto: family above all else.

She'd ceased to be shocked by his attitude – and his words also brought relief. If he really thought John was guilty, it meant Douglas couldn't be. Since they'd stopped sharing a bed – and she'd started taking sleeping pills – she had no idea of his movements during the night.

For the umpteenth time that day she examined her conscience. No – it was honestly true. She'd told the police about John because it was important to their investigation – nothing more. But in so doing, she might also have diverted attention from Douglas.

Of course, now that John was dead, it would be harder for the police to find the truth. As she left the room, she could see her husband in profile. He was smiling to himself.

CHAPTER TWENTY-NINE

It was the first time Max had conducted an interview with Jez. As before, Gilmour had insisted on doing the whole thing formally, so they were at the station with the student's solicitor. Watching Stuart sitting opposite them, worldly wise, confident, and seemingly relaxed, left Max feeling they had a battle on their hands. He wished he'd got Tara sitting next to him – they made a good team.

'We know you lied about John.' He kept his look steady.

There was an amused smile playing round Gilmour's lips. 'I don't know what you mean.'

'And we don't believe you.' Jez was trying to look as laid-back as Gilmour, but he was already riled.

The student smiled again. 'That's not something I can help.'

Max could almost see Jez's blood pressure rising. 'So you're trying to tell us Julie was involved with two men called John?' the new DC said.

'I'm not trying to tell you anything.' Gilmour dragged the words out, as though he could only just bring himself to reply.

'Were you aware of her being close to two men called John?' Max could keep his temper all right. That was one thing losing his wife had taught him. Life could throw you into the worst hell; it was worth saving your high emotion for those times, and not letting idiots like Gilmour sap your energy.

The youth shrugged. 'How would I know what Julie got up to? She was an independent woman.'

'What do you know about Julie's relationship with John *Lockwood*?' Jez said, leaning forward, his shoulders hunched. He was a big guy and Max could feel his anger in the air.

'Wait, that guy who supervised her?' Gilmour's eyes opened wide. 'Seriously? Jeez – he always looks half dead. I shouldn't think he'd be able to manage any high jinks with his students.'

It was Max's turn to smile. 'You know what he looks like, then.'

Gilmour was silent, and Max was pleased to see his smug grin fade a little.

'That's pretty interesting, given you and Julie were doing different courses, and John Lockwood isn't based at either your college or – of course – your department.'

He allowed Gilmour a couple of seconds' squirming time.

'Perhaps you'd like to tell us how you came to know about him, then. It's a coincidence that your ex was involved with one of the Lockwoods – a son of the tycoon you'd each been campaigning against. That must have hurt.'

Gilmour's look was sour now and Jez leant back again slightly, his frown lightening.

'Answer the question, please.'

The student shrugged. 'I went to find her one day. There was nothing creepy about it; I just wanted to talk, that's all. I intended to intercept her after her supervision, but she and Lockwood left together. There was something in the way they walked – all the clichéd stuff – in time with each other, shoulder to shoulder. It made me curious.'

Jez raised an eyebrow. 'So you followed? Just because you were interested…'

Gilmour rolled his eyes. 'I suspect most ex-boyfriends would have done the same. In fact, anyone who knew her might have wondered. So yes, I followed. And once they'd got off the beaten track, he put his arm around her waist, and she leant into him. They were whispering to each other, and they kissed.'

Gilmour's manner hadn't changed. Max couldn't see any fire in his eyes. His expression was still ironic, as though he thought the fuss was faintly ridiculous. It was weird: Jez looked angrier than Gilmour did.

'And then you used your secret knowledge to persuade Julie to see you? That was when she let you into her lodgings over the summer?'

Gilmour looked bored. 'Yes.'

'Did you ask her for money to keep quiet?' Jez leant forward.

'You're kidding, right? Julie didn't have any money, unless you count what she made from waitressing.' He didn't sound insulted at the suggestion, just amused at its lack of practicality.

'But presumably John had plenty of funds,' Max said, 'even if not personally, then via his family.'

Gilmour shook his head. 'As far as I can work out, he was persona non grata. And anyway, there's no way the family would cough up money over something like that. Their idea of helping would have been to set their pit-bull lawyers onto me.' He turned for a moment to his own legal representation. 'All due respect to you and your colleagues, but Lockwood's legal team is something else. They spend their entire time making sure the Lockwood family get away with murder.'

Jez was sitting forward again. 'Under the current circumstances, you might want to watch what you say. I wouldn't want you to have any regrets.'

The lawyer was on high alert again. 'We should all consider our language,' she said, with a sidelong glance, first at Gilmour, then at Jez, 'and also our tone.'

The DC had made his warning sound like a threat. His bunched fists didn't help, though only Max could see them, underneath the table.

Gilmour looked as relaxed as ever. 'You can all calm down. I'm no blackmailer; money doesn't buy happiness. I wanted to see

Julie and I used the information I had at my disposal to make that happen. It was underhanded, but it worked, and there was nothing wrong with wanting to talk.'

'Your message was threatening. You said you had evidence, and you implied you'd use it.'

The student pulled a face. 'I never had any photos of them together. Let's just say I exaggerated. Why would she see me if she didn't think I had proof? Us talking wasn't just for my benefit. We'd been campaigning against Lockwood's together. Seeing a member of the family seemed like a risk. What if John Lockwood was secretly angry about the way she was laying into his dad? He might have been a rebel, but blood is thicker than water. Family loyalty runs deep sometimes. I thought she'd be safer leaving him well alone.'

'And what was her reaction, when you passed on your message of concern?' Jez raised an eyebrow.

'She told me to mind my own effing business.' He folded his arms across his chest. 'And then she told me to let it go.'

'And what did you do?' Max watched the man's calm eyes.

'I took her advice. And – after that one visit over the summer – I never saw her again.'

'Why did you lie to us about the identity of "John" to start with?'

Gilmour smiled. 'I respect my elders. And I wouldn't want to get a university fellow into trouble.'

Max terminated the interview. He had patience, but there were limits; he needed to get out of the room. Perhaps he'd try some of that pacing that Blake seemed to find so therapeutic.

CHAPTER THIRTY

Lucien Balfour was waiting in the drawing room at the Master's Lodge. One of the housekeeping staff had poured him a glass of sherry and told Alistair he was there. The old man was keeping him waiting though, and Balfour couldn't help feeling it was deliberate. The balance of power between them was fairly evenly poised – but if the truth about Julie got out, that could all change.

At last, he heard soft footsteps on the stairs. They were thickly carpeted, so the sound was muffled, but Alistair was a large man. Balfour was sure it was him.

A moment later, the master came in through the grand double doors and closed them behind him. He walked over to the decanter on the side table and poured himself a whisky in a cut-glass tumbler.

'So, Lucien, what can I do for you?'

'I was surprised not to hear from you, what with everything that's happened.'

The older man raised his eyebrows. 'I agree, the week has been eventful so far. Have you heard about my younger son?'

Lucien blinked – what was coming?

'I see from your expression that you have not.' The man filled him in, leaving Lucien spluttering out words of sympathy he didn't really feel. How was it possible that the Lockwoods had lost a child, without any noticeable effect on their household? The housekeeping woman had said nothing when he'd entered.

'So, you'll understand that coming to chat to you hasn't been uppermost in my mind.' Sir Alistair took a large slug of his drink. 'And after all, what is there to say?'

Lucian hesitated. 'I thought you might want to tell me the background.'

Alistair eyed him. 'As a matter of fact, I was thinking the same about *you*. I'm sure you must be relieved that Julie Cooper is out of the way.'

Balfour was starting to wish he hadn't come. 'There are others who are more of a danger to me.'

The master inclined his head. 'Yes, and whose fault is that? But, thanks to me, you don't have to worry about Bella Chadwick.'

'I wish I could feel sure about that.'

'You can. Trust me.'

'Alistair, if you've—' He stopped. This wasn't going as he'd planned.

'Lucien, I don't know what you're hoping to get out of this conversation, but I think it would be wise if you reconsidered. Perhaps we should both stick to minding our manners. I'm all for keeping things civil and riding the storm until it's over.'

Balfour found himself shrinking slightly as the master walked over to him. He only let out the breath he'd been holding when the man patted him on the shoulder.

'This is just one tiny wrinkle in the smooth history of St Oswald's and of Lockwood's. It doesn't need to become anything more unless we let it. I'm assuming you haven't come here to tell me you're guilty of murder. That seems to be a little out of your league.'

Balfour shook his head, hurriedly.

'In which case I gather you've come here to see if I confess. And perhaps to make a little money on the side, if you can persuade me to give myself away. Your imagination really does run wild, doesn't it? If that's honestly what you think I've done, maybe you should watch your step.' He moved away again, over the thick rug under their feet. 'Now, drink up your sherry and go home. I've had enough of today.'

CHAPTER THIRTY-ONE

It was already mid-evening when Tara realised someone was standing over her desk. She looked up to find Jez watching her.

'Don't you ever go home?'

'I got caught up in all of this. There are so many interconnections. They must hang together somehow but I still can't see it.' She'd been making notes on a sheet of paper in front of her. He was peering down at her words now, so he'd see her train of thought. 'The Lockwoods, Stuart, Bella and the tutor, Lucien Balfour, were *all* keeping quiet about Julie's relationship with John. It's just weird – they're such a disparate group of people.'

She could see why they'd all have their reasons though. Bella, if she was scared of John Lockwood; Stuart, if he'd been trying to blackmail Julie into seeing him again; and the Lockwoods and Balfour to protect their own or the university's reputation.

But no one who'd interviewed Gilmour seemed to buy him as the desperate spurned lover, willing to use any means to get Julie back. Cold and calculating was how Max had described him. Of course, Stuart could have kept quiet about John because his affair with Julie gave Stuart a motive for murder. But that still didn't feel right; the student didn't *seem* jealous. Could he have another reason for hiding his knowledge?

She looked up and met Jez's blue eyes.

'I don't suppose I could tempt you out to the pub?' he said. He was grinning, not at all nervous at asking. 'We could pool our thoughts there. Alcohol's great for getting the creative juices flowing.'

Tara had a feeling that solving the case might not be Jez's primary motive, and it made her smile. She paused for a moment. Max and Megan had left a little while earlier. Together – she'd noticed. Maybe they'd already gone off for a conflab – or something else – over a swift half. Blake was still in his office, door closed. How would he be feeling, after seeing two corpses in two days? He'd be bound to go home to his family soon, but maybe he was putting it off. Switching from work horrors to the demands of domestic life couldn't be easy. She pushed away the thought of him, poring over his evidence, and glanced back at Jez.

'It sounds great, in theory. But in practice I'm done in.' Give the guy an inch and he'd take a mile. She was going to bide her time. His cheeky attractive smile and easy confident manner went a long way, but if he was genuinely keen he'd wait until things had calmed down. 'I think I'll have to go home in a minute. I need to get some sleep, so I can think straight tomorrow. My visitors kept me up until all hours yesterday.'

His eyes were still on hers, and his smile remained. 'All right, you win. Sometime soon then.'

She smiled herself in response to that, shut down her computer and got up from her desk.

'Are you on your bike today?'

She nodded.

'Well, maybe I'll head off with you.'

'You've got a bike now?' She hadn't thought it would be his style.

'When in Rome… and you live out towards Chesterton, don't you? I'm in that direction too – I go over the Green Dragon Bridge.'

She nodded. 'All right then. So long as you can keep up with me!' She glanced at him over her shoulder and he laughed.

Tara and Jez cycled slowly in the end. It was dark and there was a headwind which carried the sound of their words away from them.

It was only when they could ride side by side on the smaller roads that they were able to chat. Jez said he'd applied for a transfer from Suffolk to Cambridge to get a new start. She glanced at him and saw him shrug as he leant forward, his gloved hands still gripping the handlebars.

'My marriage came apart. I got hitched after a whirlwind romance. Abandoned, passionate, and very ill-advised. I didn't get to know her properly before we tied the knot. It was only once we were living together that I...' He paused, not looking at her. 'Well, anyway. These things are never all one person's fault, are they?'

Tara wasn't sure what to say to that. There was clearly more to find out. 'I'm sorry you had a bad time.'

He gave her a sidelong glance as they entered Stourbridge Common. 'It hasn't put me off relationships.'

She was glad her cottage was in sight now. Jez was easy on the eye and food for thought, but she was too tired to work out the right approach. And she certainly didn't want things to move too quickly. Taking people at face value wasn't her style.

'Well,' she paused her bike on the path, 'that's my place over there, so I'll bump my way over the grass now and see you tomorrow.'

'It's a cool house.'

'It's way more than cool – mostly freezing, in fact.' She'd already started to plough her way off the tarmac and over the tussocks. 'Crazily impractical, but I like it. And I'll like it even more after I've had a new boiler installed.'

At that moment she noticed movement in the shadows near her cottage's front gate. Her outside light wasn't on, so it was hard to discern what was going on. She stopped in her tracks and held her breath, but then a bulky shape separated itself from the house's boundary.

Kemp.

'What the?' Jez was at her side. 'Have you got an intruder?'

'Yeah, looks like it.' She laughed and raised a hand. Kemp followed suit and strode over the bumpy meadow to join them, lifting his large feet high to avoid hummocks and cowpats alike.

Kemp glanced at Jez.

'My new colleague, DC Jez Fallon,' Tara explained. 'Jez, this is my friend Paul Kemp. He's a PI.'

'And an ex-cop, though Tara's too tactful to mention it.' Kemp nodded, though neither he nor Jez put out their hands. Jez was still astride his bike and Kemp was on Tara's other side.

'Sounds as though there's a story to tell.' Jez nodded back.

'Right enough. But it's of questionable quality.' Kemp looked at Tara. 'I wanted a word, mate, if you've got a moment. I know you had a late one last night though. I was trying to call you.'

'Sorry. My phone's in my bag.' She indicated her pannier, where she'd stuffed her belongings before heading home. It was no wonder she hadn't heard it above the wind. 'But it's no problem – we can talk.'

'Looks like that's my cue to leave then,' Jez said, making off towards the Green Dragon Bridge and Chesterton.

Tara turned to say goodbye, but he was already too far away, shoulders hunched, head down.

CHAPTER THIRTY-TWO

Max was sitting opposite Megan in the Free Press. The place was just round the corner from the station but the others didn't normally go there – there wasn't much space for one thing – so they were probably safe. As he closed the door, he felt he was shutting out the horrors of the case as well as the howling gale outside. The tiny interior was cosy and welcoming.

So he'd done it. He was there, with Megan, because they'd agreed to stop off for a quick drink – but they both knew it was a date drink. It was the first he'd been on since Susie died. Five and half years. Most of his friends had implied he'd left it long enough. They meant well; didn't realise grief had no time limit. He took a deep breath.

'What can I get you?' Megan beat him to it – he'd been so taken up with what it meant to be there.

'Sorry.'

She smiled at him, put her arm through his and drew him in close. 'Don't worry. I understand. Just let me buy you a drink.'

It was funny: Max knew Blake felt Megan was less intuitive than the rest of the team, but she was bang on where he was concerned. Maybe she was more relaxed with him than she was with most people. The thought brought an automatic feeling of warmth with it. In that moment he knew he was glad to be there, even if his pleasure was mixed with guilt.

'Thanks. A half of bitter.'

Megan ordered the same. There was no chance of making a night of it. Max was glad – if they took things slowly, he could get used to the idea.

'What was it like today, doing an interview with Jez?' Megan asked, taking a seat at a table by the window.

Max wondered what was behind the question. 'He gets hot under the collar very quickly. It could have made things difficult, but in the end it didn't. All the same, I'm surprised someone hasn't drummed it out of him before now. He's the sort to leap in and say the wrong thing.'

Megan tilted her head to one side. 'I've found the same.' She sighed. 'Just a learning curve, I reckon. Next time it happens I'll have a word.'

'I noticed he was hovering round the station when we left.'

She shrugged. 'Lots to do. I felt a bit guilty heading off myself, but I'm so knackered.'

'Blake told us all to beat it, anyway.'

'I know. But he's still there, of course. I wonder if he's avoiding his family. Or keeping an eye on Jez and Tara.'

Max felt his insides sink. Why was Megan so down on their DI? 'Blake's dedicated, you know that. He minds about each and every case.'

It was only a moment before she nodded. 'Yes, sorry. That's completely true. But it doesn't mean he isn't motivated to stay late for other reasons as well.'

None of them knew what was happening with Blake and his wife. It was true that he tended to shut the topic down if anyone asked after Babette. As for Jez and Tara…

'You reckon Jez is primed to make his move then?'

Megan rolled her eyes. 'I'd say so. Something tells me he wouldn't have stayed this late if he didn't have an ulterior motive.'

Max wondered how much to say. He didn't want Megan to get the wrong impression, but he'd got the desire to confide. 'I'm a bit worried about that, to be honest.'

Megan swigged her beer. 'Really? Tara can take care of herself, Max. You know that.'

'I'm not saying she couldn't floor Jez in a fight.' He hadn't seen Tara in action, but her self-defence skills were the talk of the station. 'But Jez has got a lot of charm and Tara's had a rough time, what with one thing and another. I think the damage he could do might be more insidious.'

'So you don't think he's right for her then?' Megan gave him a nudge now, and a small smile. 'Should I be jealous, that you're so bothered about her love life?'

It was his turn to roll his eyes, but he grinned too. 'Tara's my partner on the team. I'm bound to look out for her. No jealousy required, though I'm flattered if you're bothered.'

Megan leant towards him over the table. 'I'm bothered all right.' They were an inch or so apart and he felt a flutter inside him. In a second it brought back a memory. His first date with Susie. They'd been at the cinema in Wisbech, watching *Sherlock Holmes*. He'd still been progressing towards CID at the time and Susie had teased him – said he might be able to pick up a few tips. For an awful moment he felt his eyes prickle.

Megan put her drink down, took his hand and squeezed it, then let it go and moved back in her seat a little.

'Tell me more about the interview,' she said quickly. 'What did you think of Stuart Gilmour?'

He took a deep breath and sat a little straighter too, shifting his mind back to work. 'I'd imagined a lovesick youth – I was way off there.'

Megan nodded. 'Same. I wasn't sorry to miss out on the second interview with him.' She glanced down into her beer for a moment.

'Each time I looked up, his eyes seemed to be on me.' She shook her head. 'I didn't like it. I'm not sure what he's up to, but I reckon he's wondering what we know. He's not scared, but he's wary.' She paused. 'And I think I saw him, outside the station.'

'What's that? When?'

Megan frowned. 'Mid-afternoon, yesterday, just after I saw Sandra Cooper out.' She put her hands over her face for a second, and he found himself reaching up to touch her arm, for all he'd been pulling back a moment earlier.

'I was upset.' Megan met his eyes again and he saw that she still was. 'How selfish is that, when I think about what she must have been going through? But it was so hard to watch her suffering.'

Max nodded. 'That makes you human – something to hang on to.'

'I suppose. So anyway, I went out of the building for a moment, and onto Parker's Piece. I just needed some air. I wasn't really focused on my surroundings, but after a moment I got that feeling – you know that sort of sixth sense when someone's watching you?'

Max nodded. He'd always imagined it was because you'd caught movement out of the corner of your eye, but he'd had that sensation too.

'I turned – I guess the direction I looked was based on instinct – but all I saw was the side of this guy's head as he swung round and then I got a back view of him as he walked away. But this morning, when I finally got to speak to Gilmour, I had an eerie feeling that it was him.'

'Have you told anyone?'

She shook her head. 'I'm not at all sure. I've been trying to match up the glimpse I got of him on the Piece with the guy we grilled. But if it's true it means he lied about spending the afternoon drinking vodka on Coe Fen, even though he had a receipt for the booze.'

Max nodded. And it meant he hadn't been too distraught to do something targeted too. It looked as though he'd wanted to know what the police were up to.

As they left the pub, he turned to Megan. 'I think you should let Blake know tomorrow. Just so he's aware it's a possibility – even if you're not sure.'

She nodded, her brown curls catching the light from the old-fashioned ironwork lamp that hung outside the pub's door.

He was glad they were headed in the same direction. If Gilmour had been watching Megan then, he might be keeping an eye on her now.

CHAPTER THIRTY-THREE

'Blimey,' Kemp said, as Tara got off her bike so she could bump it over the grass and talk at the same time.

'Blimey what?'

'Don't think your new DC was too chipper that I'd turned up.'

She rolled her eyes, though it would be wasted on Kemp. Even if it had been broad daylight, he wasn't one for subtleties. 'He was about to head off anyway. I'd already told him I needed to catch up on my sleep.'

'Aha! So, he *was* hoping otherwise then?'

'Oh, nice deduction, Mr Detective!'

'Well, am I right?'

She gave a deliberate sigh – also wasted, thanks to the wind choosing that moment to gust at them across the floodplain. 'Yes, you're right.'

'And you're not interested?'

They'd reached Tara's house now, and she wheeled her bike round the outside towards her back garden. It took her a moment to get the back gate open as she fumbled with her keys. At last, she shoved the bike into the tatty area of grass behind her cottage. 'I didn't say that.'

'No offence, but I wouldn't recommend dating a copper.'

'I used to date you – if you can call our casual liaisons dating. The dives you used to take me to!'

She heaved her bike into the shed, removed her bag from the pannier, and locked up.

'I did my best!'

She met Kemp's injured expression and laughed. 'I bet you take Bea to posher places.'

For a moment he looked as though he'd been caught out, but then he grinned too. 'The best pubs in Cambridge, naturally. But going back to dating police officers, it wasn't the same when we went out. I'm an *ex*-cop. Saw the error of my ways. World of difference there.'

'Hmm.' She led the way to back to the front door and let them in. 'Well, I'm a cop, and I'm all right, aren't I?'

No post on the doormat…

'Passable.'

'*Thank* you. And you've met Blake. He's okay?'

'Almost weirdly so.'

'So you can't really write Jez off after fifteen seconds' conversation. Lager?'

'That'd be great, mate, cheers.'

But when she handed him the can, his eyes were serious. 'Let's just say, I think you've got the right idea, taking things slowly.'

Bea had always been like a surrogate mum to Tara, and Kemp had looked after her too – from the moment he'd started her self-defence lessons as a teenager. He was protective. And these days there was a danger of the pair of them working as a team, worrying over her well-being from the sidelines. He opened his mouth as though he was about to say something more, but Tara held up a hand.

'Don't worry. That's why I said no tonight when he asked me out to the pub. I can take care of myself. And if he comes on too strong, I can even use one of your moves on him.'

She met Kemp's brown-eyed gaze, expecting him to laugh, but it didn't happen.

'All right.'

They were in an odd situation. They'd been in a relationship once, and they loved each other as friends. She understood his concern, but she needed to make her own way now. Kemp seemed weirdly settled (for him) and Blake was deep in some kind of complicated relationship she didn't understand. Tara needed to move on, too. She wasn't after a lasting partnership, but she ought to have some fun.

'Have you eaten?' She turned to reach a bottle of red down from a shelf, removed the screw cap and poured herself a glass.

He nodded. 'Yeah, thanks. Want me to rustle you something up?'

Now that Bea had trained him, it would be perfectly safe to accept, but she shook her head. 'I've got leftovers from Saturday night. I'll give them a reheat whilst we chat.' She pulled a plate of risotto out of the fridge and stuffed it in the microwave. 'So, what's up with you? You said you needed to talk?'

Kemp took a deep breath. 'Sorry – I feel a bit stupid bringing it up now. You'd guessed about me and Bea, then?'

She rolled her eyes theatrically. 'Uh – yeah. You're part love-struck kids, part old married couple. I find it endearing.'

He grinned. 'You don't mind?'

She didn't; she was happy for them. So why did tears choose that moment to mount an attack? 'Sorry. It makes me emotional, but I definitely don't mind. Why on earth are you asking me about this now?' She glanced at her watch. 'You're not about to *take it to another level* with her when you go back home, are you?'

He laughed. 'Nah. But we have been talking about me moving into the boarding house permanently. It's coming to a head, and I couldn't make a change like that without talking to you first. Bea felt the same.'

And she'd have been fretting about it, whereas Kemp seemed relaxed. The microwave pinged and Tara swallowed. 'I'm so glad I met you, all those years ago. You're brilliant for Bea. Two of my favourite people shacking up together is not a problem.'

'Bea would love to hear you call it that.'

She grinned. 'I know. But someone's got to lighten the mood. And I can't have you sitting there watching me eat.' She could see he'd already drained his beer. 'Bog off back to her and get planning.'

As Tara ate her risotto in silence, she thought about Jez. Had he really been fed up when Kemp appeared? She supposed she *had* told him she was too tired to go for a drink, but then agreed quite readily to chat when someone else was doing the asking. But it was none of his business what she did. If he'd been as annoyed as Kemp had implied, it was out of order. A little light disappointment, on the other hand, would be acceptable. She smiled. Kemp had probably been overreacting.

She banished the thoughts from her mind. The Julie Cooper case was all that mattered right now. When Selina had first mentioned John Lockwood she'd thought of the old boy network. Had he got his university job because of his father? Sir Alistair had been master of a Cambridge college for several years now, and the dates would fit. She'd imagined John being a chip off the old block, with a privileged existence. But now she'd seen the photographs of his body, surrounded by chaos in his tiny terraced house, and her views had changed.

Her thoughts went back to Sir Alistair Lockwood's golden cat, and its value. His family could certainly have afforded to help him, but according to her chat with Max, Stuart Gilmour had said John was persona non grata. Why was that? What had put that distance between him and his relations?

On the face of it, John looked a likely candidate for Julie's murderer. The student had told her mother she was staying in Cambridge because of him, and she'd lied about the circumstances. That made Tara think the relationship had been quite intense. Maybe John and Julie had quarrelled. Perhaps he'd wanted the relationship to continue and she hadn't. Or she'd threatened to tell someone about their affair. He'd lashed out and then—

And now he was dead too. They still didn't know if it was suicide, but it seemed likely.

The other top candidate so far was Stuart Gilmour. Under the circumstances, Tara was surprised he hadn't told them all about John Lockwood in the first place. It would have been a quick way to divert attention from himself.

What on earth was motivating his actions? Some lateral thinking was required, but it was hard after almost no sleep.

CHAPTER THIRTY-FOUR

'You should just be yourself, you know?' Stuart was lying in Bella's bed, half under the sheets, looking up at her with that lazy smile of his.

She thought back to when she'd first seen him with Julie, and how much she'd fancied him. That cocky confidence, his passion and single-mindedness. Those latter qualities were something he'd had in common with Julie, but Julie had been the big-hearted one. Now, Bella wanted to be with him the whole time, but she saw him in an entirely different light. Nothing could take away the layers of what had happened, draped over her like some kind of suffocating blanket.

'I am being myself.' She'd just got up to shower, and was standing, naked, by the bed. She'd hadn't felt quite so bare until he spoke though. Now she felt vulnerable.

He looked at her through half-closed eyes. 'No, you're not. You still dress like Julie. When you are dressed, that is. And you do the things she did.'

Bella reached for a long cashmere cardigan that had been draped over a chair in the corner. That was something Julie would never have worn. 'I got interested in her causes because she taught me about them. She opened my eyes. Now I *want* to be involved.'

He reached out a hand and took hers, pulling her back towards him. There was a lot of force behind the move, and she shivered.

'What about me?' he said. 'Have I opened your eyes too?'

She nodded.

He laughed. 'I still don't believe you really want to come out in the rain and march on Wednesday. The weather forecast is diabolical.'

She pulled away. 'I do! I want to do it in Julie's memory.'

His eyes opened wide. 'Oh, come on, darling. If you were that devoted to my ex, you'd hardly be here now, would you?'

'You're here too. If that's what you think it seems as though you're admitting you weren't devoted to her either.'

He raised himself up until he was sitting, then reached for his boxer shorts. 'We had some good times, but we fought in the end. She wasn't great at sharing.'

Bella frowned. 'What do you mean?' But she had a feeling she knew, and maybe it was good news that Julie had kept some things to herself.

He was dragging on his jeans now. 'Never you mind.'

'Shall we go and get something to eat? The burger van'll still be open.'

'With the cops all over me? Hardly. Besides, I've got things to do.'

At this hour? 'What sort of things? If you're planning for the march, I could come and help with ideas. I want to be properly involved – not just turn up for the dramatic stuff.'

Stuart shook his head. 'You should get some sleep. And besides, I like to operate independently.'

After he'd closed the door, Bella went to shower, standing under the hot water until the shivering stopped. It might be time for bed, but she'd never rest. What did Stuart really know? And where had he gone after leaving her room? She was quite sure he'd never tell her everything. The only way to find out for certain would be to follow him.

How far would she dare to go? That was the question.

CHAPTER THIRTY-FIVE

It was getting late when Blake finally arrived back at his home in Fen Ditton. He parked his car out on the lane, then walked down towards the river where his cottage lay, close to the meadows. He was still thinking about the case as he let himself in and closed the front door behind him. The sight of his mother-in-law, Sonia, her legs stretched out on their sofa, took him by surprise. But he'd known she was coming to babysit, so Babette could get out to the book club she attended – something to keep her mind active, she'd said.

Sonia made to get up as soon as she saw him.

'Don't disturb yourself.' He spoke quietly. There was no sign of Kitty. She was in the habit of listening out for his return and bounding downstairs, just when Babs had got her settled. Sonia looked very relaxed right now; she wouldn't appreciate that happening, any more than his wife did. 'They're both asleep?'

His mother-in-law nodded, recrossing her legs, causing her wide-legged linen trousers to shift and form new waves of material. Her frame, under them and her soft long cardigan, was neat. 'I've been here since school pick-up time. Babs and I took them to the park, so Kitty burnt off some of her energy. I got Jessica off half an hour ago.'

Her tone was slightly accusatory. He took a deep breath. 'I'm sorry I wasn't back sooner.'

Sonia put the book she'd been reading on the coffee table next to her, splayed open face-down at the page she'd reached. 'It is what it is. We all knew what Babs was getting herself into when she married a detective.'

He thought back to Babette's determination to give their marriage another go, after she'd decided it had been a mistake to run off with Kitty.

He perched on an armchair at right angles to where Sonia sat. 'Do you think Babs was wrong to come back to me?' He knew he was asking for trouble, but he was too tired, and too emotionally mangled, to put the social brakes on.

Sonia surprised him, moving her legs round and sitting up properly on the sofa. 'I didn't mean that. What you're dealing with is unimaginable and it needs to be done. But family life suffers. It's just the way it is.'

He nodded and got up from his seat again. 'Can I get you a drink?'

'I'm all right. There's a plateful of food for you to microwave in the fridge.'

'Thanks.' He went through to the kitchen and poured himself a beer before taking out the portion of leftovers she'd mentioned and putting it in to heat. He stared at the food as it went round and round, and wondered how much Sonia knew about Kitty's father. Had Babs confided in her? They were close, and although his wife could hide the truth with the best of them, she wasn't a strong person. He guessed she'd have wanted to offload onto someone – if not Sonia then a close friend perhaps. And that person could be the key to him finding out more.

The microwave pinged and he rummaged for a knife and fork from the kitchen drawer before taking his plateful of chicken casserole, potatoes and green beans back through to the living room. The temptation to eat in the kitchen had been strong – he'd value a few minutes to take stock – but it felt antisocial.

Sonia glanced up as he re-entered the room, but she didn't come to join him at the table.

'How are things with Babs?' she asked, after letting him eat in silence for a minute or two. 'Is she adjusting all right to being a mother again, do you think?'

Blake laughed inwardly at that. He was almost certain his wife had planned her pregnancy without his knowledge, despite her claim that she'd 'forgotten' to take her pill. She wouldn't mess up over something that had such a profound effect on her future. Once she'd known she was pregnant, instead of passing on the news, she'd tried to warm him up to the idea of extending their family. She only gave in and told him the truth when he made it clear it was the last thing he wanted, and she was starting to show. Things weren't great between them, but they both loved their daughters.

'She's adjusting well, I think.'

'And what about the two of you?' Sonia's gaze was sharp. After a moment she added: 'Babs did tell me you didn't want Jessica.'

That hurt. And if that kind of comment ever got back to his daughter… 'I adore Jessica – but before I knew she was on her way I didn't like the idea of having another child. It's different now.'

He heard Sonia sigh, even though he was across the room.

'Maybe I'm wrong,' she said. 'Maybe Babs did make a mistake, asking you to take her back. If you can't forgive her after all this time…' She let the sentence trail off.

The chicken felt heavy in Blake's dry mouth. He swallowed some whole and swigged his beer. 'We haven't stopped trying to resolve things. But there's still a lot I don't know.' He paused. 'But she's told me all about Matt Smith now.'

It was an exaggeration. Babette had told him nothing about Kitty's father except his name, the fact that the pregnancy had been the result of a brief fling, and that he hadn't paid Kitty enough attention when Babs had run off with him. Not exactly a life history.

Sonia raised her eyebrows. 'Oh, well, that's probably for the best. And I'm certainly glad she's with you, not him.' She relaxed back on the sofa again.

'Why's that?'

'I knew he was a bad lot from the moment she met him. All that on–off business for so many years – playing with each other's feelings. Too much passion, perhaps. It wasn't healthy.'

Blake felt his insides go cold. *For so many years…?*

It was just one more lie. But it was a big one.

CHAPTER THIRTY-SIX

Tara and Max were at John Lockwood's house, where the CSIs were still busy. No one was taking any chances on evidence, given the rumoured relationship between him and Julie Cooper. They'd got an appointment to speak to the man's doctor afterwards, to see what she could tell them, but Blake had already referred the death on to the coroner. Agneta would perform the post-mortem that morning, with the DI in attendance.

Tara stood in her uncomfortable overalls in the cold house. She'd finally caught up with the change in the weather and was wearing a tailored woollen trouser suit underneath, but the room was so chilly, it didn't do much to improve things. The interior of the house was just as depressing as the outside. It looked as though troubles had escalated uncontrollably for the academic, until things got so precarious that everything had come crashing down. Had John murdered Julie? She found it hard to believe, looking at his home: the unopened post piled high, empty spirit bottles under each table and on every surface, the carpet stained, the walls damp, the crockery unwashed in the kitchen. If she tried to visualise him as the killer, she could get as far as him lashing out, in a drunken haze – but the rest of it? Opting to dump her body at Wandlebury implied a level of planning she reckoned would have been beyond him. There would have been the issue of getting her there, too. They'd established that he'd owned a car – a VW Passat estate – so the journey would have been possible. But if he'd killed her here, getting her into the vehicle without being noticed would have been challenging; the neighbours were just feet away.

Max was talking to one of the CSIs and she moved to join them.

'Anything else we should know about?' he was saying.

The white-suited guy next to him shrugged. 'Not that we've discovered – as yet. We haven't unearthed a suicide note. From the position he was found in, we guess he was sitting at that table before he died. But the whisky he seems to have been drinking is unusual.'

Max raised an eyebrow.

'You'd have to get it from a specialist shop. It's sixty-five per cent alcohol by volume. That's serious stuff. And there's an empty blister pack of sedatives on the table too – no way of knowing if he took any before he passed out though. You'll need to wait for the post-mortem.'

Tara assumed John had had money troubles, but the Scotch didn't look cheap. It didn't fit with the piles of unopened bills. And presumably he couldn't have regularly mixed that much booze with sedatives either, or he'd have been dead before now. Yet he'd had both the whisky and the pills to hand. Maybe he'd been saving the Scotch for a special occasion – the last night of his life. Sadness washed over her as she went to peer at the medication's packaging. It was just the plastic blister pack – the brand name printed on the foil backing. There was nothing to show who had prescribed the drug and when.

She imagined him, sitting at the table, staring out of the window into his dark garden. Had he been consumed with guilt after killing Julie, or overwhelmed by sorrow on hearing about her death?

'One more thing,' the CSI said. 'When we came in, we noticed the phone had been dropped or knocked to the floor. Possibly thrown even. It's cracked. We'll report back on anything else we find.'

Maybe someone had called to let him know Julie was dead. 'Can we try dialling 1471?' Tara asked.

But the CSI shook his head. 'We did that, after we'd photographed it in situ, but whoever called last withheld their number.'

But they could get round that. It would be more than interesting to find out who had contacted John that night, and why they'd wanted to avoid leaving a record of their number on his phone.

After they'd finished at the house, Tara drove them towards Castle Hill, to see the man's doctor, Ava Schwarz. She sensed Max's restlessness next to her.

'Are you all right?'

'Why?'

'I could hear you huffing.'

'Huffing?'

'Or, well, sighing maybe.'

He told her what Megan had said the evening before. The news that Stuart Gilmour might be keeping an eye on them all made her catch her breath. 'Has she told Blake now?'

'She's going to, this morning. She's still not sure, but I said it was worth him knowing she'd got her suspicions.'

'I should say so.' She'd have told Blake the moment she'd had the thought. Why had Megan held back? Was it their boss or herself that she didn't trust? 'So you and she were having a little chat after work, were you?' She let her eyes slide towards him for a split second as she made the turn onto Chesterton Road. A moment later she was fully focused on the traffic. Mitcham's Corner demanded one hundred per cent concentration. Its weird layout meant cars, buses and cyclists were changing lanes at the last minute, squeezing into gaps that looked impossibly small.

Max was quiet for a moment. 'We just nipped into the Free Press for a quick drink on our way home.'

Tara smiled, despite her mixed feelings about Megan. Max sounded so bashful. 'That's nice.'

He sighed again now. 'I know you two don't get on well.'

'What, since she tried to get me disciplined for actions that led to the arrest of Freya Cross's killer?'

'Well, she—'

'I'm joking.' She couldn't do it to him. She knew she'd got a lot of things wrong on that case, even if she'd managed to pull a rabbit out of the hat at the last minute. 'I'm not surprised she was angry. She'd been shaken up.' She couldn't quite bring herself to spell out her own failings, but she'd apologised to both Megan and Blake in person.

'She's great when you get to know her.' Max's words came out in a rush. It might only be early days, but at that moment Tara could tell it was important.

'I trust your judgement. Megan and I are just on different wavelengths, that's all.'

Max was quiet, and Tara wondered what he was thinking. A moment later, she seemed to have her answer. 'What about you and Jez?'

'What about "me and Jez"?' She glanced at him, to see if he was winding her up in return for her comments about Megan, but he wasn't smiling.

'I got the impression he was about to make his move – and then when he hung around yesterday evening…'

It was true, Jez wasn't the most subtle of people, but in some ways it was nice to deal with someone who could be straightforward about what they wanted. After months of wondering about Blake, it made a change. 'We just cycled back from the station together, as far as my house. And then he went off home.'

'I trust your judgement too.' There was something about the way Max said it. He might have added *so don't let me down* onto the end of his sentence. He sounded almost as protective as Kemp. But after her comments about Megan, she couldn't really pull him up for interfering.

They met Dr Schwarz in a second-floor consulting room across the road from Castle Mound – the site of a fortification built by William the Conqueror but now no more than a low grassy hill.

The doctor pushed dark-rimmed glasses up her nose and turned her swivel chair away from her computer screen so that she was facing them. They sat on the plastic chairs reserved for patients and explained their reasons for being there.

'John Lockwood's death didn't come as a surprise,' she said, shaking her head. 'He could have gone at any time.'

'Can you tell us more about that?' Max asked.

'Under the circumstances, I'm prepared to.'

'So, he was unwell?' Tara took out her notebook.

Schwarz nodded. 'He was depressed. His mental health affected his physical health and it had done for years.'

'Did you know him before he got ill?' Max put in.

The woman shook her head. 'His family is from Cambridge – I know that much – but I didn't take him on as a patient until eight or nine years ago.' She turned to her screen. 'I can tell you who he was registered with before that though.' She called up his records and made a note on her pad, before ripping off the sheet and giving it to Tara.

'I wanted him to get help,' Schwarz said. 'Specialist help, I mean. I thought he would benefit from talking therapies and I could have referred him, but he was dead against it. I went so far as to push a little in that direction once, but he got angry and I had to leave it.'

'Was he aggressive?' Max asked.

'He shouted. I suspect he'd been drinking. But he wasn't physically aggressive.' She sighed.

'We found this packet of sedatives at his home, on his desk next to an empty bottle of whisky.' Tara took out her phone to show the doctor the picture she'd taken. 'Did you prescribe him these?'

The woman opened her eyes wide. 'Good God, no – I'd never have risked it in his state. It would be dangerous to combine them with the amount of alcohol he habitually drank. And I'd have worried he might have taken too many, too.'

Where had he got them from then? Had a friend passed them on to him? And maybe given him the unusual whisky too?

'Thank you, Dr Schwarz,' Max said. 'Before we go, did you ever get the impression John Lockwood had something specific troubling him, beyond his illness?'

The woman sat back in her chair. 'Yes,' she said. 'Every so often he'd allude to it an oblique way. He felt guilty about something. But I never found out what that was.' She hesitated for a moment, her eyes haunted. 'I think it was something big. I often wondered whether he'd tell me the truth in the end. And if he did, whether I would have to tell the police about it, patient confidentiality or no.'

CHAPTER THIRTY-SEVEN

Lucien Balfour looked around his group of students. He'd invited them all in together, and closer to the start of term than usual, given what had happened to Julie. All of the third years had known her, but there was one in particular of whom he was wary. One who might have picked up on certain things he'd rather keep quiet. Of course, there was a second who knew everything there was to know about him. But she was under control. He smiled for a moment, but then altered his expression to fit the occasion.

'This has been a terrible start to a new academic year. I know you will all be as devastated as I am at the news of Julie Cooper's death.' He slid his eyes around the group. 'She was an incredibly intelligent, driven student who cared deeply about the world around her.'

Bella Chadwick's eyes were on him, red-rimmed. He wasn't worried about what she thought, but he found her show of emotion irritating. Had she *really* minded about her friend, despite her two-faced actions?

But it wasn't Bella who was giving him sleepless nights – not any more, at least. It was the mousy girl sitting behind her. Truth to tell, he always had trouble remembering her name – but not her face. When he'd looked up that day, and seen her scared hazel eyes on his, her features had imprinted themselves on his brain. He glanced down at the calendar entry on his computer and scanned the names of the students his PA had invited. Louise. That was it.

He'd already prepared his speech: worked out what spin to put on the interaction she'd accidentally witnessed.

'I myself feel deep regret that my last words to Julie were impatient and hasty. Talented and bright though she was, many of you will realise that some of the student protests she took part in were – well – risky. Her actions could have put her future on the line – if they'd come to the attention of the police. You can't carry a knife through the streets of Cambridge – even as a dramatic prop – and not expect consequences.' He got up from his chair and paced up and down the room next to the window. It would be easier to do this convincingly if he didn't have to meet Louise's eyes. They'd been forgettable for so long. Not any more.

'As Julie's college tutor, her future was of the utmost importance to me. But also, of course, I couldn't ignore the effect her rash actions might have had on the reputation of St Oswald's, and indeed the whole university.' He glanced briefly over the room before looking away again. 'And that kind of damage would affect each and every one of you, indirectly. So' – he heaved another sigh – 'I had words with her about it. I pointed out that I'd done her a good turn by not reporting her to the authorities. And in return I asked her to curtail her political activities until she'd finished her studies here.'

He went back to his seat now and allowed himself a brief, nostalgic smile as he shook his head. 'Of course, you can imagine how she reacted to that. Fury is probably too weak a word.'

There was a gratifying response from the students: gentle, sad amusement – rueful expressions. Nods. They hadn't known Julie well, but her reputation had preceded her.

He turned his head slightly to check mousy Louise's reaction. It wasn't as reassuring as he'd hoped. She looked uncertain. And what's more, she'd seen him check her response. But there was nothing for it. And she was one of the weak ones. He'd have introduced doubt in her mind – it ought to be enough to stop her from doing anything dangerous.

'Even though we had that exchange, I honestly admired her for her convictions. I can only hope she realised that I was trying to protect her, and that underneath it all, I understood. You must all come to me, any time you have any concerns about anything – but especially at the moment if you want to talk about Julie. The counselling service is also available – they will free up emergency appointments as required. Does anyone want to talk now?'

Pathetic Louise was looking down and picking at her nails – a most unattractive action. Not that anything could have saved her from mediocrity in the looks department anyway.

One or two of the others shook their heads. They seemed incapable of simply answering his question by speaking up.

'In that case, I won't take up any more of your time, but my door is always open.'

Louise was the first to get up from her seat, and second to reach his doorway. Once the room had cleared, Balfour went to look out of his window. The gaggle of students under his care trailed off round the court below, heading in different directions.

The mouse had her head down against the rain that had started to fall. She wasn't talking to any of the others. That was good. At last he moved away, back into the shady interior of the room. Further action might be riskier than holding back.

He'd have to watch and wait.

CHAPTER THIRTY-EIGHT

Bella Chadwick was standing on the rain-washed pavement outside Fitzbillies as Tara made her way along Trumpington Street. The student's hood was down and her hair was plastered to her scalp, tendrils of it sticking to her cheeks.

Tara had worn her wool coat that morning, thanks to the recent drop in temperature. She would have been in the same boat but for a black umbrella Max had lent her. She dashed forward with the thing held out until Bella was under cover too.

'Thanks for coming.' The young woman spoke slowly, and her eyes were glassy and unfocused. It was almost as though she wasn't aware of the rain, or of the lack of it now that she had some shelter.

'No problem.' Tara nodded towards the steamed-up window of the café. The lights inside looked bright and welcoming, in contrast with the leaden sky. 'Shall we?' She manoeuvred them towards the glass-doored entrance.

It was warm inside, and Tara found them a table as far away from the door as possible, to keep out of the draught as people came and went. Bella looked as though she could do with drying out. As Tara stuffed Max's umbrella next to her chair, she wondered how long the girl had been standing there in the rain.

'Hot chocolate? Coffee?'

'Coffee, thanks.'

Bella refused the offer of something to eat, so Tara put in their order for drinks. 'How can I help?' She leant in towards the student, so that they could talk quietly and not be overheard.

Bella looked around her for a moment. It was the first time she'd seemed to focus on her surroundings. 'I wasn't completely honest with you when we spoke yesterday.'

No kidding. Her admitting it was unexpected, though. 'It's not always easy when something traumatic has happened. All sorts of competing thoughts and worries go through your head.' She waited, not wanting to influence the way Bella passed on her information.

The waitress arrived with their coffees and a small jug of milk.

Once she'd gone again, Bella took a deep breath. 'I heard this morning that John Lockwood is dead.'

Tara nodded. 'I wasn't holding out on you when we spoke. I didn't know myself, until I got back to the station. And then, of course, we had to notify his next of kin before we could make the news public.'

Bella nodded. The action looked mechanical. 'I understand.' She let out a sigh. 'This seems so wrong, but it makes a difference.' She picked up her coffee cup and took a tiny sip. 'I didn't say too much about him yesterday because I was scared.'

Tara remembered the way the student had flinched when she'd mentioned John's name.

'Why were you frightened, Bella?'

'I thought he might somehow find out if I told you things. And that there might be… consequences. But now that he's dead, I feel safer. He can't reach me any more.'

She was shivering. She didn't look like someone who'd suddenly relaxed.

'So, what was it you didn't tell me about John? You said you'd never met him.' And that still struck Tara as odd; the idea that Bella only knew of his existence because Julie had confided in her.

But the student nodded. 'That's true.'

'You never even saw them together?'

She looked down into her drink. 'No.'

If that was the case, then why avoid Tara's eyes? 'Bella – I get the impression you felt left out sometimes, when Julie went off with her other mates. If Julie regarded you as a very close friend, someone she could absolutely rely on, then she might have taken you for granted. Been a bit cruel even – without meaning to be – when it came to how much time she spent with you, and how much with her boyfriends and other contacts.' She leant in closer. 'If that happened, I wouldn't blame you for having chased after her maybe, to see who she went to meet – or to try to have a word with her. If that's how you came to know about John, there's no shame in it.' Could she get the woman to trust her?

Bella raised her eyes for a moment, but then dropped them again. 'Thanks, but that's not how I knew about him. Julie told me.'

Tara took a deep breath. She still found it hard to believe – and if it were true, there must have been something special that made Julie want to offload. Everyone kept saying how independent she was.

'So which bits of what you told me weren't quite accurate?' Tara asked. She kept her voice gentle.

'It wasn't that I lied, but what I said was incomplete.' Bella gazed down into her coffee again. 'Some of what Julie told me made me worry about John – about his state of mind. Julie liked her good causes, and it seemed to me that John had become one of them.'

'Even though he came from a powerful, wealthy family?'

'I think there was plenty of distance between him and them.' She paused. 'From what Julie said, that is.'

'Did Julie ever say why that was?'

Bella shook her head. 'I assumed it was because John had rebelled. Julie admitted he drank a lot and—' She stopped abruptly.

'And what, Bella?'

She took a sip of her coffee. 'Well – judging by him and Julie, I guess it looked as though he was into younger women. He broke the rules.'

Why that pause? 'Was Julie ever frightened by him, do you think?'

Bella shook her head. 'That's the thing, she was blind to the fact that he might be a danger to her. Even though she said he behaved erratically sometimes.'

'Erratically?'

'She said he was close to the edge, and occasionally his temper would flare.'

'Did she mention him threatening her? Or attacking her physically?'

'She implied she'd had to calm him down once or twice.'

'And what about their relationship? How much do you know about that?'

Bella looked down into her lap. 'She said they were having sex.' Her eyes rose slowly to meet Tara's. 'I think maybe he was obsessed with her.'

'What makes you say that?'

The waitress arrived to ask if everything was okay. It was a moment before she could follow up her question. 'Bella?'

The student was twisting her hands together. 'Julie was sent a few odd things in the fortnight before she died.'

Tara thought back to the contents of the dead girl's bedroom, anticipating the details. But Bella might know more than the police. 'What kind of things?'

'Creepy stuff. Someone had sent her a load of scarlet paper, cut into bits. Julie put them together like a jigsaw puzzle and they formed a heart shape. She found flowers in her bike basket one day too. A whole load of anemones.' Bella frowned. 'The heart had been coloured in felt-tip pen. And it was quite big, once she'd put it back together. It must have taken someone a while to prepare it. And to collect the flowers too. It wasn't just one or two – I saw them.'

'What made you keep all that quiet, Bella?' Tara sat back in her seat, despite her frustration. She mustn't spook the girl now. 'Even if you were scared of John, you could have mentioned that.'

'I'm sorry. It was wrong of me – I couldn't think straight. I needed to work out what I could safely say and what I couldn't.'

But Tara had other ideas. Stuart Gilmour had stayed over in Bella's room, the night after Julie's death had been made public. And Julie had thought Gilmour had been two-timing her with Bella. Just how keen was the woman opposite her to have Gilmour for herself? And how far would she go to protect him? Did she suspect he'd been the one to send Julie hearts and flowers? Was she now pointing the finger at John Lockwood as a convenient scapegoat?

'When did you get the idea that John might be behind the items that were sent to Julie?'

Bella shrugged. 'I'd always thought he was a possibility. It sounded as though he was unbalanced. And now, him dying alone in his house like that, so soon after Julie... well – that can't be a coincidence, can it?'

Tara wasn't going to learn much more. She spotted the waitress and asked for the bill.

'Thank you for telling me what you know.' She found some coins for the tip. 'But keep an open mind, okay? And if you see or hear anything else that sounds suspicious, please give me a ring.' She handed over her card. 'We're a long way from confirming who killed Julie.'

Bella's look met hers, and there was alarm in her eyes. She must know Stuart Gilmour was on their list. She clearly didn't believe he'd killed her friend, but maybe there was a sliver of doubt there. And that suspicion might just keep the girl safe.

CHAPTER THIRTY-NINE

Patrick had to spend the first part of Tuesday trailing some dumb blonde as she sashayed her way around various expensive shops. Still, his efforts finally paid off when he saw her rendezvous with her lover outside Starbucks in the Grand Arcade. He took some tacky photographs to give to her husband, then got ready for the main business of the day.

Peter Devlin had been Tara Thorpe's boyfriend through her middle teenage years. He'd been interviewed, of course, back when her mystery stalker had first got active. The police on the job had written him off, just because he'd been out of the city when one of her nasty packages had been posted. As if he couldn't have got a friend to do it! The coppers on the case would look like a pack of fools now. He hoped the original detective on the job was still around to witness his triumph.

Devlin ran his own architect's practice these days. Patrick walked down Regent Street to Devlin's office and rang the buzzer. The guy hadn't been forthcoming or friendly last time he'd visited (no wonder!) and so, on this occasion, Patrick gave the receptionist a false name. He claimed he wanted to talk to Devlin about extending his kitchen.

Two minutes later he was upstairs in the plush waiting area being plied with coffee. The receptionist even offered him a magazine to read. Did everyone find PI work this easy? Patrick was betting not.

It was ten minutes later when Devlin opened the door. The receptionist had gone to lunch. Tara's former boyfriend looked at him through narrowed eyes. It was clear he remembered Patrick's face.

'You do realise I can report you to the police for harassment if you start hounding me?' His dark brown eyes were furious.

'But I don't think you will. Shall we talk in your office?'

The guy had the temerity to roll his eyes at that. 'There's no one else here, so I don't think it's worth the effort.' Devlin had been about to throw Patrick out, he was pretty sure, but suddenly the architect paused. 'What makes you think I won't call the police?'

'I've got fresh evidence. Information that makes me certain you're guilty.'

The guy shook his head in apparent disbelief. 'You're crazy. Let's have it then! This should be a laugh.'

Patrick wasn't going to be put off. 'Back in the spring, I came to question you about Tara Thorpe's stalker. I interviewed you first. I wanted to eliminate you from my enquiries early, given the police felt you were one of their least likely suspects.'

There was a tic going in the man's cheek. 'They were right. It wasn't me.'

'In that case, perhaps you'd like to tell me why, after talking to you – and you only – Tara received the first threatening message she'd had in years, warning her to "call off the dogs"?'

For a second, Patrick seemed to have robbed the man of speech. Devlin put his hand to his mouth and stood absolutely still, his eyes widening. In fact, the man looked upset.

'Well, it wasn't me,' he said at last. 'But if Tara wants the identity of the person who's hounded her for so long, then I think I know – given what you've just told me.'

Patrick had implied that it was Tara who'd hired him when he'd first talked to the man.

'Go on.'

Devlin closed his eyes for a moment. 'There's only one person it could be. Only one person that I told…'

CHAPTER FORTY

Blake hadn't slept the night before. Sonia's words about Babette's lover had rolled round and round in his head. *All that on–off business for so many years – playing with each other's feelings. Too much passion perhaps. It wasn't healthy.*

He'd only had twenty minutes to absorb the news when his wife swept back into the house, flicking her smooth golden hair out of the way as she bent forward to give him a quick kiss. Would Sonia mention the conversation about Matt Smith to her daughter? Blake had found himself wishing that she wouldn't. He didn't want to give Babs the chance to come up with a new concoction of misleading half-truths to explain the lies she'd told him. His anger meant he'd wanted to throw her deceit in her face, the moment her mother had left, but his head told him to wait. He needed to be calm when he confronted her, and it ought to be after he'd worked out his strategy. So, when Sonia went, he'd stuck to asking Babette what the book club had thought of *In the Days of Rain* by Rebecca Stott. But inside, his mind was working, and it hadn't stopped. Wait – he must wait – and not go in all guns blazing. He took a deep breath; his heart was racing. It ought to be a measured talk, after Kitty and Jessica were in bed that night.

Once again he put thoughts of his marriage into a box. It was a skill he'd had to develop early on and the box was getting pretty full. He could feel the lid lifting, as though a creature was trying to break free. It wouldn't be long… But for now, he needed to be one hundred per cent focused on the case. Agneta must have seen something in his eye when he'd attended John Lockwood's post-mortem. For once, she hadn't asked about his family life.

Now he needed to pass her information on to the team. He glanced at them – assembled in front of him in the incident room – and took a long swig of his black coffee, which was disappointingly cool. Max was sitting next to Tara, at right angles to Megan and Jez, but the dynamics were plain to see. Max was glancing at Megan, whose look in return told him the pair were getting on well, and Jez had his eyes on Tara. Tara herself was looking at her notes and frowning. Blake was pretty sure they'd gone off together the night before. For a second, he wondered what had happened. He knew it was none of his business, but he couldn't shake his reaction to Jez's self-satisfied smile.

He stepped forward. 'So – John Lockwood's death. Agneta puts the time at around one in the morning on Monday. His blood-alcohol level was through the roof, and it looks as though the empty blister pack of sedatives the CSIs found on his desk must have been full when he started work.'

'So it was suicide?' Megan sat forward.

'We can't be absolutely sure without a note, but assuming he knew what he was taking then it looks like it. There certainly wasn't anything at the scene to suggest direct coercion. Either he intended to die or didn't care whether or not he lived. He had long-term health problems, too – associated with ongoing alcohol abuse. Agneta agrees with the assessment his doctor gave you' – he turned to Max and Tara – 'even without what he took on Sunday evening, he could have gone at any time. She did point out that the pills he took weren't a well-known brand. The CSIs couldn't find any instructions on dosage, or any outer packet, so it's possible Lockwood didn't have that type of advice to refer to. But he must have guessed swallowing that many, on top of large quantities of strong whisky, wasn't going to end well.'

They were all silent for a moment as he downed the rest of his drink. He felt appalling. At last he looked up. 'Tara – what did Bella Chadwick have to say?'

She passed on the gist of their conversation. 'I was keen to make her realise she shouldn't assume John was Julie's killer. A lot of what she thinks seems to be based on supposition. And I'm not sure she's registered that Stuart Gilmour's a key suspect.'

'I still couldn't see Gilmour sending Julie a sliced-up heart though,' Jez said. 'The guy's reptilian.'

At that point Megan raised her hand. She explained how she might or might not have seen Gilmour watching the station (or possibly her) on Sunday afternoon. Max leant forward as she spoke, as though urging her on from a distance. He nodded as she finished. She'd confided in him first, Blake guessed. Bloody hell. How could he persuade his team to work as a whole?

'You did the right thing to mention it. Next time, tell me straight away, even if you're not sure. If the information's uncertain we can take that into account.'

Megan nodded, her eyes down. 'It took me a while to put the two faces together.'

He hardly ever criticised her about anything – it was usually more about encouraging her to trust her instincts when it came to questioning. She seldom left things undone. He'd put her on the defensive.

Tara was frowning again and raised her green eyes to meet his. 'I've been thinking about the crime-of-passion angle,' she said slowly. 'I couldn't quite work out what was bugging me, but the dump site the killer used brought me up short. Why on earth pick Wandlebury? I mean, the weather's awful now, but we've had a gentle start to autumn, and families are always heading over to the Ring for weekend walks. Leaving Julie there wasn't going to delay the discovery of her corpse. They'd put her off the beaten track – just. But nothing more than that. And taking her there wasn't entirely without risk, either. The CSIs' best guess is that they drove a car up the nearest access track. It would have taken them a few minutes to get her body out, carry it to its final resting place and get clear again. And people do live in houses in the centre of Wandlebury Ring. Not many – and it's highly unlikely they'd be tramping around in the middle of the night – but it's not impossible. Assuming the killer's not stupid, they must have taken that risk for a reason. Because it fitted with their plan.'

Megan turned round to face Tara. 'You think they picked it because it's the type of place where lovers might go to make out?'

For the first time ever, Blake saw the two women connect. Tara's eyes were bright. 'It seems like a possibility. Maybe the killer was trying to paint us a picture of the sort of crime they wanted us to suspect…'

'Which would mean details like the flowers in Julie's pocket – and perhaps the cut-up heart – were planted for dramatic effect?' Blake's mind dashed through the evidence. 'And the torn underwear – despite no sign of sexual intercourse – could be part of the same scheme. As could the tearing off of the ring Stuart Gilmour gave her.' Up until then he'd been imagining Stuart yanking the thing off because Julie wouldn't take him back, or John doing so because he was jealous of Stuart.

'Casting aside that motive would throw the field wide open,' Max said.

Blake nodded. 'We can't discount the crime-of-passion theory, but this looks like a strong alternative line of enquiry. Thanks, Tara.' He put her theory together with what Bella Chadwick had said. 'So, Bella says Julie told her about the heart she'd been sent – and about some flowers in her bike basket too, which match the ones found in her skirt pocket. If that's all true, and the crime-of-passion evidence has been fabricated, then Julie's death was pre-planned. I'd been thinking of her killer lashing out in anger – causing Julie's head injury – and then putting her in a confined space, either believing she was already dead, or deciding at that point to kill her. But this might change things.'

'Someone could have hit her on the head, hoping it would kill her,' Tara said slowly. 'And then the scenario is the same – either they realised their first attempt had failed and shut her up to die, or they thought they'd managed it, hid her body in a confined space, and unwittingly killed her that way.'

'Assuming they didn't think they'd killed her straight off, why not carry on hitting her with the weapon until she was definitely dead?' Jez asked.

Max frowned. 'They might have been too squeamish. Or simply not have wanted to make a mess. That would fit with the killer being someone with a more clinical approach – and it being a carefully planned act, rather than a passionate, uncontrolled attack.'

'And we all agree Stuart Gilmour's as cold and calculating as they come – however keen he was on Julie at one time.' Megan looked pale. 'But assuming he wasn't still fixated by Julie when she died, then I can't see why he'd want to kill her.'

'He might have resented her,' Max said. 'She got off scot-free after carrying a knife on the Lockwood's march – whereas he got suspended. But there's no way he'd have killed her for that.'

It made Blake think of Balfour again. 'It's probably a side issue, but I'd like to know why Julie's tutor seemingly took no action at all over what she'd done. And deliberately kept her involvement from us.'

'He might have been protecting the college's reputation,' Jez said.

'And maybe he was lenient to avoid stoking Julie's resentment towards the master's business,' Max added.

Blake looked at them. 'Reckon that's all there is to it?' He'd got Balfour down as a serial liar, though it wasn't impossible they were right.

'If we're looking further afield, I wonder about the way Julie was digging into the business affairs of Lockwood's.' Tara turned towards Jez, and Blake watched as his body language changed – leaning forwards, arms open, expression honest. 'We know she had ambitions to make it as a journalist, and you mentioned, Jez, that she'd never manage it if her articles simply rehashed old news.'

The DC nodded.

'Well, what if she'd found something damaging? She must have got under Sir Alistair's skin when she protested against his firm. He's careful not to show it – but he's been trained for years to portray a charming public face. Maybe he was keeping an eye on what she was up to. Perhaps she challenged him even – asked him for an interview and faced him with some sort of damaging knowledge? He can't prove he stayed in London overnight.'

She'd lost Megan now. 'There's an awful lot of speculation in your theory.'

Tara nodded. 'I know. But a journalist ex of mine from uni days works on industrial stories. I could talk to him – see if he's heard any whispers on the grapevine, and whether the theory might have legs. He's based in Cambridge – handy for all the hi-tech firms – so he'll have his ear to the ground.'

Blake paused for a moment. He'd picked up on Jez's expression when Tara had mentioned an ex. 'Do it. It's worth sounding him out. From everything we know about Julie, she was focused and ambitious. I don't think any of us doubt that she was at least hoping to find something really damning, given the time she spent researching Sir Alistair's firm. Jez – can you make sure we get a look at any CCTV near the Lockwoods' London flat to check he was where he claims? Run a check on his car's plates too – see what you can verify about his journey home.'

Jez nodded, but he didn't look happy.

'Max, can you track down anyone who was supervised by John Lockwood in the same sessions as Julie? I'd like their take on how the two of them interacted. And Megan and I—'

Before he could finish his sentence, a uniformed officer slipped into the room and handed him a bit of paper.

He nodded his thanks whilst scanning it, then looked up. 'And – as of this moment – Megan and I will go to talk to Veronica Lockwood again.' He lifted the paper in his hand. 'The call to John Lockwood's landline, the night he died, was from her mobile. I'd like to know why she withheld her number.'

CHAPTER FORTY-ONE

Tara got no reply when she rang Josh Harding. It wasn't unexpected. You didn't make your way as a journalist by sitting on your backside, waiting for your ex-girlfriends to call. She texted him instead and sat at her desk, writing up her conversation with Bella Chadwick. She was reading it through when Josh texted back.

What's up? Been at a whizzy product launch in London but I'm almost back at Cambridge station now. Meet me at the Old Ticket Office if you want a quick word? I'll be 15 mins.

She rattled off a reply, then went to fetch her bike – wishing there was better parking at the railway station or less rain in the air.

Ten minutes later she was pushing damp hair out of her face in the loos at the Old Ticket Office. She'd one hundred per cent stopped fancying Josh by the time she was twenty-one, but the eleven years in between didn't mean she'd lost her pride. Once she could see to rummage in her bag she got to work with a comb. It was damage limitation, no more. After a moment she reapplied her mascara and strode back out of the bathroom, down the spiral stairs, and into the pub's main bar. She realised Josh was already there, all six foot one of him, his broad-shouldered back turned towards her as he stood, scanning the main entrance.

She slunk up behind him. 'Boo!'

'Bloody hell.' He kissed her on both cheeks. 'You've just reminded me in a microsecond of why we broke up. Too many shocks to the system.'

She smiled. They'd got together a year after she'd started her degree. A year after she'd moved away from home, and eighteen months after her stalker had suddenly stopped their campaign. Kemp had been a periodic visitor to their halls of residence and Tara had occasionally practised her self-defence skills on Josh…

'How's Theresa? And the babes?' Josh and his wife had two-year-old twins.

'Thriving. Noisy. Sleepless.'

'Is that your wife or the kids?'

He laughed. 'All of them.'

'What can I get you?'

Josh scanned the taps. 'A pint of the Brew House stout please.' He gave her a smile. 'You'll want something soft, I suppose. Ever miss being a journalist?'

'Working for *Not Now* was too high a price to pay for the odd lunchtime snifter. Besides, I never can drink in the day without falling asleep.' She put in their order, choosing a bottle of Nanny State – a low-alcohol craft beer – for herself.

Just as the bartender had finished topping Josh's stout up, she spotted a couple at a table for two gathering their coats, and made her way over to take their place. As she crossed the room, she wondered who'd chosen the green for the walls. Even if she'd gone for an alcoholic beer, the bright paintwork would have kept her alert.

'So, what gives?' Josh said as they sat down.

Tara was glad of the hubbub around them. 'I'm working on a murder. The student Julie Cooper – she was about to go into her third year at St Oswald's College. Sir Alistair Lockwood's master there.'

Josh frowned, his wavy hair falling over one eye. 'I remember that. So it's Lockwood's you're interested in?'

'Julie spent a lot of time campaigning against them.'

'Tactless, given that he was master of her college.'

'She obviously really minded about the causes she supported – there were no half measures as far as she was concerned. And we've also been told she was hoping for a career in journalism. Between ourselves' – she knew she could trust him – 'it looks as though she was spending hours on end researching Lockwood's. I mean, she had other corporates in her sights too, but there must have been something special about her college master's company. It made me wonder whether she'd got wind of something big.'

Tara pulled her phone out of her trouser pocket and opened up copies of the photos Julie had taken of the Lockwood cat. 'She'd got these on her phone when she died.'

Josh took the mobile from her and peered at the image, pushing his horn-rimmed glasses further up his nose. 'God, what an ugly ornament.'

She explained what Sir Alistair had told her about it. 'Symbolises family loyalty and love, apparently.'

'Nice! I'm glad I don't come from that sort of clan.'

'Me too.' She might find her mother difficult, but she'd take her over the Lockwoods any day of the week.

'So, when did Julie take those photos? Do we know?'

Tara nodded. 'The date stamp on them matches a day when she had legitimate access to the Master's Lodge. She was there to attend a party for students a year ago, but she'd still have had to go searching to find the cat. And I can't imagine that it was a family heirloom she was looking for when she sneaked into their private rooms.'

'You think she hoped to find something on the company?'

Tara sipped her Nanny State. 'I wondered.'

'She might have – but only if she was very naive. And if she was in the habit of homing in on corporates, I doubt that would be the case.'

'You mean there's no chance Sir Alistair or anyone else involved would have left sensitive documents around the Master's Lodge –

and Julie would have realised that?' It was a good point. But then again, you got cabinet ministers being photographed holding confidential papers that could be enlarged and read – and company employees leaving their laptops on trains. People did make mistakes.

'Well, I think Sir Alistair and his family would be extremely careful, if they were expecting an influx of students – especially as they've courted controversy recently, and young people have been the most active in protesting against them. But it's not just that. There's almost nothing Julie Cooper could have found that would stick.'

'How do you mean?'

Josh leant forward over the table and opened up a web browser. 'Name me any corporate. I'll type them into Google, add the word scandal, and see what we get.'

Tara played the game. Example after example produced pages and pages of results.

He met her eye. 'Those stories are all about household names, right?'

'Yes.'

'And how many were you already aware of?'

'A couple?'

He nodded. 'And I can see you're surprised. A lot of what we've just dug up ought to be massive stories, but by and large they pass off before long, without any major impact on the firms.'

'Some of those fines look pretty huge.' She nodded down at the last lot of headline links Josh had called up.

'Sure. To us. But each of these companies will have teams of accountants and lawyers working out just how much it would cost them to behave honourably versus how much they'll have to pay if they cut corners but then get found out. And evidently it's often cheaper to do the latter.'

'That's seriously what you think?'

'I'm afraid so. If your Julie had got a whiff of a scandal – even if it was something major – I'd say there's no way it would be a motive for killing her. Anyone from Lockwood's would simply have called their lawyer. If corporates ran about committing cold-blooded murder each time they got into trouble, there'd be an awful lot of victims.'

'Any ideas why Julie might have been so interested in the ornamental cat?'

Josh shrugged. 'It would be a good visual to go with a story if Julie had been planning to publish something. It gives the impression of a fierce family who only care about their own. And articles on corporate wrongdoing can be a bit dry. The cat would add interest. Convey the impression of a family dynasty, perhaps.' He downed a slug of his stout and shivered as a crowd came into the pub, leaving the door open. 'But who knows? She might just have marvelled at how horrible it was and snapped a pic for her own amusement. Still, the way she included a close-up of the coat of arms and the motto suggests she wanted to know more about it.'

Tara sighed and sat back in her chair. 'Julie was – apparently – in a relationship of some kind with Sir Alistair's son. Not the one that works for the business, but a younger one who's an academic at the university. I half wondered if she could have found something out from him. But to be honest, everyone's implying that he had very little contact with the rest of the family, let alone the company.'

'It doesn't sound likely then. And unless Julie had evidence of Sir Alistair killing someone with his bare hands, I just can't see him being your man.'

CHAPTER FORTY-TWO

'Take your time, Louise.'

She was already wishing she hadn't come. The face of her tutor, Lucien Balfour, kept appearing in her mind's eye. She'd probably misunderstood what she'd overheard. And even if she hadn't, it probably didn't mean anything. It wasn't at all likely to be related to what had happened to Julie. On top of all that, if she shared her worries with the counsellor sitting opposite her, the woman wouldn't be able to help anyway.

It was down to Louise. She took a deep breath. 'I just miss Julie.'

She was playing for time. The truth was they'd all been knocked sideways by the news of what had happened, but she hadn't known Julie well. Her feelings of horror, and the sleepless nights since, were down to a general pity that you'd feel for anyone, coupled with fear. It made you release how precarious life was. How you could be rushing round one minute – following your dreams, hooking up with friends, handing in an essay – and then you were gone. She kept thinking of Julie's mother. She'd seen her once or twice – visiting and dropping Julie off at the start of the second year. Her face haunted Louise's dreams.

But overlaid on top of that was the exchange she'd witnessed between Lucien Balfour and Julie. That and the way their tutor had looked at Louise that morning. He'd come out with his explanation – and it might have been true. It fitted with the words she'd heard. But then why check her reaction? Was he just scared because he realised she might have got the wrong impression? Or scared in case she'd got exactly the right one – and understood just the sort of man he was?

'That's understandable,' the counsellor said. 'And I expect you're dealing with other emotions too. What's happened is very frightening, for instance. You mustn't feel bad if your thoughts aren't just about missing Julie and what she suffered. Most people picture themselves or their loved ones going through similar events.'

Louise couldn't speak. She'd done that. And she felt guilty about it. But since this morning she'd not only imagined being attacked, and fighting for her life, she'd put Lucien in the role of her killer.

But even if he was lying – trying to cover up the truth behind his conversation with Julie – it didn't mean to say he was her attacker. He'd be scared, whether he was guilty or just looked that way.

'You don't have to tell me,' the counsellor said. 'The important thing is that you explore your feelings, even if it's only in your head. But if you can share what's on your mind, you might find your thoughts start to slot into place.'

'You won't tell anyone what I say?' Louise was surprised to hear herself speak. The thought and words had come at exactly the same moment.

'That's right.' The counsellor smiled. 'The only time we ever have to break that promise is if we're required to for legal reasons, or we believe staying quiet might put you or another person in danger.'

So many exceptions to the rule. And this was Cambridge: a small city where everyone knew someone who knew someone. The woman opposite her could be Lucien's next-door neighbour or his girlfriend for all she knew.

'I'm worried.' Louise felt her eyes prickle. She mustn't cry. 'I-I overheard something.'

The look on the counsellor's face had changed. It wasn't that she hadn't been attentive before, but there was a new alertness in her eyes now. 'Okay. Maybe if you talk to me about what that was, you might feel clearer on what to do next. Telling me doesn't commit you to anything.'

Louise swallowed. 'I heard a member of staff at my college talking to Julie at the end of last term.'

The counsellor nodded, making her bobbed hair swing forward. Louise couldn't take her eyes off it as she spoke. 'It was at a social gathering, organised by the member of staff – after exams, so the wine was flowing.' She could see the scene in her head – several students, all enjoying the free food and drink on offer. They were mostly talking to each other, but Lucien was doing the rounds. He'd spoken to her and asked about her year. She was quite convinced he couldn't remember who she was. 'I think a few people there had got a bit drunk. Including the member of staff.' She shook her head. 'He wasn't slurring or staggering or anything like that. But you know how some people get a bit more forceful when they've got a drink or two inside them?'

The counsellor was nodding, but Louise had a feeling she didn't. Louise did though. Her father was a fighting drunk. The sight of the hardness in Lucien's eyes had reminded her of him for a moment. That was what had put her on high alert. All the other partygoers were relaxed, out for a good time, but Louise couldn't switch off.

'At one point, everyone was distracted by a commotion out on the lawn, just down below Lu—' She stopped. She'd almost said his name. 'Down below the member of staff's window. Some people down there had been partying too, and they'd gone onto the grass. One of the fellows was telling them off. The students outside all had water pistols, so most people in the room were treating it as cabaret.'

She hadn't been near the window herself. The popular, confident crowd were all gathered round, laughing. There'd been no room to get close.

'The member of staff was at the back of the room, talking to Julie. I'd hung back too and when I turned round…'

'What, Louise? You'll probably feel better to get it off your chest.'

'The member of staff was sort of looming over Julie. He had his hand on her shoulder, and it looked as though he was gripping her; it wasn't just a soft touch.'

The counsellor nodded. Louise could see the seriousness in her eyes.

'He was saying, "Oh come on, Julie. Think of what I've done for you. I assumed you'd realise that one good turn deserves another." His voice was quiet but firm.' He'd sounded threatening.

'Can you remember what Julie said or did in response?'

'She shook him off. She sort of ducked down very suddenly and twisted her shoulder sharply to one side. Lu— The member of staff swore and stepped back slightly. Julie's eyes were furious. I wonder if he thought she might lash out at him.' Louise met the counsellor's gaze. 'And as he pulled away, he turned slightly and caught sight of me watching them. The other students were all still by the window, whooping and cheering the water fight down below.'

'Did either Julie or the member of staff say anything to you?'

She shook her head. 'The member of staff turned back towards Julie and said: "I'm sorry. I lost my temper for a moment there, but you do try my patience. You'll have to watch your behaviour next year." He sounded more like a normal member of staff then. He'd taken control of himself.'

Then she told the counsellor about the explanation the tutor had given the group of students that morning.

'Did you ever ask Julie about the incident?' The counsellor sat forward.

Louise couldn't hold back the tears then. Guilt had been making her insides twist ever since she'd heard the news of Julie's death. 'No.' The counsellor passed her a box of tissues. 'I was too shy. I think I thought she'd got it covered, because she was always so confident.'

'And now you're even more troubled because you don't know what to do?'

Louise nodded. Except, of course, the counsellor had been right about the effect of their session. Now Louise had spoken the words aloud, she *did* know what to do.

CHAPTER FORTY-THREE

Blake was sitting next to Megan, on a stool, at an expensive-looking island worktop in the kitchen of the Master's Lodge. They'd arrived to find that only Lady Lockwood was in. But that suited his purposes well.

He decided to begin whilst she was still preparing the drinks she'd offered. If he caught her off balance, so much the better. 'Can you tell us, please, why you called your son, the night he died?'

There was a moment when the only sound in the room was that of Veronica Lockwood putting coffee cups down on the worktop next to the Aga. Blake could see her face side-on. It was expressionless.

She didn't look at them when she spoke. She was pouring thick dark coffee from the stove-top espresso maker into tiny red cups. 'You can bypass number-withheld calls, can you? I wondered if you might.'

Blake met her eye as she passed him and Megan their cups. 'Why did you hide your identity?'

She took a deep breath. 'John would never have taken the call if he'd known it was me. I was hoping he'd be curious enough to pick up, rather than assuming it was a sales call.'

'And he did.' Blake knew the duration of the call.

She nodded as she perched on a stool at right angles to them. 'It was quite late at night. It's possible he was too far gone to even register what came up on the handset. Either way, I thought it would maximise my chances of a conversation.'

'He's not normally keen to talk to you then?'

She cocked her head to one side. 'Do you have children, Inspector?'

Blake hated it when interviewees asked him anything personal. Even admitting to Kitty and Jessica's existence felt as though he was somehow leaving them unprotected. 'Yes.' He left her to imagine the details.

'Whatever age they are, it's not uncommon for them to kick against authority – and that includes their parents.' He could see anger in her face, much more than sorrow. He was looking for the latter, but she kept it well hidden. She was of that breed – the sort who are taught to button up their emotions nice and tight. Stiff upper lip. 'I found John's lifestyle hard to take. He might have been in his thirties, but my desire to try to influence his behaviour didn't die when he reached maturity.'

Her cold eyes were on his. He couldn't help wondering if she minded more about her son, or the effect his actions might have on the family reputation.

'What made you ring him on Sunday night?'

Her eyes opened a fraction wider as she watched him over the top of her coffee cup. She might as well have called him a fool to his face – he could read her look loud and clear. 'As you're now aware, we'd heard that he'd been…' she paused, 'seeing Julie Cooper. Then I got the news about her death. I imagined the poor fool would be devastated. I wanted to speak to him, whatever our issues. Blood is thicker than water, after all, and I hoped to get him to talk. I asked him to come and stay here at the lodge. Under the circumstances it was no time for him to be alone.' Her eyes were on his again. 'I was proved correct on that score. He refused to come, of course.'

'You mentioned that you didn't stop trying to influence him when he reached maturity. Your worry over his behaviour has been going on for years, then?'

'It has.' She was literally tight-lipped – her mouth stretched taut as she spoke.

'When did it start?'

Veronica Lockwood frowned suddenly. 'I don't see what relevance this has.'

'Lady Lockwood, your son appears to have been having an affair with one of his students. A student who was murdered at the weekend. I'm sorry to cause you pain, but we do need to understand about the problems John had, and to put them in context.' He didn't know how Lockwood had gone off the rails in the first place. He'd got no record, background checks had shown that, but on occasion young people could avoid coming into contact with the police. Things could be swept under the carpet. If the man had ever been aggressive or violent, he wanted to know.

At last, the woman nodded. 'His problems started when he was twelve or thirteen. I can't remember exactly when. It's the sort of thing that creeps up on you.'

'And what went wrong?'

'I'm afraid he got in with a bad crowd.' Her frown deepened now. 'You wouldn't think there would be a "bad crowd" at the schools he attended, but there you are. And once the rot had set in, it seemed impossible to cure it. Drink and drugs. Such common problems, but with such far-reaching consequences. Both his prep and his senior school handled it internally – or thought they had. But they failed.' She sipped her coffee again. 'And there you have it. It's twenty-odd years since then, but nothing changed.'

'Did John have other relationships, before Julie?'

'One or two. They didn't last.'

'Were they with women of his own age?'

'Julie was the youngest by a long way, as far as I'm aware.'

What had made John change his habits? Had Julie targeted him after all, in the hope that he might provide a way into Lockwood's?

'When did you become aware that your son and Julie Cooper were involved?'

The woman shrugged her angular shoulders. 'It was Lucien – Julie's tutor – who mentioned the matter to Alistair. I believe it was at least a year ago.'

'It sounds as though you took the matter more seriously than your husband.'

'He tends to be more relaxed than I am. He never fully believed the rumours.'

So the Lockwoods had been alerted near the beginning of Julie's second year – when she'd photographed the cat. But the connection between the pair of them might have dated back to the dead student's first year at university. Had her affair with Lockwood started that long ago too? If it had been ongoing, it looked as though it might have overlapped with her relationship with Stuart. He needed to understand the timing.

'Lady Lockwood, you say you rang your son because you knew he'd be upset. I'm sorry to ask this, but did you also have any fear that John might have been involved in Julie's death?'

Their hostess looked at him long and hard. 'No. Not for one minute.'

But what mother would say otherwise? If pauses meant anything, then she'd found it hard to lie. For a moment his mind skipped to Tara and her mission with the journalist. He wondered what she'd discovered.

Might Veronica Lockwood suspect her husband, as well as her dead son?

CHAPTER FORTY-FOUR

Bella was meant to be in a supervision, but Dr Reynolds would cut her some slack after the news they'd had. Bella could always say she'd gone to the counselling service to try to get an appointment.

She hadn't meant to skip class, but all morning, her mind had been on Stuart. She'd texted him earlier, to ask again if she could help get ready for the protest, but he'd said no, there was nothing more to do.

What was he up to, really? He was keeping her at a distance and she wanted – needed – to know why. What had she done wrong?

She was waiting opposite his college now, hidden in a recessed gateway. She didn't think she was likely to be disturbed. In all the times she'd visited she'd never seen it unlocked. It belonged to the garden of some massive old house with high, dark windows. The place was always deathly quiet and still – as though there was no one at home. She repeated all these facts to herself as she stood there, but she was more on edge than ever. She'd never feel secure again – she knew that – but it would be a long while before she'd accept it.

She'd been in the doorway for an hour before she saw Stuart. He was on his way out, rather than in. She watched as he appeared in the stone archway that led from St Bede's porters' lodge and turned left, towards town. His collar was turned up against the rain, but he had no hood. That was like Stuart. He'd got big business to fight; he wasn't going to worry about getting his hair wet. She watched the way he walked. You could tell the sort of person he was from his gait. Confident, a bit of a swagger, and a definite disregard for anyone who didn't agree with him. She still fancied him; couldn't switch it off.

The weather meant she could use an umbrella and she was going to take full advantage of that. She emerged from the shelter of the gateway now and put it up, holding it down low so he wouldn't see her face if he turned. And she'd taken his advice for once, and stopped dressing like Julie. She'd got a smart cashmere beanie on, and a suede coat. For a second she thought of her dead friend. She was compelled to pull her phone from her pocket and call up Julie's photo on her camera roll. The almost-black hair, the clear blue eyes. Bella switched the screen off again quickly and fought back emotion. She lifted her umbrella slightly, so that she could see Stuart's legs, and adjusted her walking pace to his. He had Tuesdays free, she knew, so he wouldn't be going to a lecture.

They walked past the elegant cream frontage of the Royal Cambridge Hotel. Bella kept well back, and away from the edge of the road where endless cars ploughed through the puddles, splashing water onto the pavement. Back in the trousers her mother had bought her for her last birthday – cream, fitted, designer – she felt more restricted.

Glancing up, she saw that Stuart was crossing the road now, towards the Trumpington Street post office. Was she going to follow him only to find he bought a stamp and went back to his rooms again? She stopped and fiddled with her phone to make the pause in her journey look natural. Julie's face flashed up again. *What did you say to Stuart?* She pushed the thought away. Her quarry had walked past the post office now, and the dental practice next door. Take Five – that was where he was going. He paused at the smart red and grey frontage and then walked in. He wasn't the sort to go and sit in a coffee bar on his own, staring out of the window, thinking thoughts. He was driven, always wanting to make the next thing happen. He'd be meeting someone. How could she find out who?

If she was lucky, he'd sit near the window, and she'd be able to see his companion. She crossed the road and approached the café cautiously from one side, but it was no good. There was already a woman in a red jumper sitting at one of the two window tables. The other was occupied by a guy with a grey beard, sitting with a woman in green.

She shifted her weight from foot to foot. If she wanted to know what he was up to she needed to act, but if she followed him, he'd be bound to see her.

She inched forward, watching Stuart through the window. He was almost at the counter now.

Before she had time to think, she collapsed her umbrella and pushed the door to the café open. Stuart was just about to place his order. She needed to get past him and into the loos before he finished. And then what? What the hell did she think she was going to do after that?

She pushed the thought away. It was too late now. She moved forward on autopilot. If he turned, she'd have to pretend it was a coincidence. *It is you! I thought it was. I was just coming in to warm up...*

She held her breath. She was just drawing level with him when he looked to his left to check the menu. She paused in her tracks, avoiding the eye of the second waitress, who was free and might offer to take her order.

'The houmous and roast veg, thanks.' Bella imagined the look he was no doubt giving the woman serving him: the secret smile he'd once given her. She'd been too clingy – those days were gone.

He was looking straight ahead again, flirting, joking.

Bella moved past and found the loos. When she got inside she entered a cubicle and locked the door, even though she didn't need to go. It made her feel safe for a moment – shut off from the world. But it was no good just standing there with her heart thumping.

She needed to see who Stuart was with. It might be someone she knew too. If she was going to go and peep, she needed to make sure she didn't come face to face with his appointment at the café counter. She timed five minutes on her watch, then went to wait outside the lavatories. There was a short corridor, with a kink in it, that meant she could get a partial look at the café's interior without catching the attention of the staff or clientele.

It took her a moment to clock Stuart. He was sitting next to the far wall of the café, side on and in front of her, so that she could see part of his face from behind. And his companion was a guy. She knew the face from somewhere. He wasn't one of the protest lot. She retreated back into the corridor and tried to think – running through the various places she might know him from. College? She didn't think so. Via Stuart previously? No. Through Julie? That was it. She'd seen the guy Stuart was talking to visit Julie at her college room. He was something to do with the student newspaper she'd written for. And of course, Stuart was into journalism too. He was probably just discussing some random story. And there she was, trapped in the back of the café for no reason. How the heck was she going to get past them now? Could she wait until they left?

A woman who'd walked by her to go to the loo had come back out again and given Bella a look. She must be wondering what she was up to. Would she mention her to one of the staff? Everyone was on their guard these days. If someone was acting suspiciously, they'd probably get pulled up on it, sooner or later.

Stuart was hunched forward. He wasn't especially broad or tall, but he had presence. His stance was aggressive. She could see that the guy opposite him, from the student newspaper, felt it too. At first, he'd been shrugging in response to a lot of what Stuart said, but now he was frowning and shaking his head. He looked ruffled, and suddenly his voice rose.

'Well, she didn't, so back off.'

Who were they talking about? Julie? Maybe this was important after all. The newspaper guy was shifting in his seat and she thought for a moment that he was going to stand up and walk out. She wished he would. Stuart would go too, then, and she could escape.

But Stuart must have said something placatory. The other guy's shoulders went down a bit, and he slumped back in his chair.

And they were back to drinking and talking more quietly again. Trying to overhear what they said was hopeless.

And at that moment Bella realised that the woman who'd caught her eye when she'd been to the loo was watching her again. Watching her watching Stuart and the newspaper guy. After a moment, she got up and walked through to the corridor where Bella was standing.

'Are you all right?'

Bella nodded. 'I need to leave, but that's my boyfriend over there and we've had a row. I didn't expect to find him here and I don't want him to see me.'

A look of understanding came over the woman's face. 'Okay. How about if I walk you to the door and we keep our heads down. I'll stand between you and him. He looks quite involved in his conversation. He probably won't spot you.'

Bella hesitated, but it sounded like a reasonable plan. 'Okay. Thanks.'

They made it to the door and the woman followed her outside. 'Look, it's none of my business, but if you're that scared of him seeing you, I'm guessing he hasn't been treating you well. Maybe you should make him an ex-boyfriend?' She smiled awkwardly. 'If you need support, I've got a number you can ring. I had problems once.'

Bella was anxious to get out of the doorway. 'I'm okay. But thanks – you're right. I'll sort it.'

The woman looked after her for a moment with anxious eyes, but Bella recrossed the road and headed back towards St Oswald's. She put her umbrella back up, and pulled her hat down.

She was partway along Fen Causeway when she heard footsteps behind her. Heavy. Running. She quickened her pace instinctively, but it was only a second before she felt a hand on her shoulder.

'What the hell are you playing at? Do you think I didn't see you in the café?'

She looked into Stuart's eyes. They were fiery, like a snake's, his pupils contracted. He'd pulled her round now, and had one hand on each of her shoulders. She could tell he was fighting the urge to shake her. Or worse.

'Can you seriously not be self-sufficient for five minutes? Just forget it – okay? I've had enough.'

He did shake her then – just once. A hard, sharp movement that made a shock of pain run through her neck.

She'd had him where she wanted, but she'd thrown it all away. Would he change his mind in a few days, once he'd had the chance to calm down?

He must, surely. She could only hope.

CHAPTER FORTY-FIVE

Tara was in the Old Hall Café – a student hang-out at St Oswald's. Blake had asked her to visit on the back of a new witness statement. One of Lucien Balfour's students, Louise Fellows, had come to the station to relay a conversation she'd overhead between the tutor and Julie Cooper.

'Best if you go on your own,' Blake had said to her. 'They're more likely to chat that way.'

The move had pulled her off some background research she'd been doing on John Lockwood, but it was good to get a second solo mission. She sometimes missed the old days, when she'd operated independently as a journalist. Being able to develop her own tactics on the spot gave her a buzz.

She'd had to ask the porters to track down the people she wanted. It turned out a bunch of them were already at the café, talking about the meeting they'd had with Balfour earlier that day.

A guy with floppy brown hair was slouched back in a faded blue sofa, a coffee on the table in front of him. Next to him sat a blonde girl with a bob, and there were others too, gathered round the table. They looked pale and tired. Tara had already introduced herself – so their minds were all focused on Julie's death.

'It's just so hard to take in,' the floppy-haired guy said. 'I mean, you see horrific stuff like this on the news quite often, but you never expect it to happen to someone you know.'

Tara had ordered a plate of brownies and put them down on the coffee table now. 'I thought you might not be sleeping well. I hear you've been offered counselling?' Louise Fellows had mentioned it in her statement.

The blonde girl nodded as the floppy-haired guy helped himself to a brownie. 'There's someone there for us to talk to immediately if we want. Normally you have to wait a bit for an appointment. But I'm not sure what I feel about it.'

Tara raised an eyebrow. 'Why's that?'

'I didn't actually know Julie that well. I found her quite hard to talk to. I felt I wasn't – I don't know – trendy or radical enough, I suppose. But I've been crying almost non-stop since I heard about her death. I feel as though I'm being two-faced.'

Tara shook her head. 'You shouldn't. I appreciate it'll be even worse for people who were really close to her, but it's an appalling shock all round. People will have all kinds of reactions and none of them are wrong.' She thought back to when Greg, Bea's husband, had died. It had been Bea whose world had fallen apart, but Tara had been winded. She'd been genuinely fond of him. There'd been no crying though. She'd felt numb, and dry-eyed. The tears had come a lot later, when she'd seen how much Bea was hurting. 'If you can have a cry, and let your feelings out, I'd say that's no bad thing.'

The girl nodded and picked up her coffee.

'So it was Dr Balfour who suggested you might all like to book appointments with the counsellor, was it?' She watched their faces as she mentioned the tutor's name, but none of the students were looking at her directly.

'That's right,' the floppy-haired guy said. He'd finished his brownie.

Tara decided to keep going gently; see if she got a hint of what they all thought of him. 'It's great that someone's there with the specific job of looking out for you.'

There it was: a quick glance between the student with the blonde bob and a second female student on a chair at right angles to hers.

'Though, I must admit, I'd find it hard to confide in someone like that, unless I'd got to know them properly,' Tara went on. 'I suppose Dr Balfour must make an effort to socialise with you all, so that you feel able to go to him if you need to?'

It was the floppy-haired guy who spoke, with a sidelong glance at the student next to him. 'Oh yes. He loves to socialise, does our Dr Balfour.'

There was a moment's silence and Tara caught his eye. 'He overdoes it?'

The student with the blonde bob pursed her lips. 'Let's just say he's a man who relishes his work.'

'You think he's not just socialising for the benefit of the students?'

The blonde sat up straighter. 'He's a bit of a creep, to be honest.'

'He's made up to you?' Tara kept her voice quiet. The students were glancing around them, though she couldn't see anyone in the café that looked like staff. Or indeed, like a fellow…

There was a moment's pause. One of the other female students spoke. 'I wouldn't put it quite like that. Making up to someone implies trying your luck, to see if you get a positive response. Which still wouldn't be great, but…' She let the sentence hang.

'He's more forceful about it than that?' Tara asked.

The student with the blonde bob spoke. 'He's pretty determined.' She looked down at her lap.

'He put pressure on you to get closer to him than you wanted?' Tara held her breath.

The student paused for a moment, but then, at last, she nodded. 'I made it clear I wasn't interested, and he's had it in for me ever since.'

Tara glanced at the other females present. 'Have any of you had similar experiences?'

Slowly, they nodded. All of them.

'And you never complained to anyone?'

'It's our word against his,' the blonde girl said. 'I get the impression he's got the ear of the master, for some reason. I often see them together. I've always suspected we'd only be making trouble for ourselves if we tried to bring things to a head.'

Tara felt her chest tighten with pent-up fury. How could they be trapped like this? And why were Balfour and Sir Alistair Lockwood so close?

'And I'm afraid, once in a while, Balfour's efforts pay off,' one of the other female students said.

There were more glances exchanged.

'You're thinking Bella Chadwick?' the blonde girl said.

The other student nodded. 'Yes, I'm pretty certain Bella slept with Balfour.' She shuddered.

'Even if she seemed willing, it's not okay for someone with a duty of care to initiate that kind of relationship with a student,' Tara said. 'There's an imbalance of power that ought to make that absolutely off limits.' She was desperate to get her message across, but in the back of her mind, she was also processing the information about Bella. She'd had an affair – possibly? Maybe? – with Lucien Balfour, and Blake also suspected she was sleeping with Stuart Gilmour. What did those links mean, if anything?

The student with the blonde bob was speaking again. 'I'll tell you, I've been *very* careful to make sure I keep my nose clean. If ever I got into trouble, I have a feeling he'd use it as a lever.'

Tara felt the hairs on her arms rise. Balfour had known about Julie carrying a knife on a protest against Lockwood's, but he hadn't admitted as much to the police. And he hadn't disciplined her about it either. And then she thought of what Blake had told her about Louise Fellows' statement. She'd overheard Balfour tell Julie that one good turn deserved another. Yet Louise had seen Julie shake free of him, a look of fury in her eyes. She hadn't given in to intimidation. Had Balfour decided to take his revenge?

*

'So, based on what the students told you, we can assume Lucien Balfour is a sexual predator who tries it on with just about every female undergraduate he deals with.'

Tara was in Blake's office, reporting back. She nodded. 'Looks that way.'

He swore. 'I wish we'd got onto that sooner. You and Max had your doubts about him from the beginning. The added detail about his affair with Bella Chadwick is interesting.'

Tara had been trying to work it out too. It seemed that Bella had wanted to be like Julie – but Julie would never have given in to Balfour's advances, even under pressure. Had Balfour got something on Bella? Some bit of information that meant he'd been able to coerce her into a relationship? Her secret affair with Stuart Gilmour perhaps? Would that have been enough?

Blake's dark eyes were on hers. 'And we know Balfour was aware of the gossip about John Lockwood and Julie. Maybe he was jealous – he'd been turned down where another fellow had made headway. Or so we assume.'

'It could be.'

'We need to know where he was the night Julie was killed. And what's all this about him and Sir Alistair being best buddies?'

'I'm not sure, but I've got a theory about that. According to LinkedIn, they went to the same posh school – it's a place with a bit of an old-boy-network reputation. That might be enough to make Sir Alistair treat him differently. I doubt he'd ignore hard-and-fast proof of Balfour's wrongdoing, but it might make him happy to look the other way.' It was the worst sort of approach, as far as Tara was concerned: cowardly and lazy with it.

Blake stretched in his seat. He looked exhausted – but of all the people she'd ever met, he wore exhaustion well. She tried to think of the smile Jez had given her on her way in, and not of Blake's stubble and rumpled shirt, coupled with the exceptionally well-cut suit he was wearing that day. It must be one of the ones designed by his sister. She guessed he'd never have chosen it himself, but wore it in the same way a dutiful child wore a Christmas jumper from their parents. He'd mentioned his sister once or twice – it was clear they were close.

'Must be hard, dealing with all this and a new baby too.' Her voice had come out low and husky, despite herself.

For a long moment, Blake didn't reply. When his eyes met hers, she felt the pull of him so strongly it was all she could do to sit still in her seat. 'You don't know the half of it.'

And she never would, thanks to the way their dice had fallen.

'I'll get over to see Balfour,' Blake said. 'Are you still digging into the Lockwood side of things?'

He knew about the feedback she'd got from Josh, but although her ex had felt Julie's research wouldn't have made her a target, there was still John to consider. You couldn't ignore a man who'd apparently been having sex with a student under his care, and who'd seemingly taken an overdose just after that same student's murder.

She nodded. 'I've been trying to track down John's contacts using the records on his mobile. A lot of the numbers ended up being for work or service providers. It doesn't look as though he was the sociable sort. But I've found a couple of leads, including one guy that goes all the way back to his school days. I thought I'd start with him; find out what his teenage relationships were like.' The man might be aware of exactly when John had first gone off the rails, too.

Blake nodded. 'Sounds good.'

'And then, this evening, Max and I have an open invitation to attend the master's event for new students at St Oswald's.'

'They're still holding it, after John's death?'

She could relate to the shock in his eyes. 'I was surprised too. I got in touch to double check. Sir Alistair's PA told me the Lockwoods intend to go ahead for the sake of the students. They want to gather them together and reassure them – not cry off because there's been another death. Even if it was of their son.' She couldn't imagine ploughing on for a minute if it were her. But it seemed they could keep their emotions in check, for the greater good.

As she reached the door Blake spoke again. 'Take care.'

CHAPTER FORTY-SIX

Blake was determined not to expose Louise Fellows to any fallout as a result of the information she'd given the police. He didn't need to lead in with what she'd told them about the dynamic between Lucien Balfour and Julie anyway. He had another plan. They'd agreed that Megan would start.

'Tell us about your relationship with Bella Chadwick, Dr Balfour.'

The guy flinched, and Blake felt a tiny rush of satisfaction. It took the tutor several seconds to respond.

'I have a very good relationship with Bella, as I hope I do with all my students.'

'Yes, we heard it was good.' Blake smiled and was delighted to see Balfour squirm.

'I can't imagine who you've been talking to.' Balfour was spluttering.

Blake checked his collar for spit. Clear, surprisingly. 'Multiple people, as it happens.'

The man drew himself up in his chair, his frown deepening. Blake imagined he was trying to guess what evidence they had. The conversation could go either way.

'Well, if any of these people substantiate their accusations with proof, then I'll be most surprised.'

Blake cursed inwardly. But they could still speak to Bella Chadwick again – she might give them what they needed.

Megan took over once more. 'We understand you told Sir Alistair that his son John was in a relationship with Julie Cooper.' They'd agreed to switch tack each time a direction seemed to peter out. They wanted to stop him from predicting their questions.

'I told him there were *rumours*,' Balfour said. 'Nothing more. But it was right that he should know about them.'

'Because his son was involved, and his reputation was under threat?' Blake cut in.

'Because it was a serious accusation affecting the well-being of one of the students.'

He'd been prepared for that question all right. It didn't make his answer any more convincing, and two could play at that game. '*You* must have been upset to hear the "rumour" about Julie and John Lockwood.'

Balfour's eyes narrowed. 'What are you insinuating?'

That was a pleasingly revealing reaction. Blake raised an innocent eyebrow. 'Because she was under your care. Her welfare must have been important to you.'

The man was angry now, which was just as Blake intended. 'Indeed.'

'How did you find discussing something so personal with Julie? Do you often have to talk about sexual relationships with your students?'

His cheeks reddened. 'I didn't have to be explicit.'

'But you tackled her about it, obviously. Was she angry?'

'Were *you* angry?' Megan followed up.

'No. Of course not.'

'You were supportive? You told her it was okay for her to be in that kind of relationship?' Blake leant his head to one side.

'That assertion is preposterous, as well you know. It was wholly wrong for her to be in the relationship.'

'So you believed the rumours were true then,' Blake said. 'I'd certainly agree with you. It's very wrong for anyone to instigate sexual relations with someone under their care.' His eyes met Balfour's.

'How did you tackle the matter?' Megan said.

'I told her she was behaving dangerously.'

Megan paused then.

It took Blake a moment to recover from speechlessness, too. 'That *she* was behaving dangerously?'

Balfour looked at his hands, which were pressed hard down on his desk. 'That the pair of them were putting their careers and reputations at risk.'

Blake drew in a deep breath. 'When my colleagues interviewed you, you told them Julie was too savvy to get involved in anything that might damage her prospects. Odd, given that you were aware she'd marched through town carrying a knife, and that she was sleeping with a member of university staff.'

'There is such a thing as student confidentiality.' The man puffed out his chest, but the act wasn't convincing.

'And there is such a thing as withholding evidence. I'd like to know why you didn't ask the college to discipline Julie Cooper for carrying a knife – or instigate further enquiries into John Lockwood's behaviour.' Blake's eyes were on Balfour's the moment the man looked up.

'I wanted to give her a chance.'

'A chance to do what?' Megan's eyes were on the man too. She'd got the tone just right, Blake noticed – it told Balfour exactly what they thought of his excuses.

Balfour remained silent.

'I'll be talking to the dean to ask how you handle discipline normally,' Blake said. 'Only it would be interesting to know if it varies at all from student to student.' And from one gender to the other, too. 'Just for the record, where were you from seven on Saturday evening until seven on Sunday morning?'

Balfour opened his mouth and closed it again. After a moment, he made a fresh attempt to speak. 'I had dinner with a friend at the Chop House on King's Parade. I returned home at around ten.'

'We'll take your friend's name and contact details, thank you.' Blake waited for the man to write the information down. 'And what about after that?'

The man looked scared now. 'I went home. I live alone.'

He wasn't surprised about that. For a second, Blake's mind ran from Balfour's current students to his own daughters, who might one day find themselves dealing with a toad like the one in front of him. Whether Balfour was involved in Julie Cooper's death or not, Blake was going to make damned sure he never worked as a tutor again.

CHAPTER FORTY-SEVEN

Stuart's heart rate ramped right up when he thought of Bella. She'd texted him an hour after he'd chased her down the road. She was threatening to drop in on him later. For God's sake, why didn't she understand where to get off? For a moment he wondered if she could have overheard what he'd said in the café, but he didn't think so. He'd only noticed her when she'd walked out of the place. Although he hadn't seen where she'd been sitting, there'd been no one he knew on the tables next to him. He'd had a careful look.

He glanced down at the notepad he'd taken from Julie. It was ironic – if she hadn't accused him of stealing from her in the first place, he might never have got the idea. Her paranoia had made him so angry, he'd been prepared to go further to get what he wanted.

He thought back to when she'd first accused him of messing with her papers. She'd gone wild, turning up on his doorstep, hurling abuse. *Stupid cow.*

He looked down at the pad now. He'd gone to such lengths to get it – convinced that it would contain some hidden gems – but in fact, he'd found nothing to justify her secretiveness. She was kidding herself if she thought she'd got anything decent there. For a second, he frowned. She'd written 'Scotland?' in block caps on one of the sheets and put three circles around it, driving her pen hard into the paper. That was the one thing that didn't compute. But he had no way of working out if it was significant.

He'd have to start again from scratch, do all the research himself – he'd make a better job of it. And the potential payback, now that

Julie was dead, was way higher than it had been. Get it right, and he'd be made for life.

He'd be able to laugh in the face of the dean who'd suspended him from college. For all the risks he was taking, the prize would be worth it.

CHAPTER FORTY-EIGHT

'You don't look like a detective.'

John Lockwood's friend from schooldays – Edward Morpeth – sat opposite Tara at a table to the rear of the Cambridge Blue. Outside, the rain was still lashing down and Tara's hair was dripping. She wasn't sure if it was her unkempt appearance that had put Edward off the scent, or if it was just the usual – her relative youth and possibly the fact that she was female. *Get with the programme, Edward…*

'It helps when I'm undercover.'

He laughed. She knew he was contemporary with John, but he'd gone grey young, having that black hair–blue eye combination that tended towards that. His colouring was attractive and so was his smile, but the latter faded quickly.

'I still can't believe John's dead.'

She nodded. 'I'm so sorry. And that you had to hear it from me, too.' She'd had to break the news when she'd made contact out of the blue. 'I guess Sir Alistair and Lady Lockwood will work their way through John's friends to pass on what's happened in a more personal way, but it's bound to take time.'

Edward shrugged. 'I might hear from them. I used to go round to their house here in Cambridge when I was at school with John – in the early days anyway. But his relationship with his parents broke down. I expect you knew that?'

Tara nodded, despite having almost no details. She hoped he'd unbutton if he assumed she already understood the full story.

'I don't suppose they'll contact the friends he made in adulthood. They probably wouldn't know where to start. That's something I could do, to an extent. I'll make a list of those I'm aware of.' He shook his head sadly. 'It won't be a long one.'

'He kept himself to himself, I gather.' She'd understood that much, just by looking at his phone records.

Edward nodded. 'So why do you need my help?'

Tara would have to watch what she said, but she wanted to share enough to get him to talk. 'There's a bit of a question mark over John's death,' she said at last. 'We know he hadn't been in good health for a while, but we want to understand any other factors that might have played a part in what happened. Anything that could have made him depressed or influenced his behaviour.' She met his glance and the sad but knowing look he gave her. 'Please don't read too much into this. We're just asking as a precaution, but as an old friend, I thought you might understand why his life panned out the way it did.'

'Okay.' Edward sipped his pint of Woodforde's.

'When did you last see John?'

He grimaced. 'It's got to be three or four months ago now. You know how it is, life just takes over. We got together for a drink just before the summer break.'

'How was he?'

Edward frowned. 'Anxious. He'd got major money worries – but I think there was something wrong at work, too.'

'Did he go into details?'

Edward frowned. 'He was muttering about some research or other. Something a student was doing maybe?' He shook his head. 'I couldn't imagine why it would be important, but he was wound up about it. He didn't want them to pursue it.'

Tara felt a chill creep down her spine as she remembered the transcript of Blake and Megan's interview with Sandra Cooper.

Julie said she was doing some research to help this person out. John, I think she said his name was.

Was this what Edward had picked up on? Was it something Julie had wanted to pursue but John hadn't? Had John killed her to stop her in her tracks? She tried to refocus on the rest of her mission. 'I gather John's problems started back when he was a youngster,' Tara said. 'Do you remember him before that?'

Edward nodded. 'The change in him was marked, and sudden. He lost a lot of friends at that stage. He withdrew into himself.'

'Do you remember what year that was?'

He frowned. 'No, sorry. But we were still at prep school, and near the end. I'd guess he was around twelve years old? Something like that. Rumours went round about him taking drugs, and I got the impression some of the parents told their offspring to give him a wide berth at school.'

'Was drug taking common, where you studied?'

For a second, Edward laughed. 'Just as well their PR office can't hear our conversation. Their hair would fall out. But it wasn't unheard of by the final year. And it was more common still in our senior school. They came down hard on anyone found in possession, but kids are canny. I don't believe that was John's problem though – or not to start with. I think the drink and the drugs came later, as a result of what was bothering him.'

'He must have been grateful that you stuck by him.' She waited to see what he'd say, wondering what had made them stay close.

'I was having a rough time too, to be honest. My dad had just walked out and there was some uncertainty over whether I could stay at the school.'

'So, you and John shared your problems?'

Edward pulled a face. 'I shared mine. And John shared the results of his… his moods, his need to escape – but not what had caused them.'

'You mentioned your theory about him becoming dependent on drink and drugs because of his problems. Do you think he went off the rails in other ways? Risky relationships? Aggression? Anything like that?' Bella said Julie had witnessed him losing his temper.

'No.' Edward frowned. 'Not at all. It was all turned in on himself, and it was as though he had no energy. He didn't go wild, he went down.'

Tara nodded. 'Do you have any idea at all what might have caused him to change so suddenly? Might his parents have had trouble with their marriage, do you think?' It must have been something major to send him so thoroughly off course, but things like that could have a profound effect.

'I never heard anything about it if so, but now you mention it, that might make sense. It was around that time that I stopped going round to his parents' house. And I do remember that the change coincided with the start of a new school year. He came back troubled. If he'd been witnessing rows between his mother and father for six weeks, that might explain it.'

Suddenly his eyes darkened, and his look was far away. A frown spread over his face and he shifted in his seat.

'You've remembered something?' Tara sat absolutely still, on high alert.

He nodded slowly. 'Nothing important. I just suddenly have this image of John in my mind's eye. I remember him blanking a teacher on his first day back. It was weird, because he'd always been quite ready to take part in lessons up until then, so I was struck by it. And she was only making conversation – not even asking us about the work we were meant to have done.'

'What was she talking about?'

'Just the holidays. She was going round the class and asking everyone where they'd been. She had to ask John three times before he answered, and when he did, you'd think she'd asked him to repeat the proof for Fermat's last theorem. He spoke really slowly, as though he was dreaming.' He looked at Tara with sad eyes. 'He just said he'd been to visit his grandmother. In Scotland.'

Tara felt her stomach flutter. She thought of the odd note the tech team had found on Julie's phone: just that one word – 'Scotland' – and a question mark. And the searches the dead student had performed on her laptop, with the words Lockwood's and Scotland entered as the terms.

Scotland, where there was no branch of the firm, but where either Sir Alistair or Lady Lockwood's mother had lived.

As soon as Edward Morpeth left, she called Blake.

CHAPTER FORTY-NINE

Tara was due to meet Max at the Master's Lodge. She entered the Lockwoods' home with a gaggle of students. One of them had been in the group she'd interviewed at the café earlier. The girl caught her eye over the heads of the others and Tara met her anxious look with a tiny nod. A little way ahead she could see Bella Chadwick too, in her Julie Cooper uniform.

As she walked into the imposing hallway – long, wide, and lined with dark paintings that gave the place a sombre feel – she could hear the sound of a harp. Veronica Lockwood must be playing.

Normally, Tara might have relaxed and enjoyed it, but her nerves were jangling after her talk with Edward Morpeth. Blake had got Jez researching the Lockwoods' parents' connections with Scotland. Had something happened on the holiday that sent John off the rails? It was a leap, but Julie's preoccupation with Scotland had to mean something. She wished she was at the station, doing the research herself, but she could imagine DCI Fleming's reaction to that: *There's no 'I' in team, Tara.* It turned out people like her really did say that.

Attending the gathering at St Oswald's felt unimportant by comparison. She was only there to get an idea of how easy it would have been for Julie to sneak about the house undetected, the previous year. She wished she knew what the dead girl had been hoping to find. Unless John had told her of the family heirloom's existence, of course. That was possible. Tara could imagine Julie being seriously irked at the Lockwoods having such a valuable ornament. Maybe she'd sought it out for the reason Josh had suggested, if she'd known about it in advance. Tara's ex was right: it would make a memorable image to go alongside an article on Lockwood's.

Tara made her way through the hall and to the doorway of the grand, formal drawing room. Lady Lockwood was at one end, playing the harp, a group of students gathered round her.

As Tara watched, a man she recognised as Douglas Lockwood rounded up the onlookers. 'Do come and talk with the others,' he said. 'You needn't feel you're being rude. My mother heads off on tour tomorrow. This is the last chance she'll get to practise before her instrument's packed up.'

How must she feel, heading off after the trauma of the last few days?

Douglas Lockwood's reassurances had done the trick and the students moved off towards the sherry station.

Across the room, Tara could see Max talking to Sir Alistair. He must be saying all the right things; the master was nodding and smiling. And Tara could see Selina Lockwood too. She hesitated. She half wanted to say hello – and they had met officially, when Tara had visited the Master's Lodge about the cat – but she didn't want to worry the woman. At that moment, as though Selina had sensed Tara's eyes on her, she glanced up. Her look was shuttered.

Tara turned away, and went to speak to Sir Alistair, now that Max had moved off to circulate.

'It must be hard for you, carrying on with something like this,' she said, after they'd greeted each other, 'but I can see how much the students are enjoying the party. And it's amazing for them, being able to listen to a world-class musician play, as part of the proceedings.'

He nodded and smiled. 'I've managed to persuade Veronica to do it each year since I took up my role. I believe it encourages everyone to come along – they'd have to pay a hundred pounds or so to see my wife in a proper concert hall.' He glanced over at

Lady Lockwood. 'She tried to duck out of it this year. She's got an early start tomorrow and her harp's being shipped tonight, but I think it's best if we all keep fully occupied at the moment. When something awful happens, there's no benefit in sitting around moping. The family and its responsibilities come first.'

Family above all else. The Lockwood motto filtered through Tara's head.

'I can see Douglas and Selina are of the same mind,' she said. 'It must be a support to have them helping out.'

He nodded again. 'They always come. Again, anything I'm involved with has a potential effect on the family firm. Who knows? Some of the students here might end up working for Lockwood's when they graduate. In my business you need to make sure the show goes on, and its public face never slips.'

She nodded. She was used to putting on a brave face herself, but she wouldn't give a damn about appearances if she'd just lost a loved one.

'On another issue,' Sir Alistair said, lowering his voice slightly, 'I wanted to mention that – somewhat embarrassingly – I can now give you a witness who knows I was in London all night on Saturday.' He held up a hand. 'I understand you were only asking so that you'd dotted your "i"s and crossed your "t"s, but you might as well know, for what it's worth.'

Had he really believed they weren't genuinely interested?

'The fact is, someone came back to our London flat with me. Only with my age, and the amount I'd had to drink' – his eyes twinkled for a moment – 'I have to confess I had no memory of their presence. It was an old friend, Marcus Thompson, and I only found out he was there at all when he called me to say he thought he might have left a scarf at our place. Apparently, we sat up drinking until four.' He shook his head. 'I shall have to watch myself. I'll send his contact details over to the station later this evening.'

It seemed convenient that he'd managed to produce this person like a rabbit from a hat. Not that she had any particular reason to suspect him. Julie might have been a thorn in his side, but Tara couldn't currently see how she'd been anything more than that.

As the master moved off to speak to a group of students, Tara wove her way across the room, back towards the hall. She hadn't completed her mission yet.

The light levels were already low outside, and the upper floor of the Master's Lodge was in darkness, a clear sign that partygoers were meant to remain down below. This was only an exercise – she could explain herself if she got caught – but she wanted to think like Julie had.

She listened. Veronica Lockwood was still playing the harp in the drawing room. Downstairs, a few students were milling round between the kitchen and the large reception room, but they were all engrossed in their own conversations, some laughing, one or two looking serious – all intent on each other.

She began to mount the wide, sweeping stairway. The high-quality carpet helped her. Even if it had been silent down below, she doubted anyone would have detected her footsteps. She kept an eye out over her shoulder, moving cautiously but quickly. It was impossible not to feel a rush of adrenaline, even though this was play-acting.

At the top of the stairs, she listened instinctively. Just because the upper floor appeared to be deserted, didn't mean there wasn't some Lockwood minion squirrelled away somewhere, working by the light of a single lamp, finishing off some administrative task or other. But all was quiet and when she ran her eyes along the base of each closed door, no light shone through.

She stepped forward along the corridor. How many doors had Julie tried? It might just have been one, if John had told her about the cat and where to find it. But if she'd been on a fishing mission

– as Tara suspected – keen to find out anything she could about the family firm, then she might have tried several.

She remembered her ex's thoughts. There was no way a savvy businessman like Sir Alistair would leave evidence of damaging secrets around when the house was full of strangers. It wouldn't have stopped Julie from hoping, though. And maybe the secret she was onto had been John's, not the firm's.

She took a glove out of her pocket, pulled it on, and put her hand on the door nearest to her – the one she knew led to Sir Alistair's study. She wasn't intending to go in – only to see if they'd bothered to secure it. And they had. She wasn't surprised. It didn't follow that they had this time last year though. They'd probably be more cautious after seeing the photo Julie had taken of the cat.

She went to the door of the room that housed the ornament next. It was locked as well. For a second, at the end of the long, dark corridor, she felt claustrophobic. Downstairs she could still hear the music and chat, but at that moment, she also heard voices. Someone was coming up the stairs.

She wished she knew which door led to the bathroom. Suddenly, explaining what she was up to felt awkward. She'd just have to brazen it out as she'd planned. It wasn't as though she didn't have a good reason for looking – and you didn't need a search warrant to walk along someone's upstairs landing if you'd been invited to their party.

It was Sir Alistair who appeared. He was smiling, as usual. 'You're trying to retrace Julie Cooper's footsteps, I presume?'

She nodded. 'I'm sorry. I should have warned you, but it wouldn't have been a proper test of what she might have been able to do in secret unless I tried to operate the same way.'

He nodded. 'I quite understand. And this year we are – no doubt – more vigilant. A little bird told me they'd seen you come up here, out of the corner of their eye.'

Who could that have been? As they descended the stairs to rejoin the party, she caught the gaze of Douglas Lockwood, down below in the hallway, his expression blank.

Max left to go back to the station, but in the end, Tara stayed on. She felt uneasy – as though there was something she was missing. At last, only she and a few student stragglers remained. She said goodbye to each of the Lockwoods in turn.

Outside, a logistics lorry had appeared and behind her, as she walked along the hallway, two guys with shoulders the size of sideboards were manoeuvring Veronica Lockwood's harp case up the stairs from the Master's Lodge basement and across the hall towards the drawing room. The music had stopped. The next time the instrument was played it would be somewhere like Milan or Paris.

She walked outside, onto the gravel forecourt in front of the lodge. Through the window she could see the burly men lifting the precious harp inside its case, where it nestled in the green felt interior. Veronica Lockwood was standing next to them, monitoring their progress. At that moment, she looked up and her gaze seemed to meet Tara's. Could she see her, out there in the dark?

She heard the gravel crunch behind her, and turned. Douglas Lockwood was outside too, on the forecourt. Maybe Veronica had been staring out into the dark to see where he'd gone. He walked over to Tara now. 'Are you all right?'

She was thinking about the green felt of the harp case. What was it made of? Was it wool?

She swallowed. 'I've just never seen a harp being packed up before. It's huge, isn't it? Quite a job. Just as well the logistics guys are so burly.'

One person moving the case alone would have their work cut out. But of course, if that was where Julie had been left to die, her killer could have taken her body out again before they'd driven it to Wandlebury Ring…

CHAPTER FIFTY

In the distance, across a stretch of grass, Blake could see the lights of St Oswald's College's Master's Lodge. Sir Alistair's party would be winding up now. He'd probably enjoyed playing host, handing out drinks, offering a supportive word. He'd always say the right things.

Blake had just knocked on Bella Chadwick's door, but there'd been no reply. It was his plan to catch her as soon as she left the master's party. He was keen to speak to her, after the interview with Lucien Balfour. He was quite sure from the tutor's reaction that the rumours of his and Bella's affair were true, but he wouldn't get far on a hunch. He needed to break down Bella's defences: get her to talk, so that no other student would have to put up with Balfour's unwanted attentions.

He hovered now, watching as clusters of people left the distant lodge. He could just distinguish them in the light from the windows of the vast house, coalescing – presumably to say their goodbyes – and then heading off in smaller dribs and drabs. He'd wait for Bella's return, close to her room.

He turned back and stood near the door that led to the students' staircase. Three people walked past him in relatively quick succession and he called out to the last, a female student.

'Excuse me, have you been at the gathering at the Master's Lodge?'

She nodded, her look slightly wary, which was understandable.

'I was looking for Bella Chadwick.' He pulled his ID out of his jacket pocket. 'Do you know if she was at the do? I was hoping I might speak to her this evening.'

The student frowned. Blake wasn't sure if the effect of his badge had been positive or not. 'She was there,' she said at last. 'But I think she left a while back.'

Why wasn't she answering her phone? 'You don't know where she might have gone?'

Bella's neighbour shrugged. 'She's been seeing a lot of this guy from St Bede's.' She looked down for a moment. 'The one that Julie went out with – Stuart Gilmour. I think they might have been consoling each other.' She pulled a face. 'You know about him?'

Blake nodded.

'To be honest, Stuart's very… well, he's hard as nails – very ambitious. I don't think he cares for all those causes he supposedly champions half as much as his own future.'

'He's into journalism, isn't he?'

She nodded. 'Same as Julie was.' She sighed. 'As for Bella,' she glanced around her for a moment, as though she was checking there was no one listening, 'she's got pretty appalling taste in men.'

Blake guessed she'd had a few sherries at Sir Alistair's do, her candour brought on by booze. He raised his eyebrows. 'There are other examples, as well as Stuart, then?'

The student lowered her voice now. 'To be honest, some of my mates mentioned one of your lot had been to talk to them about Lucien earlier today. Lucien Balfour, that is, one of the college tutors. Did they mention Bella and Lucien had had a fling?'

Blake hesitated. 'We've heard various rumours.'

The young woman nodded. 'Well that's one with substance, take it from me. I'm one of Lucien's students too, and I saw him at work on Bella. I knew what he was up to; he'd tried the same with me.'

'And how do you know things went further?'

She leant back against the stone wall of her college staircase. 'Well, I didn't see them in flagrante or anything like that. But I spoke to Bella to warn her – to tell her I'd back her up if she wanted to make a complaint. But she wasn't up for that. She looked kind of resigned and said: "Don't worry. I know what I'm doing." After that I noticed her staying behind after our sessions with Lucien to "ask extra questions". Their body language told me what was going on.'

'Thank you for speaking out. We might need to come back to you for a formal statement. Would that be okay?' She didn't have proof, but her words would still carry weight if they were part of a body of evidence.

There was a moment's pause, but then the young woman nodded. 'It would. When the others told me they were interviewed earlier, I made up my mind to contact the police.'

Blake took her details, and then walked off, away from the staircase across the court, ignoring the rule about the grass. As he went, he dialled Bella's number again, and wondered. An affair with Balfour would give her a lot of power over her tutor, if she'd got concrete evidence of what had gone on. *I know what I'm doing…*

Where the hell was Bella now?

He walked through the college to the front entrance without taking in his surroundings. It was time to get back to the station.

CHAPTER FIFTY-ONE

Tara was beyond the end of the Master's Lodge's driveway and partway across the grounds when she heard footsteps behind her.

It was Douglas Lockwood again. 'I'm sorry,' he said, 'I don't mean to keep you, but we haven't heard what's going on. We pride ourselves in carrying on with our duties, but it doesn't mean we're not consumed with what's been happening underneath the veneer. I wondered if you were able to give me any news? I didn't want to ask when we were right outside the house. There are too many listening ears.'

Tara looked into the man's eyes. Was he trying to judge what was on her mind? Or was the question as straightforward as it seemed? She spent a few minutes explaining as much as she could, but her focus wasn't really on the conversation.

At last, he left her in peace and she continued her walk, glancing over her shoulder periodically, to make sure she was alone. She googled 'felt' on her phone as she went. According to Wikipedia it could be made out of natural or synthetic fibres. If it was made from the former, then wool or animal fur were given as examples…

She thought again of the green wool found under Julie Cooper's fingernails. There were many possible ways the material could have got there. The theory that she'd been trapped in a packing case containing clothes or a blanket would also work. And lots of the students had trunks or large, hard cases. But still she couldn't get the harp case out of her head – not when she put it alongside Julie's links with the Lockwoods.

Veronica said she'd been at the house the night Julie died, but that she'd taken a sleeping tablet before bed. Tara thought of her slender stature and height – around five foot three inches, she guessed. Julie had been of a similar build. Lifting a dead weight of your own body size was no mean feat. Sir Alistair was meant to have been in London, and now claimed to have a friend who could alibi him. Was there really an innocent explanation for the way he'd produced a witness at the last minute?

And then there was Douglas – alibied by Selina, who'd come forward to help the police…

She'd reached a dark path now, which led towards the side road that ran next to the college. The students were all headed in the opposite direction, making for their rooms on the St Oswald's site.

She glanced behind her again. All was quiet. In the far distance, she could still see the logistics guys, packing the harp case into the back of a lorry. The wind whistled through the trees and she shivered.

The shout came from somewhere near the road; the sound of her name made her jump. She turned and saw a shadowy figure hurtling towards her – running at full pelt. Bella Chadwick.

'Detective Thorpe! Oh God. Someone told me there were police on site.'

'What is it? What's happened?'

'I don't know.' Her eyes were huge. 'I was with Stuart earlier – before the drinks at the Master's Lodge.' She gulped for breath. 'He was acting strangely. He's been terribly short-tempered since we heard about Julie's death. I was cutting him some slack. It's not surprising – we're all on edge. But today, he – well, I don't know – he was looking at me oddly. And then asking weird questions. He wanted to know if I'd spoken to Julie on the day she died. I did talk to her briefly on the phone. It wasn't about anything important, but the look in his eye frightened me. I lied, and told him I hadn't, but he kept asking, over and over. And now…'

'Now?'

'Now he's asked me to go and meet him at Wandlebury Ring. At the spot where Julie was found.' She paused. 'He explained to me how to find the precise place.'

Tara caught her breath. But he could know that from looking at the newspaper coverage. There'd been maps showing the layout of the Ring. 'He's there already?'

The student shook her head. 'He had to do something first but then he's going to pick up his brother's car from outside that house where he stayed over the summer. You can't park by his college. He wanted to give me a lift, but I got scared. I made an excuse and said I'd meet him there.' She gave Tara a look. 'He knows I've got money, so I don't think he was suspicious when I said I'd call a cab. But really, I'm scared to go on my own.'

'I've got my car. I'll head over there. I'll call my team too, we can go in quietly, just have a word with him.'

'But what if it's not something bad at all? Maybe he's found something out. Perhaps he's got a theory, or a clue or something.' She started to cry. 'He wouldn't do anything. Not really.' And then she spoke quietly. 'I love him. He'll never forgive me if he thinks I'm on my way and a load of police turn up instead.' She took a deep breath. 'Can I come with you? Just the two of us, so we can see what's up, and decide what to do next?'

Tara paused. 'I'll do you a deal. You can come with me, but only if you swear not to get out of the car, unless I say it's okay.'

'All right. I'll text him to let him know I'm on my way.'

And Tara was definitely calling for backup – no matter what Bella said. She'd learnt her lesson. Sometimes it was worth remembering you were part of a team.

As she and Bella slammed the doors of her car shut behind them, she put the call in. The thought of the green felt flashed through her mind, but that would have to wait, at least briefly. The harp case wouldn't cross the Channel before they'd caught up with Gilmour.

CHAPTER FIFTY-TWO

Blake watched Jez exit his office, the DC's updates on Tara's whereabouts – and also those of Bella Chadwick – racing round his head. A moment earlier, he'd been anticipating going back home, and the conversation he might have with Babette. He'd allowed himself a minute to consider his words – his best chance of getting her to tell the truth about her relationship with Matt Smith. Jez's news banished those thoughts. Why the hell hadn't Bella answered her phone?

He grabbed his jacket. Fleming wouldn't want him going to give backup. And it was appropriate to send Max and Jez, given Megan was otherwise engaged. One of her contacts was in the station now with some crucial information about a manslaughter case.

He walked out of the room. It was bad timing. The DCI was just down the corridor, holding a coffee. 'Blake? What's going on? I understand Tara's requested backup as a precaution.' She peered at his coat. 'You're not going, I presume. I know she'll want people who know the case, but you can send Max and Jez and a couple of uniformed officers if you think it necessary. That ought to be enough for one jumped-up twerp, don't you think?'

She'd read the transcripts of the interviews with Gilmour. She was nothing if not diligent. She minded – but it was being on top of her team and all their activities, big and small, that was paramount from her point of view.

'I'd like an update. We seem to be following several leads, all pointing in different directions. If this business with Gilmour is a false alarm, then we need to get some perspective on where to focus our efforts. Why was Jez googling Alistair Lockwood's parents?'

He sighed. She *was* due an update, but sitting there talking, whilst everyone else drove off to Wandlebury, wasn't what he'd had in mind.

Max was in the corridor with Jez at his heels. 'Let's get over to Gilmour's summer lodgings. If his brother's car's still there we can tail him. If not, we'll make straight for Wandlebury.'

Blake had to watch them go. 'Keep me updated.'

Jez's eyes were knowing. 'Boss.'

CHAPTER FIFTY-THREE

Tara was driving Bella up Babraham Road. It was a dark evening and the trees to either side of the single lane disguised the fact that they were on a dual carriageway.

As she looked for the track that led to Wandlebury Ring, by the back route, her mobile rang. Jez.

'Gilmour's brother's car is still in the street near his summer lodgings. We haven't seen him approach. We'll wait a bit longer, but it could be that he's changed his mind. Or found another way to get to the location. Watch out. We'll follow you over soon, just to be on the safe side. We've called his mobile but he's not answering.'

Tara heard Bella take a sharp breath and glanced round at her as she made the turn towards the woods.

'Maybe it was all a trick,' the student said. 'Maybe he wanted to frighten me. Get me out here on my own.'

'We'll see.' The dirt track the killer must have used was rutted and slippery after all the rain. 'I don't want to go in too far. If he is here already, he might hear the engine. It'll be very quiet in the woods.' She found a place to pull over in a small clearing to one side of the track. The space was relatively tight; in the end she reversed the car in, so that they could drive away again fast if needs be. 'I'll get out and listen. I want you to stay where you are.'

For a second it looked as though Bella was going to argue, but at last she nodded. 'Okay.'

'I presume Stuart never replied to your text.'

It took her a moment to answer. 'No. He didn't.'

Tara opened the door quietly. What was going on? She'd seen evidence of how clingy Bella was, and how she'd followed both Julie and Stuart around. Maybe he *had* got angry with her, but Bella's theory that he was trying to get her out there on her own to wind her up didn't wash. He'd wanted to give her a lift; if she'd said yes, they'd be together.

She walked a few paces in the direction of the place where Julie Cooper had been found, peering through the trees into the darkness. The night wasn't as quiet as she'd thought. The wind tugged at the trees around her, making the leaves rustle. Those that had died floated to the ground to join the ones already at her feet.

She put one gloved hand on the trunk of the tree next to her. Had she heard something else – above the wind in the trees? She held her breath.

The sound came again. It was behind her. 'Bella,' she said turning, 'you need to stay—'

She didn't get any further. The night was dark with clouds and she only had a split second to react. It wasn't enough. Whatever Bella had been holding came crashing down, striking the side of her head. The pain was all-encompassing, but it was the force of the blow that made her fall.

She was on the ground and the student was standing over her, the object held high. She tried to focus. The 6D Maglite flashlight from the car. Tara always had it in the back of her mind as a possible improvised weapon, if the need should arise – it was the length of a baton. She hadn't imagined she'd be on the receiving end.

Bella was hesitating. She looked torn. Tara tried to struggle up but she felt sick. As she moved, the student brought the torch down again. A last-minute twist meant it was Tara's shoulder that took the blow from the aluminium. If it had struck home…

But it wasn't the end. She could see the torch descending again. It would do the job as well as any bespoke weapon – especially now Tara was down. It caught her on the side of her head again this time, and her vision blurred. She closed her eyes and lay still. Would the student give up?

Tara felt Bella's fingers on her neck. She knew how to check for a pulse, then. There was no way she'd mistake her for dead. Tara strained against the pain and fear, listening to try to get an idea of what Bella was doing. A moment later she felt the woman reach into her coat pocket for her mobile. And then she heard a step, landing on the fallen leaves. Had she moved back a little? Tara risked opening her eyes a crack.

The student was getting into the car. She was in the driver's seat. The keys Tara had been using were still in her pocket – under her hip, the other side to where her phone had been. But there was a spare set in her handbag. She'd left it in the car. Would Bella find it and escape? She wouldn't get far. She allowed herself a breath and closed her eyes again.

But then suddenly, through her lids, she registered light. Even though the car was facing away from where she was lying. The noise of the engine came to her in the same millisecond that she opened her eyes.

But the car was already lurching towards her. Bella was in reverse.

CHAPTER FIFTY-FOUR

'Excuse me, ma'am.' Blake clicked to accept the call on his phone. It was Jez.

'We're on the move towards Wandlebury now. No sign of Gilmour. We've asked the porters to check his room. He's still not answering his phone.'

'Okay. Thanks for the update.'

'We're a bit concerned. We can't get hold of Tara.'

'What?' He was up and out of his seat. Why the hell had the DC left that bit of the update until last?

'No answer from her mobile. If Gilmour's over there she might have engaged with him – or simply switched her phone to silent so that incoming calls don't give her presence away.'

Blake had worked all that out without being told. The guy must think he was a fool. He was at the door now. 'I'll meet you there.'

Fleming raised an eyebrow.

'I think there might be a problem at Wandlebury.'

CHAPTER FIFTY-FIVE

Bella Chadwick had told them she couldn't drive but she knew enough to get into reverse and put her foot down without stalling. Tara only had a split second to react. She couldn't scramble beyond the trees – there was no time.

Glancing to one side she saw a root that stuck up, well above the ground. She rolled towards it so that her upper body was protected. She yanked her legs out of the car's path as far as she could. As she did so, one of her feet came half out of the boot she'd been wearing. The car hit the sole of the boot first. Then Tara felt pain in her toes. If the vehicle carried on reversing it would crush her other ankle. She tried to pull it clear, but Bella had stopped now. Tara couldn't see anything from where she lay, just behind and to one side of the vehicle. What was Bella up to? She must have felt the car connect with something. How long did Tara have before she realised the job wasn't finished?

Bella had cut the car's engine, but Tara hadn't heard her open the driver's side door. Suddenly, she remembered the car keys in her pocket. Her hands were shaking so hard she could hardly manage to hold them. Through the panic, and the excruciating pain in her foot and her head, she tried to engage muscle memory. One click on the lower left-hand side of the remote to activate central locking. One on the upper right to set the alarm.

It was only a second before her actions had the desired effect. Bella must have heard the car's central locking and panicked. It would have been automatic to wrench the driver's door open and, as soon as she did, the car's security system was breached.

Suddenly the woods were filled with noise and light. The vehicle's hazard lights flashed, fast and bright, and the horn sounded. Loud, repeated and insistent.

Bella was out of the car. Through a haze of nausea brought on by pain, Tara could just see the top of her head. For a moment, the student stood stock-still next to the vehicle. Tara wasn't sure anyone would come. Alarms went off all the time and they weren't close to the nearest house. She could only hope that it was enough to make the student run instead of continuing her attack. If she wasn't a regular driver, she might not know how to deactivate the security system.

Her head pounding, foot in agony, Tara slithered her way between the trees, beyond the reach of the car if Bella used it as a weapon again.

A moment later, the girl followed her. She must have left the flashlight behind. She'd swapped it for something that looked more deadly. A wooden post, sharpened to a point at one end. Tara swallowed. It looked like something that had once held up fencing – chicken wire, perhaps, to keep walkers away from private land.

The stake must have been shaped to make it easy to drive into the ground. Pushing it through human flesh would be almost effortless...

CHAPTER FIFTY-SIX

Blake arrived at the Ring neck and neck with Jez and Max. Jez's driving clearly left a lot to be desired. The man stopped his car when he saw Blake appear – didn't he realise the urgency? Blake pulled past them on their inside, pausing just a second when he realised Max had his window down.

'The porters at St Bede's managed to track Gilmour down. He was in the college bar. Denied having made any arrangement to meet Bella Chadwick here. Says he thinks someone's nicked his phone.'

Blake swore. He *might* be lying, if he'd set the whole thing up as a prank. But if not… if not then Bella herself had lured Tara to this deserted place, whilst his team sat in the backstreets of Cambridge, twiddling their thumbs.

The delay in following Tara had been considerable. Why wasn't she answering her phone?

'Come on!' He put his foot down and sped away from Max and Jez down the narrow track, scraping his car on the tree branches that closed in around him.

At that moment, off ahead and to his right, he saw a flash of light. Repeated flashes. A second later he heard an alarm, blaring out into the night.

He followed the noise.

CHAPTER FIFTY-SEVEN

'Bella, think!' Talking was the only route left to Tara. She knew she couldn't run on her damaged foot and there was no other way of outpacing her opponent. 'Whatever's happened, whatever the background, there's a way of making your situation less bad. If you show remorse, and let me go, your lawyer will make the best possible case for you.'

She gasped for breath, the words not coming to mind as quickly as they should. She felt dizzy and everything hurt. For an awful moment she thought she was going to pass out and make Bella's job even easier.

She blinked hard and tried to keep a grip on reality. 'I get the impression – *we* get the impression – that you had a difficult relationship with Julie. You wanted to be her friend, and you maybe felt she wasn't there for you. Perhaps that's why you lashed out as you did. And then maybe' – she swallowed, trying to hold it together, her mouth so dry she could barely speak – 'maybe you panicked. Maybe you thought you'd killed her by accident and you didn't know what to do.'

The cloud had cleared now, and moonlight fell on Bella's face. She looked deathly pale, and devoid of expression, but then suddenly she laughed. On and on, her eyes wide.

Tara didn't dare move. Bella was at her weakest, overtaken by hysteria, but if Tara started to crawl, the unexpected movement might jolt her back to reality. She was just wondering if she had enough strength in her arms to pull the girl's feet out from under her when she saw movement.

A tiny variation in the shadows behind Bella. She fought the urge to react. If it was Stuart, come to find his girlfriend, then she might be done for, but she needed a moment to think before she put Bella on high alert too.

And then suddenly the movement came all at once. Blake seemed to go from being six feet away to being on Bella. He'd grasped the post in her hands and twisted it sharply before the student knew what was happening.

She was unbalanced and that gave Tara the advantage she needed. From where she lay she lurched for the woman's legs, bringing her down in one go.

CHAPTER FIFTY-EIGHT

The hour after Blake had found Tara had gone in a blur. She hadn't even argued when he'd told her to lie down – he could see she was in shock, her hands clammy, her skin ashen. He'd thrown his jacket over her and Max and Jez had added their outer layers. It was only when he'd tried to raise her legs to help her blood supply that he'd realised her foot was injured. He'd kept her awake by telling her what they knew so far – and how carefully Bella had set things up so that they couldn't make contact with Stuart. They'd found his stolen mobile when they'd searched her.

The ambulance came quickly – thank God Addenbrooke's was so close – as did further police backup. When he'd finally left the scene, he'd called in to see Tara's relative, Bea, to explain what had happened. He knew how close she and Tara were, and he didn't want to leave the job to anyone else. At the boarding house she ran, he'd found she wasn't alone. It had been the ex-cop, Paul Kemp, who'd answered the door. It made him see things in a fresh light. He'd often wondered if Kemp and Tara had something going together, but the guy had an air of belonging at Bea's place, somehow. Perhaps Blake had misread the situation.

He was only there for a minute – just long enough to be sure they knew that Tara was okay – and that Bea had the support she needed. Their warmth, and the way they clearly felt about Tara, made him emotional.

As he drove back to the station, he couldn't switch off the slight boost to his mood caused by guessing that Kemp and Tara weren't an item. Though of course, that left the way clear for Jez Fallon. Of the two, he'd definitely rather Tara was with the *ex*-cop, ironically. The guy might have a murky past, but he trusted him more than his new DC. For a split second his mind flipped to Babette. Suddenly, the urgency to sort out his own broken relationship seemed almost overwhelming. But there was no time now.

Back at the station he prepared to interview Bella Chadwick. Megan was going to join him. She was still at work, along with the rest of them, having finished her job on the manslaughter case.

He had his hand on the interview room door when his mobile rang. Tara.

Only it wasn't Tara on the line when he picked up. *'This is Nurse Perez at Addenbrooke's.'* Blake's heart went into overdrive. He knew shock could be dangerous, and Tara had told him Chadwick had hit her about the head. Twice. Yet he'd told Bea she was safe. He fought to keep his voice steady.

'DI Blake speaking.'

'Tara's very unwell.' There was a pause. *'I've told her she shouldn't be trying to deal with work issues until she's fully recovered, but she's extremely agitated and she's been insisting that she be allowed to speak to you. Please can you keep it short? I'll hand you over now.'*

Blake leant against the corridor wall. He felt as though all the breath had gone out of him.

'Yes?' His voice sounded harsh and irritable with anxiety. He cursed inwardly.

'Lovely to speak to you, too.' She sounded reassuringly Tara-like. *'Thank God they finally let me ring. When I was lying on the ground, you told me Bella had stolen Stuart's phone – yes?'*

'Yes.'

'It's just come to me. As we drove off towards Wandlebury, Bella said she'd text him to let him know she was on her way. And then she took out her phone and got busy.'

Blake paused. She must have been bluffing, except why bother? It wasn't as though it would have looked suspicious if she hadn't. 'You think she was really contacting someone else?' A tingle ran down his spine.

'I can't think of any other explanation. And there's one more thing, Blake.'

'Shoot.'

'The green wool that Agneta found underneath Julie's fingernails. Could it have been felt?'

Blake listened as Tara spoke of seeing the harp being loaded into its lined case, ready to be shipped off to Veronica Lockwood's next concert.

'I googled harps,' Tara said. *'Seven stone. Six feet tall.'* He heard her swallow. *'I don't know, but they – one of them – could have fitted Julie into that case. Tonight was weird, Blake.'*

That seemed like quite an understatement, under the circumstances.

'I don't think Bella really wanted to kill me – at least not at first. I've been running through it all in my head. If her heart had been in it, I'd be dead by now.'

Suddenly the line went muffled. *'That's quite enough.'* Nurse Perez was back on the phone. Her words were harsh, but her tone wasn't. He'd never seen Tara cry, but in the background, he thought that's what he could hear. He wanted to ask the nurse to pass on a message, but his feelings weren't anything he could convey via that route. And Megan was by his side, waiting for him. 'Please tell DC Thorpe I'll be in to visit her.'

'And you'll be warmly welcomed… during visitors' hours and only after she has had a chance to recover.'

Blake was prepared to pull rank over that one if required. But now, he had work to do. He went to find Bella's phone. Through the evidence bag that contained it he pressed the home button.

A message flashed up immediately, requesting a PIN. It wasn't unexpected.

A moment later he was in the interview room with Megan, Bella and Bella's solicitor.

'Bella, before we begin our talk, I want you to unlock your phone for me.'

The girl seemed to shrink back into herself.

'If you don't do it, our tech guys will. You'll just save us a few minutes, that's all. You won't gain anything by being obstructive.' In fact, the ease with which it could be done was variable. With some phones, it would depend on guessing the number she'd used, but with any luck she wouldn't know that. The models that needed fingerprint ID could be even more problematic, if the owner had done a runner.

At last Bella took the instrument and unlocked it.

Blake took the mobile from her and went to her text messages. The one she'd have sent when travelling with Tara said: *I don't know how to do it.* There'd been no response.

As Bella, Megan and the solicitor watched, Blake redialled the destination number. It rang three times before the call connected.

'What's the situation?

Blake recognised the clipped, upper-class voice. It was Veronica Lockwood.

CHAPTER FIFTY-NINE

An hour later, Blake was sitting opposite Lady Lockwood at the station. The solicitor next to her looked very well-heeled. He was clearly making way too much money out of his privileged clients. Megan sat to Blake's left.

Chadwick had shut up like a clam after he'd made contact with Veronica. She wouldn't confirm that the woman had been involved, but she couldn't tell them how she'd managed to get Julie's body to Wandlebury without her own transport.

He'd left her to stew whilst he found out what the harpist had to say. The harp itself was being brought back to Cambridge. He was well aware there'd be hell to pay if they'd got this wrong.

'Can you explain to me, please, why Bella Chadwick texted you this evening? What did she mean by "I don't know how to do it"?'

Lady Lockwood raised an eyebrow. 'I spoke to her earlier today when she came to attend the student party at the lodge. I sensed something was upsetting her. When I asked what was wrong it was clear it was boyfriend trouble. I advised her to finish the relationship she was in. I assume she must have been hoping for suggestions on how to go about that.'

'Do you know Bella well, Lady Lockwood?'

The woman's eyes were cold. 'I try to involve myself in the lives of the students as much as possible. If they need a listening ear or a shoulder to cry on, I consider it a privilege to provide that service.'

Blake found that very hard to believe; he didn't have the woman down as the touchy-feely sort. 'You must have done an excellent job, if students feel they can text you for relationship advice when you're trying to pack for a trip to Italy.'

She didn't bother commenting on that.

'The number Bella texted you on isn't the same as the one you gave us. Why is that?'

She raised her eyebrows. 'You surely don't imagine I'd give my personal number out to the students? I support their welfare, but I need to keep some distance too. If I'm working I keep my normal mobile switched on, but silence the one that Bella used.'

'I'd be grateful if you'd let us examine the phone you keep for students.'

'I couldn't possibly allow that. As you can imagine, it contains messages that were sent in confidence.'

'I'm afraid I'll have to request a warrant then. As well as one to take a sample of the lining of your harp case.'

He watched as she blanched. She didn't know about the wool under Julie Cooper's fingernails, but if she was involved, and the student had died inside the case, she must know they were almost certain to find her DNA there.

'We'd better add the boot of your car to the list too. I'm sure you must want to help us with our enquiries.' He caught the woman's eye.

'It's the principle I object to. You have no grounds to suspect me of anything.'

Blake leant back deliberately in his chair. He'd wanted to do the opposite but knew the solicitor would complain if he 'used intimidating body language'. 'Lady Lockwood, you seem to know Bella Chadwick quite well, and it appears – from her text – that when she set out to murder one of my officers, she came to you for advice. This was shortly after my officer left your premises, having commented on the size of your harp case. She'd put two and two together and I think that you – or one of your family – realised that.'

He did lean forward slightly now. 'I think you and Bella Chadwick put together a hasty plan for her to intercept Tara Thorpe before she had the chance to call the station and update us.'

He sat back again. 'If I'm barking up the wrong tree, do let me know and give me access to the areas I want to search. But one thing's for certain, there was no way Bella Chadwick was making plans to dump her boyfriend when she texted you this evening. She'd got other things on her mind. And we have records of other calls she made to you too – before this evening, when you claim she told you about her boyfriend trouble.' Thank God that Bella had unlocked her phone. It had saved a lot of time. 'I expect she'll tell us more soon. If you'd like to get your story in first, I suggest you start now.'

CHAPTER SIXTY

Veronica Lockwood's solicitor had asked for a few moments alone with her client after Blake had summed up his thoughts.

Fifteen minutes later they were all assembled again. Once the recorder was going, Blake turned to the woman.

'You've got more to tell us?' He could see from her face that she was building up to something.

She took a deep breath. 'I can see I need to let you have the full story. I've been a fool, and I'll have to leave it to the authorities to decide what to do.' She pursed her lips. 'Bella Chadwick seems to have had a strange relationship with Julie Cooper. As I said to you before, I try to involve myself with the students, and I couldn't help noticing the pair of them around St Oswald's. Bella followed Julie everywhere, dressed as she dressed, pretended to be interested in the causes Julie championed. Anyone will tell you. I think she wanted to *be* Julie – it was clear she was after Julie's ex-boyfriend, Stuart. I only found out about that triangle by talking to Bella and Julie's tutor, Lucien. He has his ear to the ground.'

What would he have felt about Bella and Stuart, Blake wondered, if he and Bella had been sleeping together at one point? Where did that fit into all this? 'Go on.'

Lockwood inclined her head. 'I managed to get Bella talking – I thought she might need help. That's why there are lots of calls on her mobile to my "student" number. Once she started to confide, it all came flooding out.'

Blake looked at her steadily, waiting, letting her know he was judging her every word. 'Go on,' he said at last. 'Tell me what happened on Saturday.'

Lockwood sighed. 'I wish to God I'd gone with Alistair to London now. As it was, I went for a walk around the college grounds after I'd practised my harp for a couple of hours. I needed the fresh air. I bumped into Julie and Bella out there. I assume they were coming to see where their new accommodation was, before moving their things back in. Anyway, I could hear from a distance that they were arguing. Something about their interaction set my alarm bells ringing. I sensed Bella was close to the edge, and in the end I decided I'd have to intervene. It was the last thing I wanted – I needed more time to practise – but I invited them into the Master's Lodge to talk about their differences.' She shook her head. 'It was over that lad, of course – Stuart. I couldn't calm either of them down. It was evening, and I thought I'd offer them both a stiff drink, see if that would help. But when my back was turned, Bella picked up a heavy decanter and smashed it side-on into Julie's head.'

Blake mentally added the item to the list of things forensics would need to examine.

'I was so shocked that I just stood there. Julie had dropped to the floor – her head was bleeding and she was deathly still.'

She put her hands over her face.

'I knew Bella had problems. I should have called the police – but I felt for her. She'd killed Julie as a result of losing control in my house. If I hadn't invited them in, it would never have happened. Bella had used one of my possessions as a weapon. In that moment, I realised two things. If I called the police, it wouldn't save Julie, and equally it would ruin the rest of Bella's life. Whereas if I helped Bella cover up what she'd done, I could make it my duty to ensure she got the help she needed. Then at least one of the two of them would have a future.'

She met Blake's gaze. 'I can see it was wrong now – but at the time it seemed logical. I think I was in shock. And of course, once the die was cast, it was too late to go back.'

'So you thought Julie was dead?'

Veronica Lockwood blinked. 'What do you mean?'

Surely she'd have checked for a pulse, under the circumstances? 'You didn't look for a heartbeat, or realise that Julie was still breathing?'

'She wasn't.' Lockwood caught her breath. 'I mean, I'm sure she wasn't. You only had to look at her—'

Blake didn't reply. 'What did you do next?'

He saw her swallow. 'We carried her down to the basement and put her in my harp case. I just wanted to get her out of sight until we'd worked out what to do. It was too early to move her – too much of a risk that we'd be seen. And if anyone had come calling… So we moved her down there, and then came back upstairs again. Bella went back to the house where she and Julie had been lodging, but we agreed we'd meet up later to get Julie's body away from the lodge.'

'What time did you ask her to return?'

'Two a.m. It took a while to get Julie's body back upstairs and out to the car. We covered the boot with bin liners before we lifted her.' She looked down into her lap. 'I already knew then that I'd made the most horrific mistake in deciding to protect Bella in that way. Looking down at Julie as we carried her – feeling her dead weight – brought it all home. But it was too late by then.'

'Whose idea was it to put flowers in her pocket, and to remove Stuart's ring? It threw suspicion onto Gilmour, specifically.'

Lockwood shook her head, slowly. 'Bella's. She was still jealous. I tried to stop her, once I realised what she had planned, but she was crazed. She must have collected the flowers on her way over to the lodge. It was clear to me then that she'd been obsessing about the best way to cover her tracks, as well as to get her revenge by directing the police's attention towards Stuart. It was one more thing that made me realise saving Bella would be much more complicated than I'd thought. Fatally injuring Julie hadn't been an isolated action or a tragic twist of fate. Bella is unbalanced.'

'What about the flowers Bella says she saw in Julie's bike basket before she was killed? And the heart that was sent in advance of her death?'

'I don't know about those. Could Bella have invented them?'

Blake didn't answer that one. He thought of the text Bella had sent to Veronica Lockwood when she was sitting alongside Tara. 'If your story is true, perhaps you'd like to tell me what Bella meant by her text: "I don't know how to do it."'

The woman sat up stiffly. There was no emotion in her eyes. 'Bella was consumed with guilt about what she'd done – and I felt the same. I'd begun to think the whole thing was unsustainable. The idea of admitting to the part I'd played was horrific – but living with the guilt was worse. I managed to have a quick word with Bella at this evening's party. She mentioned she'd met a detective that she liked – someone she felt she could talk to. I said—' She paused a moment and closed her eyes. 'I said maybe she should find a way to tell her the truth. I'd got to the point where I felt we'd have to, but I wanted Bella to be the one to admit her own guilt. I'm afraid her text was a cry for help. She couldn't work out how to confess. I couldn't think how to respond to her, so I did nothing. And instead of managing to be honest, Bella clearly attacked your officer. I don't know why she would have done that.'

'If you were ready for the whole thing to come out, why not just tell me all this the moment we brought you in?'

'I was worried you'd think I was involved in the attack on Tara Thorpe. Everything was suddenly out of control. I should have just trusted in the law and explained. In fact, I should have done that from the start.'

Fine words. Blake might even have believed them if he hadn't had access to Julie Cooper's phone and laptop – and heard about the trip the Lockwoods had made just before their younger son went off the rails. The woman opposite him was intelligent and rational. And cold. Not the sort to put her own future and the name of her family on the line to protect a troubled young student.

He thought of the call she'd made to her son John, just before he'd taken the pills and drunk himself into a permanent oblivion.

'That's all very interesting.' He sat back in his chair. 'And now, perhaps you'd like to tell me about Scotland.'

CHAPTER SIXTY-ONE

Tara was lying in her hospital bed. It turned out the injuries weren't as bad as they could have been. Breaks that would heal in time. The painkillers she'd been given weren't perfect, but she felt a hell of a lot better than she had. There was still a dull ache in her head though, and the staff were watching her like hawks, despite the reassuring scans.

It was late, but Kemp and Bea had been allowed in to see her as immediate family, even though visiting hours were long since over. Bea had already passed on the news that her mother had been on the point of heading over too, driving across from the Fens. Cue a spike in blood pressure. Only she'd been told by the hospital staff that tomorrow really would be better. Tara wouldn't have to deal with Lydia until the morning.

'Is there anything you need from home?' Bea asked.

'A change of underwear and a random selection of books would be wonderful, if it's not too much trouble.'

Her mother's cousin nodded. 'Will do.'

Kemp scratched his chin. 'Shame I never covered "action to take when some maniac tries to run you down with a car" in my self-defence drilling.'

Tara managed a half-smile. 'You gave me back my fighting spirit – and I sure as hell needed that this evening.' She still felt shaky. Each time she closed her eyes she saw Bella towering above her, holding the stake. She needed to focus on something else. 'I can't believe I'm stuck in here whilst they're trying to wrap up the case.'

Bea leant forward. 'They'll do it. You need to rest. You're no good to them in future if you ruin your health now.'

Tara reached to give her hand a squeeze. 'Don't worry. I'll be fine.'

'Yeah.' Kemp leant forward. 'You'll be good.' He turned to Bea. 'And you can see Tara's point. If you're going to take a beating over a case, you don't want to be shut out when things come to a head.'

Bea gave him an exasperated look. 'You are no help at all.'

Kemp grinned. 'Always happy to hinder. So, what would you be investigating, if you weren't stuck in here?'

'The Scotland connection. John went off the rails when he was a boy, after a family holiday there, and Julie seems to have minded about him – as well as having it in for his father's firm. I don't know what happened, all those years ago, but I think she was onto it. She'd been googling for information, and she'd noted "Scotland" as something to look into on her phone.'

Tara thought back to her ex, Josh's, words. *Unless Julie had evidence of Sir Alistair killing someone with his bare hands, I just can't see him being your man.*

'I wonder if the Lockwoods somehow got wind that a very old secret was in danger of coming out. Perhaps that's what made Julie a deadly threat.' Her headache was getting worse and she frowned. 'But then I don't understand Bella's involvement. Jez was investigating the Scotland angle – just to find out whether it was Veronica or Alistair's mother who lived there, for a start. But I don't think he'll have got far. He and Max were busy giving me backup instead.'

Bea was looking furious, her ire directed towards Kemp. 'This is making her worse.' She nodded at Tara.

'I'd feel worse still if I didn't get it off my chest – honestly.' But a nurse was on her way over too now, a stern look on her face.

'Don't worry, mate,' Kemp said. 'I'll look into it for you.'

Tara had been wondering how much information she could get on her phone, but as she sank back against the pillows, she suddenly realised that, for once, she was going to have to stop being a control freak. 'Thanks, Kemp. I don't know what year it was. The summer when John was twelve, maybe? Something like that. Let me know, but above all, keep Blake up to date. If it was something that happened in the family home, we might never find out. But if it caused any kind of public ripple, there's just a chance.'

Bea was bending down to give her the gentlest of hugs. She didn't have far to lean, she was so tiny. Kemp followed suit, rather more clumsily. She made every effort not to wince.

As they walked out of the door she felt tears well up. They were both there for her – each in such different ways, but both gave her comfort. As for the Scotland connection, she hoped Blake wouldn't mind her confiding in Kemp. She was using him as an extension of herself.

But would he find anything, after so many years? It seemed like the slimmest of chances.

CHAPTER SIXTY-TWO

Now they had two witnesses who weren't talking. Blake was in Fleming's office with Megan.

'What's your opinion?' the DCI said.

Blake flexed his shoulders, trying to reduce the tension in them and think straight. 'Veronica Lockwood's story doesn't ring true. We need to get Bella Chadwick to give her version of events. Then we can start to pick the evidence apart.'

'You think Lady Lockwood's indulging in personal and family damage limitation?'

Blake nodded.

'Why would Chadwick clam up? And if you think Lady Lockwood is lying, what's your theory about the real course of events?'

That was the problem. Blake wasn't sure. 'Bella might be staying silent because she's protecting the Lockwoods for some reason. Or because they have a hold over her, that's worse than everything that's coming out.' Hard to imagine. 'Or' – he frowned, marshalling his thoughts – 'they could have promised her something for taking the rap. Sir Alistair's worth a fortune. Maybe they've convinced her she can get off lightly for saying she killed Julie on the spur of the moment, and claiming diminished responsibility.'

'It's not impossible.' Fleming frowned. 'Equally, it's not impossible that Lady Lockwood *is* telling the truth. A lot of her statement ties in with what we know about Bella and her relationship with Julie and Stuart.' She held up a hand. 'I know what you're going to say, there is this point about Scotland, but that's thin, Blake. And we have no proper evidence.'

But Blake had seen Veronica Lockwood's reaction to that word. There was something there.

'Go back in and have another go at Chadwick,' Fleming said. 'Make her realise that no one can protect her, and her best defence is to tell the truth. Use what we know. If Tara's right and Bella didn't really want to kill her, playing on her emotions might work.'

They were back in the interview room. The recorder was running again, and Chadwick's solicitor was standing by. Her client certainly looked a lot more emotional than Veronica Lockwood had.

'We've just had word from the hospital, Bella.' It was Megan who spoke, as they'd arranged. Blake had got the impression Bella had warmed to her, the day they'd all first met. His DS was doing better than he'd given her credit for. 'Tara's in a bad way. They've been running lots of tests to see what damage you did when you attacked her.'

There was silence.

'She's been in and out of consciousness,' Blake said. *Well, she'd probably dropped off once or twice since she'd been admitted.* 'She was so shocked as well. To be honest, I think she felt you'd almost become friends. I know she was worried about everything you were going through.'

More silence, but he could see a tear run down Chadwick's cheek.

'And she was convinced you were genuinely upset about Julie's death.'

'I was!'

The words came out in a rush, and Chadwick looked shocked at the sound of her own cracked voice. Of course, if Lockwood's story was true, that wouldn't stop Chadwick being sorry for what she'd done. They needed to choose their next words very carefully.

He nodded. 'Tara will be glad to know she was right. If we're able to tell her.'

The student's eyes met his, full of tears now. 'You think she'll die?'

'She's been badly injured. We're reliant on the hospital doctors to update us on her prognosis. She was conscious when I arrived at the scene.' And afterwards too, in fact. 'She told me she didn't think you'd wanted to kill her.'

Chadwick sat up straighter. 'I didn't.'

'Bella,' Megan's voice was gentle, 'whatever anyone's told you, your best option here is to explain why you did what you did. You're sad that Julie is dead, and you didn't want to hurt our colleague Tara – we can see that. That makes me feel that you've been forced into this situation. Whatever you think about the future, whatever options you imagine might give you the best chance, you've got to believe me that telling the truth now is actually what will help your case the most.' She paused a moment. 'Not only that, but it's the right thing to do. You look to me as though you want to do the right thing.'

Megan's tone was spot on. He couldn't fault her words, or the way she said them. He applauded inwardly. He must make sure he told her how good she'd been, afterwards.

'You do want to do the right thing, don't you, Bella?'

At last, the student nodded.

'Why don't you start at the beginning? Tell us what happened on Saturday.'

But Bella shook her head. 'The beginning is way before that.' For a second, she buried her head in her hands. 'It all started when Lucien Balfour made a pass at me after one of the student socials he ran.'

CHAPTER SIXTY-THREE

Bea had gone to bed, though Kemp was willing to bet she wasn't asleep. She was going through the wringer. It was different for him: he was protective of Tara too, but he saw her as an equal. Bea might only be five years older than him, but she treated Tara as a mother would treat their child.

Kemp owed it to Tara to investigate what had happened in Scotland. Besides, he was just as consumed with curiosity, and the thrill of the chase, as she was. For a moment, he thought of her, bruised and weak in her hospital bed. The fact that she'd been willing to hand this job over to him made him emotional – both because it showed how ill she was, and because of her trust in him.

In reality, Kemp didn't rate his chances of success. Whatever had happened up there, it was years ago now. And it might have been something that took place in private. It was probably only Julie Cooper's connection with John that meant she'd got wind of it.

But if it provoked so much fear in the family, it must have been something serious, which meant there might be evidence left behind, if the incident hadn't happened behind closed doors. He'd found the name of the village where Veronica Lockwood's mother had lived: a remote place in the Highlands. It was lucky that it was mentioned on Veronica's Wikipedia page – she'd spent some of her childhood there.

Now he started to search for online records, but it was hard to guess the right terms to use. In the end he settled for 'unsolved', 'crime' and 'scandal' together with the name of the village. It was a start. Shame he didn't know exactly which year to home in on. And the internet had been much less well used back then, too.

He went to get a beer from the fridge and sat back down, frowning at the page of results, which included a local story about a missing sheepdog.

No one had said it was going to be easy.

CHAPTER SIXTY-FOUR

'It wasn't just me,' Bella Chadwick said. 'Lucien Balfour tries it on with all his female students.'

'We've heard similar reports, whilst we've been investigating this case,' Megan replied.

'Most of my friends got upset, but they weren't confident enough to complain. If we'd all banded together it might have worked, but everyone was worried about the effect Lucien could have on their lives at the college.'

Blake felt his blood pressure rise once again.

'When Lucien started work on me, he made subtle hints about how he could make sure my grades improved, if we "spent some time together" so he could give me some more "intensive help".' She looked down at the table for a moment. 'He used the fact that I hadn't been doing well in my classes. He said he could talk to my supervisors, explain I was having emotional problems and that they should make some allowances when marking my work.' She hung her head. 'I'd been so worried about my parents' reaction when they found out how badly I was doing, academically. I knew he just wanted sex. As for his promises of help – the approach might work for the odd essay, but not when my annual exam papers went off to some unbiased marker.'

'But you still agreed to sleep with him,' Blake said.

She nodded, and a tear rolled down her cheek. 'It meant I could put off the confrontation with my parents, even if it was only for a few months. I hoped that I could somehow turn my grades around before things came to a head.'

Trapped by three authority figures, each of whom had had such an unhealthy effect on the decisions she'd made. Blake felt like crying himself. 'What happened then?'

'Lucien kept his side of the bargain. I could tell, because some of my supervisors took me aside to ask about my problems, and occasionally I'd get a note on my work, saying my grades had been "adjusted" because of my circumstances. It wasn't done subtly. I was in Lucien's room one day, feeling utterly disgusted with myself. He was asleep next to me, and it suddenly occurred to me that I could take a photo of us together. I was scared, but the feeling of revulsion took over, and made me braver than I might have been. It wasn't right that he was getting away with it.'

She shuddered. 'After that, I started to plan ahead. I didn't think the photo would be enough – I could have been a willing participant in the affair. So, the next time we met, I nerved myself up and recorded our conversation on my phone. I just left it going in a zipped jacket pocket, but the results were clear enough. The file gave away how he coerced me. I was planning to turn everything over to the police. I wasn't sure I could trust the college authorities to act.'

'What happened?'

'Lucien had another go at getting me to sleep with him before I'd got as far as bringing my evidence here. I told him to leave me alone and, when he pushed me, I let on about the evidence I'd got.'

'You must have been frightened,' Megan said.

She nodded. 'The moment I said it, I wondered what he might do. I thought he'd hit the roof, but I think he was actually scared himself. He asked me to give him twenty-four hours before reporting him; he'd make it worth my while.'

'What happened then?'

She pressed clenched fists against her forehead. 'I waited, like he said. My parents are expecting big things from me, but I only got into Cambridge by the skin of my teeth. I've been struggling ever since. I think I'll fail. My family will be furious, and who gets a job when they've failed their degree? Lucien's foul but he's not stupid. He knew what mattered to me. Before the day was up, he told me he'd got a solution that would solve my worries, and if I surrendered the evidence I had on him, he'd take me to Alistair Lockwood, who would tell me all about it.'

'What did you think was coming?'

She swallowed and shook her head. 'I didn't know. But I'd already realised that Lucien and Sir Alistair were close – they went to the same school, and our tutor left us in no doubt about who the master would believe, if we went running to him with our complaints.' Her tone was bitter. 'I should never have bargained with him. It was wrong.'

'What happened next?'

Chadwick licked her lips and Megan pushed the glass of water they'd poured for her further towards her side of the desk.

After taking a sip, the student went on. 'It turned out there was room for a sort of three-way deal. We each had something the other two wanted. I wanted security – a way of ensuring I wouldn't fail in life. Lucien wanted my silence, and the master – he wanted my help.'

Blake frowned. 'What were you able to do for him?'

'I was close to Julie, and she was a threat to him. At first, he just wanted the information I already had on her. She'd crossed his radar when she went on various marches against Lockwood's, and then he got word that she was in an illicit relationship with his son, John. He thought it was that way round, and that she'd maybe hooked up with him to try to find out more about the family. But I was able to tell him it had been the other way about. Julie's protests against the business became more extreme *after* she'd met John. I can remember telling Sir Alistair that, the day when I went to meet him at the Master's Lodge. And the fact seemed to worry him. I think he suspected John had shared personal information with Julie that had made her feel sorry for him. She seemed to want to fight his corner, against his parents.'

She took another sip of water and blinked. Her eyes were dry now, but wide. She recounted events as though she was in a trance.

'He made me an offer. I was to watch Julie: stick to her like glue, get myself into the same friendship groups as her and onto the same marches. He wanted me in her room, looking at her papers, peering over her shoulder to see what websites she was browsing. I was to report it all back to him – secretly, regularly. And if I did all that, so that he knew how far she was getting with her research on his firm and his family, he promised me there would always be a job for me with Lockwood's. Not just something junior – a really well-paid executive role. I wouldn't have to worry about passing my finals, or any of that. The only other thing he asked of me in return was to drop any idea of complaining about Lucien. It's possible Lucien had some idea of what the master was getting out of the deal, and Sir Alistair bought his silence by making me stay quiet too.'

The building bricks Blake had erected when assessing Bella's character and motivations had started to wobble as she spoke, and one by one they'd come falling down. 'You dressed like Julie to try to fit in with her crowd?'

The student nodded. 'It came across as false. I overdid it, but I'd got no experience of trying anything like that before. It was akin to working undercover, acting as a spy.'

'Didn't you feel guilty, for betraying your friend?' Megan asked.

Bella winced. 'It didn't seem that harmful. And, to be honest, I always thought she went completely over the top with her protests and causes, so I could understand Sir Alistair being irritated by her efforts. It never occurred to me that anything I did would affect her future. But going along with Sir Alistair's wishes secured mine – and that was a huge deal to me. Julie would have got top grades. She never had to worry. Or at least,' her voice cracked, 'that's what I thought.'

Her sense of priorities made Blake's insides contract. He paused for a moment. 'Did your brief from Sir Alistair expand to include Stuart Gilmour?'

The girl nodded. 'The master wasn't sure how much Julie had shared with him. Or how much information he'd managed to acquire, rather.'

Blake raised an eyebrow. 'What do you mean by that?'

'That's what split them up. They both wanted careers as journalists.' She took a great gulp and a sob escaped her. 'Julie wanted to do some good – unmask wrongdoing – all that kind of thing. Sometimes I felt I couldn't ever be PC enough for her. But she cared. I shouldn't have mocked her.'

'But Stuart's different?'

She shivered and nodded. 'He's just driven by his own ambition. He'd worked out that if he could break a really huge story, he'd be made. Probably get a top job on one of the national newspapers. All of that. He got the idea that Julie was onto something big about Lockwood's. At first, he tried to persuade her to share her research. When she refused, he took to bullying her.'

'Yet she agreed to see him over the summer.'

Bella nodded. 'I knew he'd visited. And afterwards Julie said she thought he'd taken some notes of hers, so I guess that was his reason for worming his way in. I tried to find out what was going on, as part of my work for the master, but I never got to the bottom of it.'

Blake remembered the text Gilmour had sent Julie. *Read this! I know about John. And I've got evidence. Now tell me you don't want to talk.* Had he meant evidence about their relationship? Or had he been trying to tell her he'd got the information that she'd been looking for? If so, had it been a bluff? Either way, he'd known how to blag his way into Julie's room.

'Gilmour's been pretty cagey with us each time we've interviewed him,' Blake said. 'Is he involved in what happened to Julie at all?'

Bella's eyes were desolate as she shook her head. 'I followed him just recently – so I could make my report to Sir Alistair. I saw him talking to the editor of *Uncovered*, the student paper Julie worked on. They argued. My guess is that he's still trying to find the story he thinks Julie was onto. And maybe to work out for himself who killed her. He could sell the scoop to one of the nationals.'

There was a moment's silence.

'So, bring us up to date,' Blake said. 'It's going to be hard, but you've done really well so far. What happened in the run-up to Saturday? Did something occur that put Sir Alistair on high alert?'

Bella shook her head, not meeting their eyes. 'That's not exactly how it was. I went to see Julie in her room, and she'd been doodling on her pad. She'd written Scotland and another name – a place name it looked like. I asked her what that was all about. She just shook her head and said nothing, but I noticed, after that, that she covered the pad up with a pile of books and shut her laptop lid. She was being secretive, and I got the impression it was far from nothing.' She shrank down in her chair as she spoke. 'When she went to the loo, I took a photo of the pad on my phone. I wasn't due to see the master that day, but he'd been pushing me to find out more. He didn't believe I was digging deeply enough. And suddenly, here was something fresh.' Her eyes were welling up again. 'By that time, I was scared of him, instead of my parents. So, I went to the lodge, but he was away. Lady Lockwood invited me in, and I could tell she knew exactly what I'd been asked to do. She wanted me to pass on my news to her, in case it was urgent.'

'So, you showed her the photo you'd taken?' Megan said.

There was a long pause before she nodded. 'I knew the moment I saw her face that I was right – I'd hit on something crucial. She went very pale, and I could see how hard she was gripping my phone. Her knuckles were white. She asked me if I knew why Julie had written the words, but I had no idea.'

Blake was guessing that fact had saved Bella's life.

'She told me to call Julie that evening. I was to tell her that Lady Lockwood needed to confide in her, and when she knew the truth she'd understand. I wasn't to go back to our lodgings, but I should offer to meet Julie outside the lodge so that we could see Lady Lockwood together, for safety and moral support.' Bella gulped back a sob and shook her head. 'I actually thought Julie would be pleased – that Lady Lockwood was going to pass on some kind of secret.'

Blake felt sick to the stomach.

'I called Julie and she came straight away, as I'd asked. I understand now why Lady Lockwood arranged things as she did. If anyone saw Julie leaving our lodgings, she wanted to make sure they saw her alone. And she wanted her to leave for the lodge in a hurry, so she didn't have time to tell anyone else what she was up to.' Bella shook her head. 'She wouldn't have, anyway. She always worked independently.'

'So, you went into the lodge together?' Blake's own throat felt dry now.

Bella nodded. 'Lady Lockwood poured us a gin and tonic each, then went back to the drinks table. I thought she was about to pour one for herself. But instead of doing that she swung the decanter round and smashed it into the side of Julie's head.'

Bella buried her head in her arms, down on the table. 'I still can't believe it! I went from having some kind of job and a future, to seeing my friend killed. I had no idea what she was planning.'

'Julie wasn't dead. Not at that point. Why didn't you raise the alarm?'

'I couldn't speak.' She lifted her head slightly. 'I was shaking all over and Lady Lockwood was still holding the decanter. She looked wild. She told me I must have realised what would have to happen if Julie found out something important. She said I was an accessory. It was my evidence that she was acting on, and I'd brought Julie to her. No one would believe I was innocent if it was her word against mine. Everyone knew I was obsessed with Julie and that I wanted her boyfriend.' Her voice was muffled as she put her head back down on her arms again. 'She'd done her homework, you see. That was how it looked. And I genuinely had fancied Stuart. We'd been having sex for a while.'

'So, she persuaded you to help her?'

Bella nodded. 'Julie was unconscious, so we carried her down to the basement and put her in Lady Lockwood's harp case and fastened the lid.' She sat up again now, her eyes wide with horror. 'We went back upstairs but after a minute we could hear her, struggling down below. Lady Lockwood told me to leave. It was too late now. She made it clear that if I said nothing, the Lockwood family would always look after me, but if I told, she'd put her own spin on what had happened.'

She'd done that all right, but Bella could still have done the right thing. If only she'd gone for help immediately. The situation could have been so different...

'I had the keys to Julie's room. I removed the page of the notepad with the place name on it. Lady Lockwood had made me promise to take it to her that night, so she could see it was destroyed. And then I planted the heart, cut up into tiny pieces. She had various ideas about how to make the murder look like a crime of passion. She'd got it all planned. She must have worked quickly after I showed her the photograph of Julie's notes.' Bella's hands were shaking.

'You made it up, then, about Julie being sent the heart in advance, and about someone putting flowers in her bike basket?'

She nodded, once again not meeting his eyes. 'Lady Lockwood thought of various… refinements that would help build up the right picture. It was she that suggested I should tell Tara Thorpe that I suspected her son, John, of being guilty of the murder, too.

'On the night Julie died, in the small hours, I went back to the Master's Lodge. The basement was quiet by then. I helped Lady Lockwood carry Julie's body from there to her car. We lined the boot with bin bags before we put her in.' Blake couldn't imagine the memories in Bella's mind. 'We drove to Wandlebury Ring and heaved her body into the clearing. It looked like the sort of place where lovers might meet in secret. Lady Lockwood had collected some flowers from the college gardens. She put them in Bella's pocket, and tugged off Stuart's ring. She was violent about it. She even messed around with her underwear – yanking at it.' Bella was shaking her head sharply now, as though the action could rid her of the images that were stuck in her mind.

'She said it was because it would make it look as though a boyfriend had done it in a fit of anger, but it was she who was furious. She blamed Julie for sticking her nose in. That was how it seemed. On the drive back into town she said she should have been practising her harp all evening.'

'And you never saw Sir Alistair that night, or made contact with him?'

She shook her head. 'Lady Lockwood was expecting him, but in the end he didn't come home. She was nervous the whole time, thinking he'd turn up at any moment – or that he might have been back whilst we were over at the Ring – so she must have been worried about acting without his input.'

It seemed he really had stayed in London, as he claimed.

'Does he know what went on now?'

'I don't think so.'

'And what about tonight?'

'Lady Lockwood thought Tara had clicked. Apparently, she said something to Douglas Lockwood about the harp case. His mother saw them talking and asked what had been said. The moment she heard, she called me and told me we were under threat. She said I had to get Tara Thorpe somewhere remote and get rid of her. I couldn't believe what she was asking of me, but I felt trapped and utterly alone. I hadn't got a clue what to do, but Wandlebury came to mind again. I'd left the party at the lodge early and I was with Stuart when she called. I came up with a story, and pinched his mobile, so no one would be able to reach him to verify what I said. I was very short of time, but Lady Lockwood said she'd sent Douglas after Detective Thorpe, to hold her up.'

'He was in on the plan?'

She shook her head. 'I don't think so. She just asked him to check if there were any updates. I ran, hell for leather, to make it to St Oswald's in time to catch Detective Thorpe. I was genuinely panicking – I could hardly breathe – so when I told my story, my fear was real. But it wasn't Stuart I was frightened of – it was Lady Lockwood, and my own situation. I was having to make split-second decisions and I tried to go through with Lady Lockwood's instructions. I felt as though I had to – I was in too deep. But I've never wanted to kill anyone. I could have done it. I had the chance – especially when I was standing there with the stake. But in reality, even if you hadn't turned up and taken it off me, I'd never have gone through with it.'

Her principles hadn't saved Julie though – and Tara's head injuries could have killed her. Even before the scheme had turned violent, she'd been prepared to sell her friend down the river for the promise of a well-paid job. But perhaps her mind had been twisted by parents who cared about results and status more than they did about their daughter. He swallowed back all he wanted to say and glanced at Megan, who came to the rescue.

'You still don't know the significance of the words written on Julie's pad?'

'Scotland? And the other place name?' Bella sagged in her chair. 'No. I caused the death of my own friend, and I still have no idea why.'

And given the inconclusive search results in Julie's internet history, Blake had a feeling she hadn't known either. It made his heart ache.

CHAPTER SIXTY-FIVE

Blake stood in his kitchen, back in Fen Ditton, nearing the bottom of a large measure of whisky. It was past 3 a.m. now, but he couldn't bring himself to sit down, much less go to bed. The case sent him pacing round the room. That place in Scotland – what did it mean? And swirling in amongst the questions that remained came thoughts of Tara in hospital, and of Babette, upstairs in bed, and the words between him and his wife, as yet unsaid.

Battening down his feelings during the day, and quashing the desire to rehearse questions about Matt Smith and his wife's relationship, had left him full of pent-up anger. How could she have told him such a fundamental lie? Let him think Kitty's father had been a fleeting connection – a fling who didn't live up to expectations when she ran away with him?

Now, with the whisky warming his insides, and the lack of sleep loosening the control he might have hung on to, all his frustration came to the surface. The lid of the box he kept his feelings in was off.

And at that moment, he heard the stairs creak.

A second later, Babette was standing in the kitchen doorway, her hair tousled, eyes sleepy, a pout on her lips.

'I thought I saw a light on down here. You could at least come to bed and lie next to me, now you're in the house. It wouldn't compensate for never seeing you in the day, but it would be a start.'

If it hadn't been for the whisky, the case, and the late hour – or for her lies, her selfishness, and her cowardice – he might not have thrown his glass down onto the tiles, watching it smash into what looked like a hundred pieces.

He heard Babette gasp, and she took a step back. 'Garstin – what the hell?'

But it had given him the release he needed – brought him back to reality. For an anxious moment he listened for any sound from the children, but all was quiet upstairs.

He walked behind Babette, crunching shards from the tumbler underfoot, and closed the kitchen door. 'We need to talk.'

'How can we possibly talk? I can't even walk to sit at the table now you've covered the floor in glass.'

'You don't have to sit to talk. I got into a conversation with your mother about Matt Smith.' He watched her eyes, saw the uncertainty there. She'd have no idea how much had been said, so she wouldn't know how to frame her lies.

'So you know…'

He nodded. 'I know.' He wasn't going first.

'Garstin.' She tiptoed round the fragments of his whisky tumbler. 'I let you think he was a brief fling, little more than a one-night stand, because it seemed so much more hurtful to admit the truth. It doesn't alter the facts. When I ran off with him, I realised I'd made the most massive mistake of my life. It was you that I loved.'

She put her hand up to his cheek. He put his hand on hers, then wrapped his fingers round it and yanked it away.

'Not good enough. I can't be in a marriage that's built on lies. It's too much. You knew him for *years*, Babette.' He caught his breath; paused to stop himself from shouting. 'Your mother said the relationship was too passionate to be stable – on–off for all that time. So forgive me if I don't believe your story about why you came home again. If you'd been in love with him for that long, there's no way you'd have given up on your relationship after two weeks, because he wasn't being sufficiently attentive to Kitty. You'd gone to bloody Australia, for God's sake. You'd have told him how you felt, and you'd have worked at it. You came back for another reason. And frankly, I don't even care what that was any more. This is the end. I can't live with someone who lies to me in such a casual way.'

Babette dropped into a chair at the table, her eyes wide, face white. 'I've left out information to protect you. We can be happy.' He could hear the desperation in her voice. 'We *were* happy.'

Blake's heartbeat was in overdrive. 'We were, but that was a long time ago. It's over, Babette. I'll always want to be a part of Kitty and Jessica's lives, and we mustn't expose them to this any more than we have to – but staying together would be worse for them now. No one benefits from growing up in this sort of atmosphere.'

Babette was looking down at the table. There was a long pause before she lifted her head. 'You never got past Kitty being another man's, did you?'

Was that really what she thought? She didn't know him at all. That was the one part of all this that meant nothing. He was too angry to speak. The kitchen was silent apart from the noise of his own ragged breathing. A second later, he was aware of a slighter sound: that of Babette crying.

'Garstin, you're right. I've tied myself in knots. I should have told you everything, properly, from the moment I asked you to take me back. I—' She gulped for air. 'I just didn't know how. The truth is…' She paused again and put her head in her hands. 'The truth is, Kitty *is* yours.'

For a second he felt winded. It was as though time had stopped and all he could feel was a sort of pressure, pushing at his head and body, stopping him from moving or breathing.

'What?' But the effect only lasted for a moment. Of course, this was just one more lie; one more last-ditch attempt to get him to stay, and a wild one at that.

Babette took a deep breath. 'You remember I got a DNA test done? Matt had been away for a while, traveling, but when he came back he got interested in Kitty. He said if she was his that I should leave you. We could make a new life together. He's always been very… mercurial, I guess you'd say. Suddenly he was all for making us a permanent thing, and he loved the idea of being a father. He'd never wanted to commit before – and I thought he never would.'

Which was why she'd decided to marry Blake, presumably. A second-best option.

'I took a sample of Matt's hair, but I got two tests done: one using yours, from your hairbrush, and one using his. It was yours that came back positive. He didn't know what I'd done, and there were no names on the test of course, so I just showed him the positive result – same as I did you. And you both believed me that he was the father.'

His eyes felt wide and dry. The breathlessness was getting worse. 'And you told me to stay out of Kitty's life and let her be with her natural dad. You said it would be selfish if I tried to follow you, or make contact with her. You made me believe that I had no place in her future, and it was my duty – for her sake – to let her forget me.' He could hardly see the room around him. Everything blurred with his effort to contain his anger.

'It was colossally stupid – a dreadful mistake. And I was the one that was selfish – I can see that now, Garstin. I was a fool. That's what I've always told you. I've regretted what I did every minute of every day since. But at least you know Kitty's yours now.'

Far from it – she'd say anything – but it was irrelevant. It was all he could do not to shake her. 'I've never cared about that! I've always loved her and I always will, whether she's mine, Matt Smith's or the milkman's!' He'd let his voice get louder, but he managed to rein it in. 'Babette, it's your deceit I can't stand. Your attitude to me. Can't you see that?' He thought for a moment. 'So, let me guess. He found out? Is that why you came home?' It was the logical conclusion – big enough to send her running after two short weeks in Australia.

She hung her head. 'You've got to believe me, Garstin – I realised I'd made a mistake on my way to the airport before we flew out in the first place. I kept thinking of your face as I took Kitty away. And on the flight out, Matt had no patience with her at all. It was awful. The draw he'd always had for me, over the years, always unattainable, always desirable, started to fade very quickly.'

How touching.

'Kitty kept crying for you. Each time she asked for "Daddy", Matt kept saying, "I'm your daddy". She was so confused and upset and he didn't get it at all. Then one day, he overheard me talking to Kitty. She was asking for you again and I said, "Matt's going to be there as your daddy now." I didn't even know he was in the flat. I must have missed the sound of his key in the door, what with Kitty's crying. It wasn't much, that one small sentence, but he saw the truth. Maybe he'd started to think how easy it would have been for me to lie about the DNA test. He confronted me – and I was in a state, worn-out and crying myself. When he threatened me unless I told the truth, I admitted what I'd done. He hit me. I was scared, Garstin, and I really knew at that point that I'd been an utter fool.'

CHAPTER SIXTY-SIX

Blake had only had an hour's fitful sleep in a chair after his row with Babette, but the wakeful thinking time had allowed bits of his personal life to slot into place. It wasn't helping with his concentration at the station though. He was currently trying to understand what Paul Kemp was doing in his office.

'I've got to be honest with you,' the ex-cop said, his roguish grin splitting his rugged face, 'Tara told me just a tiny bit about the case.' He held up a hand. 'Never normally does, she's as tight as a— well, anyway, this time I guess her mind was wandering a bit. You know, after the bump on her head.'

Blake gave a hollow laugh. Tara couldn't leave the case alone, and if she was stopped from investigating personally, Kemp was the next best thing. They might not be in a relationship – not now, anyway – but they were as thick as thieves. All the same, he couldn't help respecting the guy. Being instrumental in getting rid of Patrick Wilkins had to count for something. And he trusted Tara's judgement, anyway. He was as sure of her as he was of anyone.

'I might have to let her off, just this once,' Blake said. 'And all information gratefully received.' At that moment he felt as though he was wading through treacle. He'd been back at the station since dawn and as well as Bella Chadwick and Lady Lockwood, he now had Sir Alistair on site too. He'd spent the last two hours trying to get the man to slip up and admit to the job Bella said he'd given her. So far, he'd had no joy at all.

'I've not got much as yet,' Kemp said hastily. 'Circumstantial and all that. It might not help. All I had to go on was Scotland

and the name of the hamlet where Lady Lockwood's mother lived. I managed to find that online – she spent some of her upbringing there, according to Wikipedia. Though the main family home was in Surrey.'

Blake nodded.

'I couldn't find any hint of a scandal at the hamlet itself, but then I looked at the route the Lockwoods would have likely taken if they were travelling up from Cambridge. I found an unsolved crime, here.'

He took out a road atlas he'd got with him and pointed to a tiny village, south of Veronica Lockwood's mother's hamlet. Blake caught his breath. Lady Lockwood had deleted the photo Bella had taken of Julie's notepad, but the tech guys had managed to retrieve the file. The name of the village on Kemp's map matched the name Julie had noted.

'What happened there?' he asked.

'Hit and run – not in the village – a little way outside. End of July the year John Lockwood would have turned twelve, judging by his school dates on LinkedIn. Late at night, the investigators reckoned. Bad weather. Two people killed, travelling in a small, rusty Mini.' Kemp's eyes met his. 'The reports reckon the car was hit by another, larger vehicle – there was a scrape along the Mini's side – which sent it off course, straight into a tree trunk. The driver was a mother, travelling with her daughter. The reports reckon the woman would have died instantly, but the girl – she was only eight – probably hung on for hours. The medics said she could have been saved, if she'd got the right attention. Whoever sent them careering into the tree made the conscious decision to beat it and save themselves instead of doing the right thing. From the tyre marks on the road, the investigators concluded the other car involved must have skidded to a halt before being driven away. They'd have been well aware of the accident they'd caused. Not pretty.'

'No.'

Kemp shrugged his huge shoulders. 'It might not help. And I could be duplicating. Tara said that Jez was looking into the Scotland connection, but she reckoned he might have got distracted.'

'He did.' He'd been busy with the haulage company transporting Lady Lockwood's harp, and liaising with the CSIs examining the woman's car, stairs, sitting room and drinks decanter.

There'd been something in Kemp's eye when he'd mentioned the new DC's name. 'Have you met Jez?' If he had, that must have been round at Tara's place, surely?

'Briefly.' Kemp's tone said it all.

'Ah.' Blake let his eyes convey his own views.

They exchanged a look.

Kemp handed him a printout of the articles he'd found. 'The web addresses are there for reference, too.'

'Thanks – I appreciate it.'

'Think it'll help?'

'I think it might.'

Kemp rose to his feet. As Blake showed him out, he imagined the accident as viewed from the Lockwood's car. Two children sitting in the back – John and Douglas. They'd kept their parents' secret buried for years. And they must have shared their guilt for what had happened, too. The position they'd been in didn't bear thinking about. If they'd been on their way to their grandmother's, they might have been out of contact and off the grid for weeks. Shut up with two adults who had left a child to die – and a grandparent who maybe knew nothing. He imagined Sir Alistair and Lady Lockwood speaking to their children. Had family loyalty been enough to keep them quiet? Or had they used threats to drive home the need for silence? If the boys had spoken up, they might have been told they'd lose their family home, their school places, their friends, their future.

No wonder John had gone off the rails. He was beyond their reach now, but Douglas – a chip off the old block though he

seemed to be – might crack under questioning, if all this speculation was true.

Blake could face him with one of the news articles. Douglas
would be mystified if they were on the wrong track – but he was
sure they weren't. And if the story was all too familiar, he'd assume
the police knew more than they did. That would be the key to his
mother and father's undoing.

CHAPTER SIXTY-SEVEN

Blake felt uncharacteristically nervous as he entered Tara's hospital ward a little later that day, clutching a bunch of scented stocks. He'd got some in his cottage garden in Fen Ditton, though these were from a florist. They were his favourite and he thought they might help mask the hospital smells of disinfectant and rubber flooring. But as he approached her, he realised his offering would be dwarfed by a showy bouquet of roses and lilies.

'Someone beat me to it,' he said, taking a seat by her bed, and feeling that he'd like to be closer to where she lay.

She shifted to pull herself more upright. 'Jez.' She raised an eyebrow. 'I have to confess, he's gone to town.'

He felt his insides sink. 'A grand gesture?'

Her cheeks coloured slightly. 'The stocks are lovely.' She took them from his hands and sniffed. A nurse appeared with a vase filled with water a moment later. She put the flowers in the shade of his DC's bouquet.

There was an awkward silence. 'It's lucky I ended up with a bed here,' Tara said at last. 'There are no flowers allowed on the orthopaedics wards, but they were full.'

Tara never made small talk. Blake looked at her closely. 'Are you okay? Apart from having a broken foot and head injuries, that is?'

She seemed to come to, and pasted on a smile. 'Dandy, thanks very much. So, tell me what's happening.'

He wasn't entirely convinced, but he ran through the events up until the point that Kemp had come to see him. At the mention of the ex-cop's name, Tara looked down.

'Sorry. I shouldn't have told him what was going on, but the nurses were breathing down my neck. I knew they'd have a go at me if I tried to call work again, and Kemp came to visit with Bea, so…'

Blake gave her a look. 'A law unto yourself – as usual.'

'At least I told everyone where I was going this time, when I went off with Bella.' Despite her light words and ironically raised eyebrows, her voice had a slight shake to it.

'There is that. And I have to confess, Kemp's information was invaluable. He told you what he found, I presume?'

She nodded. 'He dropped in earlier to bring me some bits and pieces from home.'

'On the back of his research we brought Douglas Lockwood in for questioning. We'd already got his mother and father on site, so it was starting to feel like a game of happy families. Only they're all a lot less chirpy than they were this time yesterday.'

Tara leant back against her pillow. 'That sounds promising. The questioning went well, then?'

'We told Douglas we knew what had happened on the way to his grandmother's in Scotland – and then I showed him the newspaper article Kemp found. I said at this stage, under the circumstances, it was far better for him to tell the truth. I made the point that he wasn't personally guilty – and that people would look leniently on a schoolchild who'd been put in that sort of position. Though in fact, I think he's just as hard as his parents – it seems to have been John who really suffered. Anyway, it worked. He was all too keen to put himself in the best possible light, once he thought the whole story was bound to come out anyway.' He met Tara's eye. 'He says his father was at the wheel that night. They'd set off for the journey later than planned. The weather was stormy and Alistair Lockwood was driving like a demon. He rounded a bend in the middle of the road at high speed in his expensive four-by-four and caught the side of an oncoming car. The blow sent the other vehicle off the road and straight into a tree. Lockwood managed to keep his car under control, and got out to see what had happened. He even opened the door of the other car, apparently – Douglas says he always wore driving gloves. His father told them the woman was dead and the little girl as good as. Then Veronica Lockwood turned round to her kids and said it was too late. She claimed there was nothing anyone could do, and if they called an ambulance the child would still die, and their own lives would be in ruins. Douglas remembers that his father had had a whisky or four at the pub where they'd stopped mid-evening. As he grew up, he realised their secret was vulnerable. It's clear the pub landlady told the police about Sir Alistair, when she heard about the accident. She had no name or number plate, but she knew he was with a family, and had an upper-class accent. The Lockwoods were safe, so long as the rest of the jigsaw puzzle pieces were missing. But if John had talked, the evidence on file would probably have been enough to put them in the frame.'

Tara was very still. 'They condemned that child to a certain death, just as Veronica did Julie.'

Blake nodded. 'Douglas said Alistair got back in the car and put his foot down. Their vehicle wasn't that badly damaged. He drove it back to Cambridge just as it was, two weeks later, and got it fixed by a local garage, so no one would make the connection. He told the mechanic they'd hit a deer.'

'Did Douglas seem upset?' He could hear the horror in her voice.

'At what's happening now, yes. But at what happened back then?' He shook his head. 'Not genuinely, though he went through the motions. He claims he believed his parents, that the girl couldn't be saved – as though that makes what they did all right. He said John seemed stunned. He hardly spoke the entire time they were staying at their grandmother's house. And so his parents were able to persuade him that he was complicit – he hadn't protested when it counted, so he'd clearly been happy to go along with the plan.

They were all in it together. It had been a terrible accident, but they couldn't have altered events once they'd been set in motion.'

'Family above all else,' Tara said.

'I'm afraid so. I wonder how much Julie had managed to find out.'

'I don't think she can have got as far as Kemp; we'd have seen it in her search history if she had. I guess she was stopped in her tracks.'

'I agree. I wonder how she came to have the place name of the village nearest the hit and run.'

'Did she?'

Blake explained about Bella's photograph of Julie's notepad.

'If she was looking at it the day she died, that makes it sound like a recent discovery,' Tara said. 'Maybe John let the name slip when he was drunk – or talked in his sleep. He might not have told anyone about what happened, but it sounds as though it was forever on his mind. I'll bet he looked up all the press coverage of the accident at some stage and knew the details inside out.'

'It's possible. What's your guess about Julie's motivation, then?'

Tara bit her lip. 'I reckon she was in love with John and could see how much he was suffering. I guess she didn't know why, but she saw how he'd distanced himself from his parents, and imagined they were to blame in some way. She would have wanted to investigate Lockwood's anyway – she had that sort of company in her sights. But then perhaps, as she got to know more of John's history and his preoccupations, she began to realise whatever had destroyed him was something unrelated to the business.' She raised her eyes to Blake's. 'I'd guess that's why she went snooping round the Master's Lodge when she found the cat. She was probably hoping she'd unearth some kind of clue as to what had left John so broken. The statue didn't provide the answer, of course, but maybe she photographed it for the reason my journalist contact suggested. It would have been the perfect illustration to bring a dry story about

Lockwood's to life, if she ever finished her article about them. So, what happens now?'

'Douglas's evidence makes Bella Chadwick's version of events look much more likely than his mother's. The two women and Sir Alistair are all under arrest. We're onto the garage that fixed the family's four-by-four, all those years ago, as well as the former landlady of the pub where Sir Alistair drank his whiskies.

'On Julie's murder, the felt interior of Lady Lockwood's harp case has been matched to the wool found under her fingernails. DNA's being worked on – evidence built up. Oh, and we found that the sedatives John Lockwood took the night he died were the same sort that his mother has been prescribed.' He still felt sick when he imagined what the woman might have said to her son on the evening of his death. Had she really wanted to offer solace? Or had she left the wherewithal for him to take his own life at his house, then called to make him feel as low as possible? Maybe she'd convinced him everyone would think he'd killed Julie. Or perhaps she'd suggested her death was actually John's fault. She might have hinted that Stuart Gilmour had found out about his and Julie's relationship and killed the student in revenge. They'd never know for sure, but John had been the most likely family member to give away his parents' secret. It gave them a motive for wanting him out of the way.

Tara was shivering, despite the heat of the hospital ward.

'Are you all right?' He looked up for a nurse, but Tara put a hand on his arm.

Her touch made him lean in towards her. He was conscious of Jez's flowers again.

'I'm okay. It's just the case.'

He took a deep breath. 'Have you been having nightmares?'

There was a slight quaver to her voice – something almost unknown. 'The odd one. Didn't get my solid eight hours last night.'

'We can arrange counselling, of course – but if you ever want to talk to some untrained idiot, you know where I am.'

Her eyes looked damp. 'Thanks, Blake. I appreciate it.'

But she'd probably rather share with Jez Fallon. It was understandable. No baggage, no kids, charming, carefree... He thought of the decision he'd made at three o'clock that morning. But it didn't make any difference. He'd finally come to his senses, but it was too late, and he'd have to live with it.

'Take care, Tara.' He squeezed her hand for a moment.

'You too.'

As he turned away, she was looking down, her hair falling forward, hiding her face.

CHAPTER SIXTY-EIGHT

Patrick Wilkins was sitting opposite Giles Troy, editor of *Not Now* magazine, in the Mitre, enjoying a lunchtime pint of IPA.

'You look very pleased with yourself,' Troy said.

Patrick would have bristled, but he was in too good a mood to be wound up by the man today. He was well aware that the editor had written him off, but he'd shortly be eating his words. That was compensation enough.

'I've identified Tara Thorpe's stalker.'

Troy frowned, disbelief written all over his face. 'How the hell did you manage that?'

Patrick wasn't going to give him the full details. He was hardly planning to highlight his botched attempt to solve the mystery earlier in the year, or how it had *accidentally* led him to the right answer. And then there was the part Shona had played in his success... No. Troy needn't know any of that.

'Through hard work and diligence,' Wilkins said instead, giving a slow smile. 'I found an old boyfriend of Tara's, Peter Devlin, who gave me some useful information. After that, I went to the suspect and presented him with what I knew. I managed to record our conversation secretly, so we're home and dry.'

Troy was holding his pint halfway to his mouth, his eyes wider still now. 'You're seriously telling me we can unmask the guilty party?'

'*I* can,' Patrick corrected him, 'and I'll give you your story – for the fee we agreed, of course.'

'Of course.' He shook his head. 'So, you picked up on clues that a team of police officers – and no doubt that bastard Paul Kemp – all missed when they investigated the case first time around…'

Patrick felt his pulse quicken at the incredulity in the editor's tone. So what if the particular set of circumstances that had set him on the right track could never have occurred back then? Investigators relied on serendipity the whole time. It was what you did with your good fortune that made the difference.

Troy licked his lips. 'What's the truth? How much will it hurt Thorpe?'

Wilkins' mood lifted again. 'Oh, it'll hurt all right – and the scandal will be huge. It turns out the culprit was her own father, Robin.'

Troy's smile was broad. 'That's one of the best bits of news I've heard in a long time. She mentioned him once or twice, back when she worked for me. An architect, isn't he? I always got the impression he despised her, but I didn't think his hatred ran that deep.'

'It's more complicated than you imagine.' Patrick had been astounded at the story that had come out. 'And when I say he was responsible, I have to qualify that. He was responsible for every delivery after the first one. And also, for killing her cat.'

Troy frowned. Patrick himself wasn't best pleased that he still didn't know who'd sent Tara her very first item of hate mail. Now he understood that it had been a one-off, he doubted he'd ever get at the truth. It might have been a school friend that she'd upset, or an ex-boyfriend perhaps. Some weirdo. Tara Thorpe was just the sort to attract them.

The editor of *Not Now*'s eyes were cold. 'Explain.'

'The news of Tara's first poison pen, with the delivery of a load of dead bees on her sixteenth birthday, made the press quite quickly. Lydia Thorpe was at the height of her career, and several national papers picked up on it, as well as some glossy magazines.'

'I can imagine. If *Not Now* had existed back then we'd have been all over it.' Troy sipped his beer. '"Bizarre hate mail sent to film star's daughter" would draw the readers in nicely.'

Wilkins nodded. 'Meanwhile, it turns out Robin's architects' practice hadn't been doing well. He was struggling and wondering if he'd have to close it down. It was bad timing: he and his wife were trying to start a family, so he needed the cash.'

Troy yawned. 'Cut to the chase, for heaven's sake.'

'Robin was interviewed in almost all of the press coverage. His name – and the odd photo of his work – got included as added colour when the hacks went into Tara's colourful family background. And before Robin knew it, he was getting more clients.'

Troy's jaw dropped. 'I don't believe it! He sent the next package just to prolong the associated publicity?'

Patrick nodded. He was lucky to have got the information out of Tara's dad. He'd blagged his way into the man's house and accused him of being Tara's stalker in front of his current wife, Melissa. The woman had been so horrified at the idea of her beloved husband victimising his own daughter out of hatred, that Robin had ended up defending himself by detailing the rather more 'practical' reasons for his campaign. Melissa hadn't looked any less appalled, once her husband had spilled the beans. As for Wilkins, he wasn't fooled. Yes, the man might have acted for the sake of material gain, but he'd seen his eyes. He hated his daughter all right. And no one who knew what he'd done would doubt that.

Patrick smiled. 'I looked at some of the press cuttings from the period. The deliveries got more and more creative, so they continued to capture the newspapers' imagination. Maggots, a pig's heart, piles of feathers. It was all weird, dramatic, attention-grabbing stuff. By the time the press covered the killing of Tara's cat, Robin was being described as a "society" architect and, along with quotes expressing his heartfelt concern at his daughter's torment, were his firm's contact number and little thumbnails of his latest high-end commissions. They did the same for Lydia, of course – little boxes with her photograph and details of her most recent film. Only she didn't need the publicity, whereas for him, free advertising in a range of upmarket publications was a massive bonus. He told me he stopped once he was sure his business was secure.' Patrick shook his head; he'd made that last statement in defensive tones, as though it showed he'd got some principles.

'Remarkable. A man after my own heart, in many ways.' Troy laughed. 'I'm sure he'll understand that we need to use publicity to keep our pockets lined, just as he did. How did Tara's ex come to put you onto Robin, by the way?'

'He became a family friend – another architect who once did a stint in her dad's practice.'

'Excellent.' Troy raised his glass to Patrick's. 'I'll see that the story's drafted as soon as possible. Come into the office when you're ready, and bring the recording you made.'

'I'll want to hand it over to the police too.' They'd see his worth then. They'd be kicking themselves for forcing him into resigning.

'Of course, but only as we go to print with what we know so far. They'll probably slap restrictions on us once they've got your report.'

Patrick nodded. He intended to write to Tara with the news direct, too. He *could* leave *Not Now*'s coverage to come as a surprise, but that really would be low. And besides, he was enjoying mulling over the wording of his letter…

'Oh,' Troy raised his drink again, 'and watch your back. If there's any hint you got your information dishonestly, it won't affect me – but I think it's a fair assumption that Tara and her allies will find out. If you've indulged in malpractice – letting your "source" think you were working for Tara, for example – then I'd say you're in for trouble. It would be a shame if your PI business went down the pan so rapidly.'

As they left the Mitre, Troy was smiling, but Patrick wasn't.

CHAPTER SIXTY-NINE

Blake had felt a moment of peace after he'd got the truth out of Babette. He'd finally acknowledged that breaking up with her was the right thing to do. Far from protecting the kids, staying in the marriage was exposing them to a poisonous atmosphere. After doing some googling during the night, he was confident the courts would support shared care for them.

Three days later, on Saturday, he was sitting in the kitchen at the house in Fen Ditton. He'd already told Babette what needed to happen and had begun to sort out his possessions, ready for the move. His biggest anxiety had been finding somewhere local to live, so he was buoyed up at having secured a place to rent just up the road from the family home. Kitty and Jessica would be able to run in and out of both houses as they grew up.

He'd expected Babette to go into the same routine she had in the past when he told her about his plans – sobbing, pleading and making excuses – but something in her eye told him she knew there was no going back this time. She'd gone to talk to her mother, but the kids were in the room with him: Kitty making fairy cakes – with some help – and Jessica in her bouncy chair, flipping the pink and blue plastic rabbits that dangled from the frame he'd put over it.

He'd sent off a fresh DNA check to try to match him to them both – not because he cared, but because he wanted them to know who their biological father was, one way or the other. He needed to be prepared too, in case the truth had any bearing on custody decisions in the family courts. But he hoped to God it wouldn't, if it turned out Babette had lied yet again. He was the one who'd been there for them and he'd fight to the death to protect them if need be.

All in all, things were a lot more certain than they had been – he felt more grounded than he had in years.

But no matter how important all that was, he couldn't entirely stop his thoughts from straying to Tara and Jez. He pushed the images away, but they sprang back at him with worrying regularity.

Tara was still in Addenbrooke's – they'd decided to operate on her broken foot. It was just before hospital visiting time that evening that he realised he'd have to take action. Babette was back home, so he made an excuse and left the house.

Tara had been transferred to a new ward. Half an hour later, he approached her hospital bed once more. He'd bought her some chocolates from an eight till late. It took her a moment to realise he was there. She'd been looking at an envelope, a frown traced across her brow.

'Everything all right?' He nodded at the letter.

'I'm not sure. This was delivered by hand earlier – it's just made its way through the internal system to me.' She held it up, and he recognised Patrick Wilkins' handwriting.

'There should be a law against Wilkins writing to people whilst they're in a reduced state of health. Do you want to open it now?'

She shook her head. 'I don't want to open it all, if I'm honest. I'll leave it until later. Or chuck it in the bin. One or the other.' She sat up straighter in bed and glanced at the chocolates he was holding. 'What's all this? Are you trying to butter me up for some reason?'

He managed to give her what he hoped was a casual grin. 'They're just to keep body and soul together, in case the hospital food's not up to much.'

She raised an eyebrow. 'As a matter of fact, I just love beetroot, mystery meat and wilting lettuce leaves – but I'm prepared to accept your kind gift anyway.' She took the box, opened it and offered him one. 'So, what's the news? Is the case wrapping up okay?'

He nodded as he ate the white-chocolate-covered praline and took a seat in the chair for visitors. 'We've got testimonies now from witnesses dating back to Alistair Lockwood's hit-and-run. The woman from the pub was able to match the family she remembered with a photograph of them from that period. She still remembered Sir Alistair drinking more than he should. The car mechanic was helpful, too; we were hoping he might vaguely remember encountering Sir Alistair or someone from Lockwood's, but he still had all the paperwork for the job. Over twenty years' worth of invoices, all neatly filed away. The evidence against both Lockwoods senior is going to fill a briefcase.'

Tara shuddered. 'What about Bella?'

'She'll have to answer for what she did. However manipulative Veronica was, and however much pressure her parents put on her, she was complicit in the most terrible of crimes. She might have been able to save Julie. She's going through psychiatric assessments though, and the jury will see how she was used.'

Tara nodded. 'And how are the team?'

'Max and Megan were behaving like a pair of love-struck kids last time I looked. The whole station's enjoying their romance. Even Fleming's gone all dewy-eyed.'

'It's about time Max had some joy in his life.'

Blake nodded. 'I know you haven't always seen eye to eye with Megan, though.'

'I was probably too hasty.' She gave him a look. 'If Max has fallen for her then I'm convinced. He knows what's what.'

The team was beginning to gel, Blake realised. Megan had relaxed a little, and Tara had begun to see the benefits of receiving backup, as well as giving it. Fleming had said much the same when they'd met to discuss the investigation into Julie's death.

'And I suppose you don't need an update on Jez.' There were no flowers allowed on Tara's current ward, which saved him from having to look at the DC's showy bouquet. It was still fresh in his mind though. 'Are you and he an item?'

Her eyes narrowed and her mouth formed a thin *what's it to you?* line. 'He's asked me out, once I can walk again. I wouldn't be hot on the dance floor right now. Why?'

He took a deep breath. 'I didn't just come in here to pass on gossip from the station. I wanted to say that if you and Jez ever part company… I'm waiting in the wings.' He felt the heat rise up in his face. 'I appreciate you might not want me anywhere near the stage, but – well – I wanted you to know.'

She frowned. 'And what makes you think I'd date a married man?'

'It's finally over between me and Babette.' He hardly knew where to start. Tara – and most people at the station – knew his marriage had had its ups and downs, but most of the details were still secret. 'I haven't loved her for years. I kept hoping I could save our marriage for the children's sake, but it wasn't working. We've been doing them more harm than good.' He sighed. 'Things are really complicated just at the moment, but I wanted you to know how I feel, just in case, once I'm in my own place…' She was quiet, and his mouth went dry. 'I've finally realised what matters and how life isn't a dress rehearsal. Obviously, if you did ever go out with me, you'd have to put up with my corniness and clichéd phrases… But,' he hardly dared look her in the eye, 'perhaps you could just bear it in mind?'

She cocked her head. 'Okay.'

There was an awkward pause.

'Right. Well, I'll see you sometime then.' He got up to leave. At least he'd got the words out.

He was just unlocking his car when the text came through.

Following in-depth consideration, I plan to tell Jez I'm washing my hair. A date with him would have been a laugh, but being with you will be complicated, messy, and full of drama, which is much more my scene…

He stood there in the chilly concrete multi-storey car park, grinning like an idiot. It was a minute before her second text came through.

Damn it – I'm being flippant because I find emotions hard. But it's always been you, Blake; you know that, don't you? x

Within three minutes, Blake was back on Tara's ward, facing a nurse who was telling him visiting hours were now over. He showed his warrant card and asked for sixty seconds, which met with a roll of the eyes, but also precious permission for one last minute with Tara that night.

When she looked up at him, her eyes were glistening. His own felt just as watery. He took her hand and held it tight, then raised it to his lips and kissed it: a promise until he was finally free.

A LETTER FROM CLARE

Thank you so much for reading *Murder in the Fens*. I do hope you enjoyed it as much as I liked writing it! If you'd like to keep up to date with all of my latest releases, you can sign up at the following link. Your email address will never be shared, and you can unsubscribe at any time.

www.bookouture.com/clare-chase

I got the idea for this book after thinking about people's sense of right and wrong and how that might vary, according to their priorities and their backgrounds. For my story, I imagined one of my characters gradually getting sucked into a situation where they were behaving in an immoral way, but one that might just about be forgivable – or at least understandable – under certain circumstances. And then I imagined how that situation might develop, so that the same character was gradually blurring right and wrong to a greater and greater extent, until, ultimately, they crossed a horrifying point of no return. Of course, if you've read the book now, you'll see that the character in question is surrounded by others with a total lack of morality and that also had its effect.

If you have time, I'd love it if you were able to **write a review of *Murder in the Fens***. Feedback is really valuable, and it also makes a huge difference in helping new readers discover my books for the first time.

Alternatively, if you'd like to contact me personally, you can reach me via my website, Facebook page, Twitter or Instagram. It's always great to hear from readers.

Again, thank you so much for deciding to spend some time reading *Murder in the Fens*. I'm looking forward to sharing my next book with you very soon.

With all best wishes,
Clare x

 www.clarechase.com

 @ClareChaseAuthor

 @ClareChase_

ACKNOWLEDGEMENTS

Loads of love and thanks to my immediate family as ever: to Charlie for the eagle-eyed pre-submission proofreading, to George for the encouraging witty banter when I got the jitters, and to Ros for the fab feedback and later corrections. (I hope you like Tara and Blake's ending!) Much love and thanks also to my parents for their most excellent cheerleading, and the same to Phil and Jenny, David and Pat, Warty, Andrea, the Westfield gang, Margaret, Shelly, Mark, Helen, Lorna and a whole band of family and friends.

Thanks also to the fabulous Bookouture authors and other writer mates both online and IRL for their friendly support and insights. It makes so much difference. I'd also like to express massive appreciation to the book bloggers and reviewers who've taken the time to pass on their thoughts about my work.

And then crucially, thanks to my fantastic editor Kathryn Taussig, who's steered me through this first series for Bookouture with inspiring feedback, excellent ideas and friendly support. It's been a hugely enjoyable experience and I'm so thrilled to have the chance to work with her again on a new set of books. Massive thanks too, to Maisie Lawrence, Peta Nightingale, Alexandra Holmes, Fraser, Liz and everyone involved in the editing, book production and marketing process at Bookouture. And enormous thanks as ever to Noelle Holten, for the phenomenal promotional work she does – above and beyond the call of duty – alongside the amazing Kim Nash. I feel hugely lucky to be published and promoted by such a wonderful team.

And finally, thanks to you, the reader, for buying or borrowing this book!

Manufactured by Amazon.ca
Bolton, ON

19409859R00182